LAMP BLACK,
WOLF GREY

LAMP BLACK,
*W*OLF GREY

Paula Brackston

THOMAS DUNNE BOOKS

ST. MARTIN'S GRIFFIN

New York

THOMAS DUNNE BOOKS.
An imprint of St. Martin's Press.

LAMP BLACK, WOLF GREY. Copyright © 2015 by Paula Brackston. All rights
reserved. Printed in the United States of America. For information,
address St. Martin's Press, 175 Fifth Avenue, New York, N.Y. 10010.

www.thomasdunnebooks.com
www.stmartins.com

Designed by Ellen Cipriano

Library of Congress Cataloging-in-Publication Data

Brackston, Paula.
    Lamp black, wolf grey / Paula Brackston.—First edition.
        pages ; cm
    ISBN 978-1-250-06968-9 (trade paperback)
    ISBN 978-1-4668-5986-9 (e-book)
    1. Married women—Fiction. 2. Merlin (Legendary character)—Fiction.
3. Man-woman relationships—Fiction. I. Title.
    PR6102.R325L36 2015
    823'.92—dc23

                                                    2015016278

St. Martin's Griffin books may be purchased for educational, business, or
promotional use. For information on bulk purchases, please contact the
Macmillan Corporate and Premium Sales Department at 1-800-221-7945,
extension 5442, or write to specialmarkets@macmillan.com.

First Edition: July 2015

10 9 8 7 6 5 4 3 2 1

For Tad and Skyla

LAMP BLACK,
WOLF GREY

PROLOGUE

$\mathcal{I}$N THE DARKNESS something scuttled. The girl shivered in the chilling damp of the small room. The dead grey stone of the walls seemed to drain the warmth from her body. Even in her heavy velvet gown she felt naked, exposed, vulnerable. She ran her hands over the dress, as if she might gain some heat from the rich, fox-red fabric. She looked down at the unfamiliar garment, puzzled, in her distress, to see such fine clothes on her body. The feeble, flickering light from the entrance to the room caught the amethyst on the ring finger of her left hand. Its brilliance jarred in the frightening gloom. The girl worked at the ring, struggling to free it. Her hands were cold, but made clammy by fear, so the ring clung to her flesh as she pulled. Panic began to rob her of air. Fear tightened its grip around her throat. She took a steadying breath, but it left her in broken gasps which clouded in the bitter air of the room. Her nostrils filled with the musty smell of the wet walls, of a space unused and unlived in. A space that rejected human presence. A space that spurned life.

The workman in front of her labored at his task without once looking up. With every scrape of his trowel the girl flinched as if he were administering blows. She watched him work on, at once both fascinated and appalled at his detachment, his lack of compassion. But then, she knew he was no more free than she. That his life was ransom in the same way as hers, should there be any person living whom he cared about. Whom he loved.

He will find me, she told herself, *he will come. He must come.*

The sound of approaching footsteps shocked the girl from her thoughts. The dim light was momentarily brightened by the lantern in the hand of the man who now stood in the doorway. He held up the light, its rays falling on his face, casting heavy shadows beneath his eyes.

The coldness of this fearful place, the girl thought, *is as nothing when compared to those eyes.* And though the sight of the man worsened her state of fear, it also brought hatred. And anger. And in these she found a small, powerful kernel of strength. She straightened her back. She would not show her suffering.

"I see that even in this wretched gloom," said the man, his voice low, "your radiance remains undimmed. Such a waste."

He took a step toward her, his gaze sliding the length of her body. The girl stepped back, feeling herself trapped against the rough wall. Nowhere left to run. The man sighed.

"Just remember, my dear, in the long hours to come, remember who is responsible for the . . . *lamentable* position in which you now find yourself." He turned to leave, then added, "I know you are certain he will risk all to come heroically to your rescue. I suggest sightings of him riding west from here an hour ago indicate otherwise. How will love fare when a lonely death comes close, I wonder? Will you cry out for your precious lover then, d'you think? Or will you curse him for abandoning you with such ease?"

The girl held her breath as the figure stepped out of the opening and disappeared without a backward glance.

The mason quickened his pace, as if eager to be done. The girl felt fear growing to unmanageable terror. The horror of the fate that had been chosen for her was too much to bear. Her knees weakened as if they could no longer support the weight of her dread. As the last stone was put in place the mason's eyes met hers for a brief, painful instant, then he was gone, and with him the last of the light. A scraping sealed the gaps around the rock and the deathly, suffocating blackness swamped her. In the unnatural silence and stillness she was left, shaking, alone.

❧ 1 ❧

"ⒶND THROUGH HERE, we have the fourth bedroom, again with the exposed beams and rather charming, sloping ceiling." The estate agent pointed as he spoke.

Laura wondered if he thought all viewers needed hand signals as well as endless commentary to fully appreciate a house, or if he were making a special effort because they were from London. She still hadn't forgiven Dan for letting slip the fact they were selling their house in Hackney. She had seen the way the agent rubbed his hands together at the thought of getting commission on the full asking price.

"A small room, but plenty big enough for a nursery." The man was unstoppable.

She could feel Dan looking at her but refused to meet his eyes. Did he think she was going to fall apart every time someone mentioned babies? It was ridiculous.

The agent tried another tack.

"And, yet again, gorgeous views, I think you'll agree."

Laura and Dan stepped toward the little window, both having

to stoop to avoid the low beams. Even if Laura had not been tall, she would have had to duck. Dan took her hand and gave it a firm squeeze. She smiled back at him, a practiced, stop-fussing-I'm-fine smile. She gazed out at the seductive vista. The countryside was dressed in its prettiest May garb—everything budding or blooming or bursting out in the exuberance of late spring. For Laura, the landscape at thirteen hundred feet up a Welsh mountain was the perfect mix of reassuringly tamed and excitingly wild. In front of the house were lush, high meadows filled with sheep, the lambs plump from their mother's grass-rich milk. Their creamy little shapes bright and clean against the background of pea green. A stream tumbled down the hillside, disappearing into the dense oak woods at the far end of the fields, the ocher trunks fuzzy with moss. On either side of the narrow valley, the land rose steeply to meet the open mountain on the other side of the fence. Here young bracken was springing up sharp and tough to claim the hills for another season. Beyond, in the distance, more mountains rose and fell as far as the eye could see. Laura undid the latch and pushed open the window. She closed her eyes. A warm sigh of a wind carried the scent of hawthorn blossom from the hedgerow. She breathed in deeply. The breeze moved the wisps of dark hair at the nape of her neck that had escaped being tied back. As they tickled her skin she felt a sharp quiver travel over her scalp. She stood for a moment, eyes still closed, listening to small birds toiling to feed their young, and the far-off mewing of a soaring buzzard.

This is what I'm going to paint, she thought, *not just this place, but the* essence *of this place.*

She felt Dan's breath on her ear.

"Go on, admit it, you're in love."

She opened her eyes slowly. His boyish, familiar face wore a knowing grin. She smiled back at him, a genuine, connecting smile this time. The first in a long while.

"This is the place," she said.

"You really want to live here?" he asked, raising a doubting eyebrow at the idea.

"I *really* want to live here," she said. Then, seeing his reluctance, she took his hand. "Please?" she said quietly. "I need to try this."

Dan hesitated, then sighed and shrugged. He nodded toward the fidgeting estate agent, "Come on, then," he whispered. "Let's make his day."

Laura was about to step away from the window when a movement outside caught her eye. She squinted against the light, down into the far corner of the meadows. A figure—a man—was striding toward the woods. He was tall, dressed in dark clothing, and carried a heavy stick which he pushed hard to the ground with each step. He walked purposefully, head down, intent on his destination, and beside him loped a shaggy grey dog.

"Laura?" Dan touched her arm. "Are we going to do this thing?"

She turned to look at him, nodding decisively, "Yes," she said. "Let's."

As she moved from the window she glanced back, but the walker had vanished into the dense woodland.

THREE MONTHS LATER, sitting cross-legged on the wooden floor of her London home, the chaos of last-minute packing around her, Laura was doing her best to stay calm as she swaddled yet another wineglass in bubble wrap. Despite a ruthless purge of all cupboards and several trips, laden, to the local Red Cross shop, she remained overwhelmed by the endlessness of the packing. She sighed. Sorting and organizing and efficient planning were not her strong points. She had always known the major part of the move would fall to her, and it niggled her that Dan would have done a better job of it. But he couldn't possibly take time off. She frowned as she thought of him now, happily ensconced in the Blue Boar with his work cronies, enjoying his habitual Friday-night wind down. It was just typical of him to have worked up until the last minute, and yet not be here now to lend a hand. The moving van was due early the next morning and there was still a daunting amount to do. Her shoulders sagged as she gazed at the mess that had been their living room. To make matters worse, she could already hear Daniel berating her for not labeling things properly. Unpacking was going to be equally stressful. Well then, he shouldn't have left it all for her to do. He was the one with the organized mind, the one who liked order and logic and everything in the right place. And he'd have a hangover on moving day. How sensible was that, for heaven's sake? It was as if by carrying on as normal until the actual moment of leaving, he was putting off accepting that they really were going. This was her dream, her idea, her choice. Dan had paid lip service to the plan for weeks before having to declare his true feelings when Laura had started to push property details under his nose at mealtimes. He had admitted, then, that he couldn't imagine living out of London, moving to somewhere remote and rural, starting a new type of life. But Laura had been as persuasive as she knew how. She could work anywhere, and he could take his time finding the right job near their new home, staying in a rented studio flat on weekdays in the meantime. He would get used to the idea; he would surely come to see how much better, more relaxed and less stressful their lives could be. And how that might, just might, give Laura a chance to conceive. And hadn't they tried everything else? Could they really give up without trying this one last thing?

She swore under her breath and picked up another glass. As she leaned forward her hair swung down, wet and heavy. She had found a moment to wash it, and now it hung about her shoulders in glossy black ringlets. It would take hours to dry naturally, but she hadn't the time to deal with it, and in any case, the hair dryer was already nestled in the bottom of a box somewhere.

The telephone rang. Cursing the interruption she searched for the handset, eventually spotting its flashing light peeping out from under a pile of newspapers.

"Hello, Laura, darling. Just thought I'd ring to see how you are." The tension in her mother's voice was unmissable.

"I'm fine, Mum. Just sorting out a few last-minute details." She wedged the phone under her ear and continued to wrap as she spoke. "How was your lunch with Miriam?"

"What? Oh, noisy and fattening. I can't think why she insists we try out a new restaurant every time we meet. Will someone tell me the point of enormous plates when you are given a silly little table? We had to put the cruet on the floor . . ."

Laura let her mother chatter on, relieved she had so easily deflected her from talking about the move. She knew Annabel hated the thought of her only daughter leaving London, and she was having to learn to live with niggling guilt at moving so far away from her lone parent. It would have been easier if her mother had been more open in her objections, but she confined herself to the well-placed sharp observation. To this she added a near-constant expression of hurt and quiet insistence that she would get used to the idea. In time. Laura closed the box of glasses and walked over to the mantelpiece. The room was clear of breakables now, save for a heavy vase and a photo in a silver frame. She picked up the picture and gazed at it. Younger, happier versions of herself and Dan beamed back at her. She remembered it had been taken just before they had started trying for a baby. Before they had realized there was a problem. Before her heart had been broken.

"Laura? Laura, are you still there?"

"Yes, Mum, I'm here. Look, I'd better go. There's still a bit to do. I'll ring you before we leave, OK?"

Even after she had hung up, the sadness in her mother's voice as she said good-bye lingered. Laura bit her lip and closed her eyes. Were they doing the right thing? Giving up everything they knew, everything comforting and familiar, to chase some flimsy notion that a more peaceful, rural environment might just convince her stubborn body that it was safe to make a baby? Non-Specific Infertility. With those few words the doctor had finally shrugged, sighed, apologized, and sent her away. It seemed a cruel trick of nature to condemn her to childlessness with something so vague. Of course, they had tried every possible remedy, from crackpot diets, through medication, meditation, homeopathy, and psychotherapy, to the emotional trauma of IVF. As wide and varied a course of treatments as it was possible to have, all with one thing in common: They hadn't worked. Laura found a space in a box for the photo and was brushing away an infuriating tear when the doorbell rang. She had never been more pleased to see Steph. Steph, whom she had known since she was five years old. Steph, whom she had shared digs with at University. Steph, who had supported her so stoically over the past, long, barren eight years.

"Thought you might be in need of this by now." Steph waved a bottle of champagne under Laura's nose as she stepped into the hall.

"I always said you had a spooky talent for mind reading." She led the way back into the sitting room and unpacked two of the wineglasses she had just wrapped. "Don't ask me to find a champagne flute, unless you want to see a grown woman cry."

"I can slum it, for a good cause." Steph kicked off her sandals, ran a hand through her choppy magenta hair, and curled up on the leather sofa.

Laura popped the cork and poured the drinks, handing a glass to her friend.

"Most people would rush round and offer to help pack at a time like this, not come here and get me sozzled with the job half done."

"As if you'd care about a bit of muddle, Laura Matthews. I'm surprised you're here, actually. I felt certain you'd still be fiddling about in your studio—you never know what day it is."

"I resent 'fiddling about.' Mmm, half decent bubbly. I'll have you know the studio was packed up, done, and dusted ten days ago."

"You mean to say you haven't picked up a paintbrush in all that time? My God, this is the end of life as we know it. First you decide to take to the hills. Next you stop painting so that you can wrap up knickknacks. It'll all end in Laura Ashley, you mark my words. Just as well I came to get one last look at the chic, city you before you go bush."

Laura laughed, reassured to find that even now Steph could rid the room of tension in minutes. Many times her friend's ability to get her to lighten up and not take herself too seriously had just about saved her sanity.

The two drank in companionable silence for a moment until Laura said with a small smile, "I'm going to miss you."

"Now, before you go getting all slushy on me, I have to warn you this is not waterproof mascara. I don't want to be frightening taxi drivers out of their socks on the way home." She took another swig of champagne, then added, "Besides, you won't get a chance to miss anybody. Me, Angus, and the Terrible Two will descend on you with alarming frequency. In fact, you'll probably see more of us than you do now. It's a win-win situation—Angus will be leaping out of bed early to drag the kids up some craggy rock or other, so yours truly can fester under the duvet until noon. Then your Dan can cook us up a full English, or full Welsh, whatever the hell that is . . . . I can't wait. Come on, don't hog the booze."

Laura passed her the bottle. Steph topped up both their glasses then looked at her, frowning a little.

"So, you're sure this is the right thing for you both, yes?"

"No. How can I be sure? But it does feel . . . worth doing. We need to change something."

"You've had a rough trot these last couple of years, Laura. I only hope this isn't going to prove more difficult than you expect. And you've worked so hard to get the recognition you deserve as an artist. Are you sure you're going to be able to work properly, stay in touch and, in fashion, keep networking and whatever it is you do in your arty circles?"

"Of course. In fact, I expect to be able to raise my prices once I'm a bona fide harum-scarum artist living in the wilds! And besides, Penny is not known as the bossiest artists' agent in Chelsea for nothing. She's invested too much time in me to stop nagging now. She won't let things slide. She's determined I'm going to have a show before Christmas." Laura wished she felt as confident as she sounded. That the move might have an adverse effect on her career was a secret fear she was loath to admit even to herself. She was already missing the thrill of starting a new painting. That suspended moment before beginning, where the image lived in limbo, somewhere between the reality of the subject and the realms of imagination. It was a moment of perfection, which no artwork could ever hope to live up to. All that could be done was to strive to get as near to that early vision as possible, and feel blessed if the result came within a hundred miles of it. How long would it be before she could settle enough to produce worthwhile work again? And would being out of the loop of the London art scene cause problems? She refused to be cast down by the thought. She waved her glass at Steph. "And before you ask, I'm already resigned to the fact I won't be able to get a decent latte or watch a good movie or find any clothes I'd want to buy." She smiled. "I'm ready to give it all up for . . ."

"For? What, exactly?"

Laura raised her eyebrows and shrugged, not quite able to meet her friend's questioning gaze. "We'll just have to wait and see, won't we?"

❧

BY THREE O'CLOCK the following afternoon Laura was weary from driving and on the point of losing her temper with Dan. The loading of the van had taken an age, and Dan had been working at half speed, nursing his inevitable hangover. As she negotiated another roundabout, Laura squinted into the strong summer sun, reminded that they were most definitely heading west. She thanked God and Audi for the car's efficient air-conditioning system. Beside her Dan flapped and crumpled the map as he tried to fold it.

"Dan, if you're not going to be any use at reading that thing for pity's sake put it away. You're driving me mad with it," she told him. "I thought women were supposed to be the ones who couldn't navigate."

"You're the one who wanted to do the driving."

"Because you're the one probably still over the limit, judging by the amount of aspirin you've had to take so far today."

"All right, don't go on. We must be nearly there by now, anyway."

"Nearly *where?*"

"Oh come on, it's not that bad. Look, we've been through Abergavenny . . ."

"Yes, thanks for that. Always wanted to sit in a traffic jam beside an abattoir when there's a cattle market on. Who wants to just sail round the bypass?"

". . . and we've done another twenty miles or so. I reckon that puts us about . . . *here.*" He stabbed decisively at the map. "Very close to a pub, as it happens."

"Don't even think about it."

"Just my little joke."

"Very little."

Laura changed gear pointedly and overtook a smoking Land Rover. Dan reached out and put a hand on her knee. She took a deep breath and made a conscious effort to be more tolerant. They were doing this because of her, a fact Dan was not above reminding her of with irritating frequency. She wanted him to want it, too, but that would take time. And patience. She was so bewitched by Penlan, so excited at the prospect of settling there, it was hard for her to deal with Dan's lack of enthusiasm. But it was up to her to win him over.

"Never mind," she said with a smile. "We'll soon be in our lovely new home, starting our lovely new life, on this lovely sunny day."

Dan forced a thin smile back.

"How . . ."

"Lovely?" Laura suggested. She grinned at him now and felt his hand work its way up her leg. She must not let him see how daunted she was beginning to feel. However much she wanted to start afresh in this wonderful place, she still harbored doubts and questions of her own. Suddenly, everything seemed very real and irreversible and daunting. She was tired and hot and fed up with driving, and completely flattened by the thought of all the unpacking and sorting that lay ahead of them. And under it all was the nagging dread that neither of them dared talk about. The continued longing. The rekindled hope. The aching wish for a child that might, just might, by some bucolic miracle, be granted. Or might not. She wouldn't let herself think about it. That was a tactic she had become pretty good at lately. There were plenty of other things to keep her occupied right now. Keeping busy was just about the only strategy for coping she knew of that actually worked.

"Turn left here," Dan told her.

"You sure?"

"Sure I'm sure. Left fork, up steep hill, over small bridge. This is it. I recognize it. A few more miles and we're there."

For once Dan's directions were accurate. They drove through the village and pulled up the hill, following a narrowing lane which seemed to twist back on itself every few yards. At last Penlan came into view. Laura and Dan fell silent as the place cast its spell over them once more. The low, white house nestled at the top of the meadows, its back against the hill that rose behind it, protecting it from the north winds. The slate roof shimmered under the late August sun. Honeysuckle twisted up over the front door, knitting its way across the wall, heavy with butter-yellow blooms. A barn and a short run of stables formed a farmyard, which had mostly been put down to grass. Foxgloves grew at will. Dog roses spilled from the hedges and tumbled over the Payne's grey of the stone walls.

Laura slowed the car as they skirted the oak woods before the final stretch of bumpy lane. Fractured light fell through the high

canopy of leaves, picking out lemon yellow celandines and glow-
ing violets on the dry forest floor. She felt tension and doubt melting away as she stopped the car in front of the house. She turned
to Dan, beaming.

"We're going to be happy here, Mr. Matthews. I feel it in my
bones."

Stepping out of the car she felt the strength of the sun on her
bare arms. They could not have chosen more glorious weather for
their first day at Penlan, and she knew this moment would be im-
printed on her memory forever. The thought of painting this
magical place excited her.

Dan fumbled with the chunky key in the old lock. At last it
worked, with a satisfying clunk, and the weathered door swung
open.

Laura squeezed past him, barely able to contain her excitement at crossing the threshold of their new home. Inside the house
was a blissful temperature, the dense walls successfully keeping
out the heat. It took a moment for her eyes to adjust to the low
level of light, so that the room revealed itself to her slowly, as if
in a dream. The front door opened directly into the living room,
which looked even bigger now without any furniture. She walked
over to the cavernous inglenook and ran her fingers along the
gnarled beam above it. There was still a smell of wood smoke, so
distinctive she could almost taste it. Kicking off her sandals, she
let the smooth flagstones refresh her tired feet. She wondered
about the person who had laid those stones, and the man who had
built the fireplace, and the one who had found the oak for the lintel, all those hundreds of years ago. The house had been dated as
being built in the thirteenth century, and Laura found endless

fascination at the thought of all the people who had lived there before her. So much time, so much history. So many lives, and loves, and losses. So many secrets, all stored in the fabric of the house, in the two-foot-thick stone walls, in the worn flags, in the charred fireplace. How many women had stood as she was, gazing into the hearth, wondering what life at Penlan held in store for her?

Behind her, Dan was flicking a light switch repeatedly.

"Ah," he said. "Seems we do not, as yet, have power." He went to the telephone on the floor in the corner of the room. "No, nothing here either. I thought this was all supposed to be working."

"I was told it would be."

"Did you check?" Dan wanted to know. "I mean, did you chase after them? You can't just expect people to do this sort of stuff. You have to keep on top of them."

"Like I said, I was told everything would be connected. If it was so important to you, why didn't you chase them?" Laura folded her arms defensively. Here he was, Mr. Organized, with a hangover, about to pick holes in everything she'd done.

"You were dealing with this sort of thing," Dan pointed out. "We agreed. You know it was impossible for me, being in the office."

"Oh yes, of course. Your job had you in an office, sitting right next to a telephone, but you couldn't possibly pick it up and call the estate agent, or the electric company. My work, on the other hand, could be interrupted anytime. It was the sales from my last two exhibitions that made this move possible. Wouldn't hurt you to admit that, you know."

"Seems only fair," he snapped. "As you were the one who wanted this so much."

Laura opened her mouth to speak but thought better of it.

Dan ran a hand through his hair with a sigh.

"OK, OK, let's not bicker. Let's just sort it out, shall we?" He looked at his watch, "Four thirty. I suppose someone might still be working, even on a Saturday." He took his mobile from his pocket and switched it on. "Great. No signal." He frowned at Laura, who stared back levelly. "Right," Dan said. "I'll drive back to the village and call from there. OK?"

"Fine. You do that."

She watched him go, biting her lip, cross with herself for getting short-tempered over nothing. She didn't want anything to spoil this special day. Taking a steadying breath, she decided to explore. She climbed the stone spiral stairs, which led up out of the sitting room. Upstairs was warmer, being in the roof, the windows set low. She had to walk slowly, ducking to avoid beams, not yet accustomed to the layout of the house. The main bedroom was light and roomy, with two south-facing windows and a small, working fireplace. Plenty of space for her beloved four-poster bed, so long as they positioned it in the center of the room, where the ceiling was highest. Laura wandered around, arranging furniture in her mind. As she reached the far side of the room, she sensed rather than saw a movement near the door. She turned, half expecting to see Dan standing behind her, but there was no one. No sound, no shadow, nothing, save for the persisting feeling that she was not alone. She found herself contemplating the strange experience with some detachment. She didn't feel scared, or even spooked, just quietly curious. She held her breath, standing as still as the house itself, waiting. Though for what she did not know.

Then, quite distinctly, she felt someone stroke her cheek. It was mad, impossible, ridiculous, but she was absolutely certain that was what it was. She raised her hand to her face and found a coolness, but nothing more. She had a second to wonder why she was not terrified before another sensation startled her. A scintilla of excitement, raw, real, sexual excitement, shot through her body. Laura gasped at both the strength and the unexpectedness of the feeling. She turned, searching the room, wanting to leave, and yet, at the same time, not wanting to. Then, as suddenly as it had started, the feeling went, and she knew she was alone again. She stood motionless, waiting for her ragged breathing to return to normal.

The sound of a blaring horn pulled her from her stupor. Looking out of the window, she saw Dan driving back up the hill toward the house, flashing his lights, the moving van growling up behind him. She realized she had lost all sense of how much time had passed since he went. She shook her head and hurried back down the stairs, putting the incident down to fatigue and the excitement of the move.

Four exhausting hours later, Laura sat on a heap of rugs, cushions, and throws in front of the inglenook and gazed into the dancing flames. They had pushed through the exhausting process of unloading of the van and crucial unpacking for as long as the light lasted. Then they had watched the men driving the empty lorry away, squeezing down the narrow lane. The thought of assembling beds was too much, and they opted instead for a night sleeping in front of the fire. Dan arrived at her side clutching wine and glasses. He sat down next to her.

"Voilà!" he said triumphantly, pulling a corkscrew from his pocket. He set about opening the bottle.

Laura snuggled into him. "How's this for a romantic first night?" she asked. "Crackling log fire . . ."

"Logs being an old chair you found in the barn."

". . . wine, finger food . . ."

"Two Mars bars and a packet of cheese and onion crisps"

". . . and animal skins to recline on. Well, OK, a picnic rug and a random selection of cushions. But, hey, how much perfection can a man stand?"

The idea of bedding down in front of a real fire had seemed lovely, but now Laura feared an uncomfortable night lay ahead. She took the glass Dan was offering her and downed a thirsty swig. Dan slipped his arm around her waist and they sat quietly together. Laura considered telling him about her strange experience in the bedroom earlier but decided against it. She knew it would sound silly and didn't feel like having him laugh at her. As the wine began to do its work she felt herself relaxing once more.

Dan put down his glass and began to rub Laura's shoulders. She closed her eyes, enjoying the soothing, sensual feel of his hands. He undid her hair and let it fall loose and heavy. He stroked the back of her neck softly, then pushed her T-shirt straps to one side, letting them fall. He kissed her tanned shoulders, moving slowly around until he was sitting in front of her. He took the wineglass from her hand and put it to one side, then leaned forward and kissed her throat, wandering slowly down toward her breasts as she let herself fall back against the cushions.

Laura lay passive, allowing herself to take pleasure from Dan's attentions. It seemed the right thing to do, to make love now, here, like an affirmation of their new life. A wordless statement of intent. Unbidden, her thoughts strayed to what she had experienced upstairs that afternoon. There was a world of difference between the comforting, familiar nature of her arousal now, and the powerful intensity of the mysterious sensations that had so surprised her earlier. The memory of it excited her, and she responded more eagerly to Dan, aware of a peculiar sense that she was in some way being unfaithful to him. Then pleasure took over, and all such thoughts vanished.

❦

THE FOLLOWING MORNING, Laura awoke soon after dawn, as light fell through the uncurtained windows. She slipped from beneath the throws, leaving Dan sleeping peacefully. She pulled on jeans and a T-shirt, stepped into her sandals, and went outside, shutting the door as quietly as she could.

The air was pure and still, and early sunshine sparkled on the heavy dew. In the valley sat cotton candy mist, and the distant hills stood softly, their edges blurred and colors muted by the moist air. Swallows and house martins swooped and dipped, hungry for their breakfasts, catching the first rise of insects of the day. The honeysuckle and roses had not yet warmed to release their scent, so the strongest smell was of wet grass and bracken. Laura smiled, breathing deeply, and walked lightly through the gate into the meadows. She hadn't the courage to head off onto the mountain on her own just yet but could not wait to explore the woods at the end of the fields. By the time she reached the first towering oaks, her feet were washed clean by the dew. She felt wonderfully refreshed and awake. As she wandered among the trees she had the sense of a place where time had stood still. Where man had left only a light footprint. Here were trees older than memory. Trees that had sheltered farmers and walkers for generations. Trees that had been meeting points for lovers and horse dealers. Trees that had provided fuel and food for families and for creatures of the forest with equal grace. As she walked deeper into the woods she noticed the quality of sound around her change. Gone were the open vistas and echoes of the meadows and their mountain backdrop. Here even the tiniest noises were close up, bouncing back off the trunks and branches, kept in by the dense foliage. The colors altered subtly, too. With the trees in full leaf the sunlight was filtered through bright green, giving a curious tinge to the woodland below. White wood anemones were not white at all, but the palest shade of Naples yellow. The silver lichens which grew in abundance bore a hint of olive. Even the miniature violets reflected a suggestion of viridian.

Laura followed a narrow, meandering sheep track. Passing through a sunny glade she was surprised to find the ground muddied and churned. Looking closer she could clearly make out the tracks of a small-wheeled vehicle.

Who would be driving around in here?

Her silent question was soon answered, as the peace was broken by the roar of an approaching engine. She was suddenly conscious of the fact that this was not her land. She had no idea where the public footpaths might be, if indeed there were any. She thought of disappearing into the undergrowth, but within seconds a quad bike sped into view. Its driver slewed the ugly machine to a halt in front of her. A sheepdog with a matted coat kept its precarious grip on the back of the bike.

Laura felt wrong-footed at being discovered somewhere she had no business being. She had intended to talk to the local farmers and ask permission to walk on the land near Penlan. She did not want to upset her neighbors on day one. She put on a sunny smile.

"Good morning," she said brightly, raising her voice above the noise of the engine.

The man on the quad stared hard at her. He was small and wiry and, Laura reckoned, would not see seventy again. His scrawny face jutted out beneath a grubby flat cap. Despite the time of year he wore a heavy tweed jacket, tied around the middle with baler twine. His hands were as gnarled and wrinkled as the roots of the trees around them.

Laura tried again.

"It's a beautiful day, isn't it? I couldn't resist exploring. Sorry if I'm on your land." Still he did not answer, so she added, "We've just moved in up at Penlan."

The man's face twitched slightly. He leaned forward and switched off his engine. The peace of the woodland was even more noticeable now. Laura stepped forward, hand outstretched.

"I'm Laura Matthews."

The man stared at her hand, then cleared his throat with a stomach-churning gurgle and spat at the ground, thankfully on the other side of his quad bike from where she stood. She dropped her hand awkwardly. He frowned at her, and when at last he spoke his voice was as thin and spindly as the man himself.

"There aren't any footpaths through these woods," he informed her.

"Oh. I see. I haven't studied the map yet." She was beginning to feel cross now. There was no need for him to be so rude. She had hoped for friendly locals. This was far from what she had imagined.

The man looked around, then turned back to her.

"'Ave you got a dog? I see a dog near my sheep, I shoot it. I'm tellin' you now."

"No. I don't have a dog."

The old man stared at her again, then turned on his engine once more. He nodded toward the fields.

"There's a path across the top of the meadows. You can walk there. Without a dog," he said, then tore off into the woods, sending up dust and twigs and stones in his wake.

Laura watched him go, not moving until he was out of sight and the noise of the quad was fading into the distance. The mood of her walk was ruined. Still seething at his unnecessary rudeness, she turned and strode off in the direction of home. As she did so her swinging hand grazed against the bark of an enormous, slanting oak.

"Ow!" she cried, instinctively sucking at her knuckles. When she checked the wound, it was bleeding quite heavily, as knuckles can. "Damn," she said, fighting back stinging tears. She glanced up at the tree, barely noticing the curious angle at which it stood. Cursing herself for her carelessness, and her new neighbor for his rudeness, she headed for home.

⤳❧⤲

Megan leaned back against her favorite oak, gazing up at the sky through its sloping boughs. She closed her eyes and listened to the birdsong and the laughter of the two boys as they played nearby. It was wonderful to be out of the dark castle, to have some time away from Lady Rhiannon, and to be well out of the way of Lord Geraint. She opened her eyes and scanned the trees for the children. She always enjoyed spending time with them without their parents. Watching them now she could almost forget what family they belonged to.

"Don't go too near to the edge," she warned as they dropped sticks into the stream. It would be a rare outing where at least one of them did not get wet or muddy or both. Out here, in the woods where she herself had played as a child, they weren't the sons of the most powerful noble in the region, they were just two little boys having fun the way all little boys should. Megan stepped away from the oak, brushing down her long skirts, seeing that the hem had collected moss as green and as soft as the worn wool of her dress. She noticed wild garlic growing a few paces away. She stooped to study it closer. A good garlic plant was a valuable part of her herb store; the stronger the specimen, the better its calming and cleaning effects on the blood. No doubt her father would have need of it for one of his animals soon enough. As she bent forward her waist-length plait of copper red hair fell over her shoulder. She flicked it back absentmindedly. People often commented on her glorious hair, but to her it was only important as a reminder of the mother she had lost when only a small girl.

The wistful way her father looked at it sometimes tore at her heart. Not for the first time she wished that one day she could know a love like that.

Megan walked across the dry woodland floor to where Dafydd stood holding the horses. He, too, seemed to enjoy these outings, and he looked relaxed and happy leaning against his bay mare, watching the children. He straightened up as Megan approached. She would never get used to people reacting like that to her. Her position in the household was, technically, superior to his, but she could not think of herself that way. Besides, to her mind, his job was wonderful. If she had been born a boy she would have spent her life with horses, as her father had done. She smiled at Dafydd, taking the reins of her palfrey from him. The old courser was plain and brown and unremarkable, but had a good nature and a willing heart. She patted its neck.

"Now, Hazel, how about a quick trip across the meadows to pay Father a visit?" She raised her eyebrows at Dafydd as she spoke to the animal, not asking his permission, but seeking his agreement.

"Right you are, Mistress Megan," he said with a nod as he set about tightening girths.

"Huw! Brychan! Come, now, boys. It is time to leave," she called to her charges, who ran to her, giggling, and climbed aboard their patiently waiting ponies.

In moments they were out of the shade of the woods and under the strong summer sun. Megan let Hazel plod slowly across the fields, both of them savoring the warmth and peace of the moment. Now she could see Penlan, the low white farmhouse that had been her childhood home. The sound of ax on wood echoed around them, and she could soon make out her father in the yard, chopping and stacking fuel for the coming winter. As if sensing her approach, he stopped his work and raised a hand to shield his eyes from the sun, as he looked toward the meadows. Megan waved, and the boys kicked their ponies into bumpy trots.

"Well, well, well, who are these two fine knights I see charging toward me? Why, it is young Master Brychan and Master Huw!" Twm laughed as the boys came to untidy halts beside him. "I feared for a moment I might be under attack."

The children jumped down and hugged the old man, having grown close to him during their visits with Megan.

"Can we go and search for eggs, please, sir, can we?" asked Brychan, his younger brother clamoring behind him.

"You'd best ask Megan about that," Twm told them.

Megan nodded.

"Go on then, run along," said Twm. "But don't go finding fleas' nests and mice, mind, or you'll have us all in trouble."

As she watched him with the boys Megan thought how much he must have longed for a son of his own. It still warmed her heart that he had shown no disappointment at his only child being a girl, and that he had treated her with no less love and respect than he might have shown her brother, had she had one. Megan slipped lightly from the saddle and embraced her father. She was never more homesick than when he held her close and tight, as he had done for so many years, being all the family she had.

"Let's look at you," her father demanded, holding her at arm's length again. "As I thought, paler and thinner than last time. Is Lord Geraint short of food this summer? I've a barn full of corn."

"Which you would rather burn than give to anyone but your precious horses, Father."

"True enough. Ah well, come inside and have a bowl of cawl at least. Will you join us, Dafydd?"

"Thank you, no, Twm. I shall stay with the horses."

"As you will. Now, daughter, while you eat I shall tell you of my bay colt. You have never seen such a fine animal in your life," he said as he led her indoors. "Though the silly creature tore his stifle on a briar. The wound is healing, but I fear the scar will be a bargaining point for a buyer come next spring. But I'll wager you can work your magic on him for me."

The thick walls of the old house kept the rooms wonderfully cool in the summer heat. Megan was always impressed at how clean and tidy her father kept his home, and a pot of cawl was always ready, hanging above the fire in the broad, low fireplace. He had had to be father and mother to her, and he had taken to his tasks with determination, seeking perfection in everything he did. Now, as an adult, she realized how hard her mother's death had been for him, understood the enormity of his loss. The love that her parents had shared had been a beacon of light for her in a dark and dangerous world. She wondered if she would ever have the chance to find such a love herself. As her father talked excitedly about the latest young horse he had bred, Megan saw the years fall away from his face and the lingering sadness lift a little. She owed him everything—her resourcefulness, her skills as a horsewoman, her knowledge of medicinal herbs, as well as her undeniable stubbornness. Leaving him to take up her position at Castle Craig had been hard, but she had, in truth, had no choice in the matter. When Lord Geraint took an idea into his head it was not wise to go against him. It was he who, while inspecting a new courser one day at her father's home, had seen Megan and suggested she would make a good nursemaid for his young sons. Lord Geraint was not only the most powerful noble for many miles, he was Twm's landlord, and as such held great power over him. Twm had no sons to inherit the tenancy, but it was his wish, and Megan's, that she be allowed to take it on, with her husband, should she be married by then. It was her dearest hope that she would one day be permitted to return to her true home and breed and train horses as her father had done. But she recognized this could only happen with their landlord's goodwill, and she was worldly enough to see the precarious position in which her employer's interest placed her. In the meanwhile, Twm paid his rent promptly and gave his landlord first pick of his best mounts, at a reduced price, naturally. Almost two years had passed since Megan had moved to Castle Craig. She had grown up quickly and had learned that her wits were all that stood between her and Lord Geraint's baser desires.

As if the thought of the man had summoned him, the sound of approaching horses jolted Megan and her father from their precious moment together. Twm squinted out of the window.

"Riders. It is Lord Geraint."

They hurried outside. The sunlight seemed harsh now, its glare illuminating Megan, leaving her no place to hide her awkwardness at being found visiting when she should be taking the children home.

Dafydd struggled to hold the horses and ponies as the entourage thundered into the little yard. Lord Geraint had been out hawking, and the mounts in his party were slick with sweat. They made a spectacular sight, a sudden carnival of color, jangling tack, and regal birds. He reined in his destrier a few feet from where Megan stood. He rode one of his favorites, Midnight, a colossal black stallion with arched neck and flowing mane. This was a mount built for speed and endurance, trained for sport and battle. It fidgeted as it stood, restless, ready to be off, listening for the slightest signal from its master. As it tossed its head foam from its mouth flecked Megan's dress. She made no move to wipe it away but stayed still, waiting for Lord Geraint's reaction to finding her there. He gazed down at her, a small smile playing on his lips, enjoying her discomfort. Even now, at his sport, he looked every inch the nobleman. His clothes were of the finest leather and wool. The saddle on which he sat so proudly and at ease would have taken a year to make and cost more than Megan's father would earn in twice that time. The hawk on his gauntlet was one of a number kept for his amusement and trained to kill. He held out his arm and an aide took the bird from him. He shifted in his saddle, leaning back, reins in one hand, relaxed, taking no notice of the nervousness of his horse.

"Megan, I must say I am surprised to find you here. I understood you were taking my sons out riding. But then, you must have gained permission for your visit from Lady Rhiannon, am I right?"

Megan kept her voice level. "No, my Lord. That is, I did not think to ask for permission."

"Oh. Is that so? Then you thought it of no account where you wandered with my children in your charge."

"I would not have brought them here had I believed this to be in any way against their best interests, my Lord. We were pass-ing on our return journey."

"Indeed?" Lord Geraint dropped the reins and swung his leg forward, springing down from Midnight's back with casual ease. He stepped forward until he was close enough to Megan for her to feel his breath on her face as he spoke. Although she was tall he loomed above her. She stood firm but lowered her eyes, not wishing to provoke him further.

"Have a care, my dear Megan. Liberties taken may one day have to be paid for," he said. He placed a finger beneath her chin and tipped her face up. Now she looked at him, her defiance visi-ble to no one else but clear to him.

Megan held her breath, letting the silence between them be her only answer. At that moment the children came running from the barn.

"Father! Father!" they cried as they ran to him.

His harsh features softened as he smiled down at them and ruffled their hair. "Ahh, my little princes, what have you been about?"

"We've been searching for eggs, Father, look," said little Huw, holding out his finds.

"And there are swallows nesting in the roof. I climbed up to see them," said Brychan.

"Did you now? Such courage deserves a reward, wouldn't you say?" With that he swung the boy onto his saddle and sprang up behind him. Brychan's face lit up with pleasure and excitement. Huw backed away as his father's horse began to prance.

"Don't look so disapproving, Megan. A son may ride with his father, may he not?" And with that, one arm clutched around the boy, he wheeled his horse around, dug his spurs into its flanks, and galloped away, his men charging after him.

Megan looked down at Huw, whose scowl and brimming tears gave away his hurt and jealousy. This was not the first time he had been overlooked by his father. Megan was certain the favoritism shown for his older brother would one day cause a serious rift between the boys.

Twm stepped forward and patted the boy on the shoulder.

"'Tis a pity your brother could not stay longer," he said. "For I was just about to tell you of the kittens born in the woodshed last week."

Huw's face was transformed. "Kittens!" he breathed.

Megan watched them cross the yard together, trying to put from her mind the man who would be waiting for her back at Castle Craig.

2

MEGAN HURRIED ALONG the narrow passageway that led through the back of the castle and up the winding staircase toward the solar, which was Lady Rhiannon's bedchamber. The candle she carried spluttered as she walked, caught in thin drafts from the narrow window in the north wall and the glassless loopholes in the stairwell. The castle had been built for strength and security, and there were few spaces within it that afforded comfort. The hour was late, and Megan had the sense she was the only person moving around the castle on this moonless night. She reached the top of the stairs and paused for a moment outside the ornately carved door. She could hear low laughter from inside the room. She knocked and the door was opened by a lady's maid. Megan hesitated on the threshold, letting her eyes adjust to the further gloom. Candles and lanterns illuminated corners and decorative features, but the overall effect was one of dancing shadows and low light. A fresh layer of herbs had been strewn over the floor. In the center of the room was a magnificent bed, its four posts draped with elaborate tapestries and trimmings. More laughter drifted out from the curtains, which were half drawn around it. The maid stepped forward and informed her mistress of Megan's presence.

"Ah, is she here at last? Come closer, Megan. I wish to talk to you." Lady Rhiannon's voice had a sharpness about it that was not softened even now.

Megan did as she was told. As she neared the bed, she was shocked to find her mistress was not alone. Lady Rhiannon reclined against a broad-shouldered young soldier. Both of them were naked, and their skin glistened with sweat. Megan recognized the youth as one of Lord Geraint's soldiers. He seemed completely at ease with the situation, stroking Lady Rhiannon's hair as he cradled her head on his chest. In his other hand he held a goblet of wine, which he drank from deeply before putting it gently to his lover's lips.

Lady Rhiannon sipped, then smiled. "Llewelyn, darling, you see to my every need," she cooed, stroking his face, seeming to forget Megan's existence.

Megan could do nothing but stand and wait. She fixed her gaze on a detail of the tapestry behind Llewelyn and tried hard to ignore the unmissable smell of sex. At last Lady Rhiannon dragged her attention away from her lover.

"I hear you visited your father yesterday. Is this true?"

"Yes, my Lady."

"Lord Geraint mentioned it before he was called away for a few days." Still she ran her fingers along Llewelyn's arm as she spoke, not bothering to look at Megan. "Don't be frightened, girl—I care not where you take my boys for their riding, so long as you bring them back safe to me. Nor have I the slightest interest in your family. No, it is in another matter that I believe you might be of use to me. I have heard that there is a stranger recently moved in to the croft above your father's house. What news does your father have of this man?"

"Why, none, my Lady."

"He has not seen him?"

"He did not mention it. Our conversation was short."

With an irritated sigh, Lady Rhiannon sat up and beckoned her maid. She slipped a silk robe around her shoulders and stepped from the bed. Behind her Llewelyn made no effort to cover himself up. Megan blushed at the sight of his nakedness and his obvious state of arousal. Lady Rhiannon saw her uneasiness but put a hand on her arm to prevent her turning away.

"I have not dismissed you," she told her, wine and sexual languor slowing her words but not lessening their force. Lady Rhiannon was at least ten years Megan's senior, but was still a strikingly beautiful woman. They differed from each other in so many ways. Lady Rhiannon was womanly and curvaceous, Megan was lean and angular. Her features were strong and stern, Megan's were fine and delicate. Her hair was a black, straight veil, whereas Megan's was a cascade of red waves. And her nature was cruel while Megan's was compassionate.

Megan knew they were amusing themselves at her own expense, but there was little she could do about it.

"He is beautiful, don't you agree?" Lady Rhiannon teased.

She looked at the floor, struggling for an answer.

"Why don't you look at him, girl? Look at him!" the older woman snapped.

Megan raised her head and kept her face impassive as she was

forced to look at Llewelyn. To her shame she felt sensations of excitement and arousal stirring inside her. She fought to think of
other things, to at least place her mind in some other, better place.
Lady Rhiannon stood behind her now, her hands firmly on her
shoulders, banishing all chance of escape.

"I want you to do something for me, Megan. I want you to
go back and visit your father once more. Ask him about the
stranger. I have information that he is the seer Merlin. I wish to
have this verified, and your father can do this for me. Discreetly,
do you understand? No doubt my husband will have his own spies
out the moment he returns and hears the news. However, I wish
to conduct my own inquiries. Naturally, this is a private matter,
and Lord Geraint does not need to be informed of my interest. It
would be best you do as I bid before his return the day after tomorrow." She leaned closer now, her voice a wine-fumed whisper
uncomfortably close to Megan's ear. "Fail me in this, and you may
not see your father again until the spring."

Megan opened her mouth to speak, but her mistress waved a
hand in dismissal as she turned her attention back to her lover.
Megan needed no further bidding, and hurried from the room.

❦

LAURA BRUSHED HER hair from her face with her forearm.
Her brow was damp with sweat, and she felt the grittiness of dirt
rub over her skin. She straightened up and contemplated what
progress she had made. The barn attached to the house had
not been used for years. She and Dan had spent all the previous
day clearing out ancient, rotting hay, broken bits of furniture,

and rusting farm implements. Hours of toil had at last produced a clear space. Now, after a further morning's work, she could begin to see her new studio taking shape. There was no floor in the upper part of the building, so the room was open to the roof. The rafters at the rear still retained old Welsh slate, but the front half had been replaced with see-through corrugated plastic. While un-attractive, this did at least allow in plenty of light, making the barn the obvious place in which Laura could paint. It had been weeks since she had sat before a canvas, and she was impatient to start again. Laura had always painted and always known that was what she wanted to do with her life. She only ever felt truly her-self when she was creating new images. And now that pictures seemed to be the only thing she would ever be capable of creat-ing, they had become even more important to her. Too much time away from her art and she began to feel maudlin, restless, and unfulfilled. Even now, just the sight of her canvasses stacked against the wall cheered her. She could scarcely contain her ex-citement at the thought of squeezing out fresh paint onto her pal-ette once again. She stepped over to one of the crates containing her artist's materials. She pulled out a bottle of turpentine, run-ning her thumb across the label. A dried smudge of ultramarine reminded her of her last picture. She leaned forward and sniffed the bottle and the smell took her to another place, another state of mind, where reality was what she created with her own skills and imagination.

"Hmm, sniffing toxic substances, eh?" Dan came to stand be-side her. "Surely that's a city habit? You'll have to find some other vice now we're out here in the boondocks. Magic mushrooms, per-haps, freshly picked."

"I can't wait to get painting. It's going to take a while to get rid of all the dust in here, though. I might try doing some work outside while the weather's good."

"Maybe you could just incorporate dust and bits of hay into your next batch of paintings."

"Oh, very bucolic. Not quite what I had in mind, though." She paced about, picking up a broom and sweeping ineffectually at the floor. "These cobbles are beautiful but not very practical. Setting up an easel is going to be a challenge."

"Don't get too settled in. We'll have to have some fairly major work done before winter, or you'll freeze to your paintbrushes out here. God knows where one finds a reliable builder in these parts."

"I'll start asking around. There's bound to be someone local. But I don't want them to change it. I love it just the way it is, dust and all."

"OK, you can keep the 'authentic features,' but you will need more than one lightbulb. And some heating. Not to mention a sink, water, doors, that sort of stuff. Probably cost a fortune. Sure you wouldn't rather take up flower arranging and work in the kitchen?"

"Dan, you have the soul of an accountant. Don't worry. It won't cost much. Besides, it'll be an investment. I'm going to do my best work here. I can feel it. My next exhibition is going to blow people's minds, you wait and see." She smiled at him and could see her own excitement and happiness reflected in his face as he watched her.

He stepped forward and put his arms around her, nuzzling into her neck. "Mmm, you smell deliciously warm and . . ."

". . . grimy?"

"I was going to say dirty, but I thought I might get my face slapped." He kissed her forehead gently then looked at her levelly, his face serious.

"Don't look so worried," Laura said. "We are going to be happy here, you know that, don't you? Whatever happens, whatever *doesn't* happen, you and me . . . this is going to be good for both of us, yes?"

Dan nodded, "Of course," he said. "Come on," he took her hand and pulled her toward the doorway, "let's go for a walk together."

"What, now?"

"Yes, now."

"But Dan, we haven't finished here yet. I want to get everything set up."

"Just a couple of hours, come on. It's a gorgeous day, we've views waiting for us that come straight out of *National Geographic.* If I'm going to live halfway up a bloody mountain I have to at least have a go at walking on the thing. We've been here four days and we haven't so much as trodden in sheep shit yet. I've got to go back to work on Monday. What am I supposed to say to everyone in the office when they ask me how much yomping I've done?"

"I don't think it's actually called yomping."

"Whatever. Let's get on with it. I know what you're like. Once you get dug into your studio, such as it is, I'll never get you out. You can hole up in here once I'm back in London. OK?"

Laura smiled, glad Dan was at least trying to show enthusiasm for something their new home had to offer, and keen to encourage him.

"OK, but wait a minute. I'm not going without my sketchbook."

She rootled through a box and pulled out a small, leather shoulder bag. She checked there were plenty of pages left in the block inside, slipped some fresh charcoal and another pencil into the front pocket, and slung the bag over her shoulder. She and Dan were both equipped with all-terrain sandals. The weather continued to be reliably hot, and they had both quickly become accustomed to wearing shorts and T-shirts. Dan fetched a hiker's plastic container of water, which he clipped to his belt. They didn't bother to lock up the house before setting off, so complete was the illusion that there was nobody else for twenty miles around. They climbed the bank behind the house following the footpath signposted. Within moments they were through the boundary gate and onto open hill. The bracken was fully grown now, chest high, forcing them to stick to a narrow sheep track that traversed the hill. After twenty minutes' steady walking, they broke free of the ferns and found themselves on short springy grass. Farther on low whinberry bushes jostled for space with tough heathers. The sun was high and hot, and Laura realized she should have grabbed her hat before they left. She stopped, turning to take in the vista that stretched out for twenty miles below them. Dan let out a low whistle.

"Wow," he said. "Just bloody wow."

Laura's mind was already racing with the creative possibilities presented to her. She whipped out her sketchbook and started to work away with a stump of charcoal, trying to capture the sweep of the hills and the patterns made by the blocks of light and dark. She half closed her eyes, the better to appreciate the variations in tone and depth. She was astonished to find just how brash and vivid and wonderfully discordant colors in nature could be. At this time of year there was no sense that things were attempting to blend or mingle or go unseen. Every tree, bush, and flower seemed to be shouting out its presence, each one louder than the next. On the lower slopes the leaves of the aged oak trees sang out, gleaming in the heat. On every hill bracken screamed in solid swathes of viridian. At Laura's feet the plum purple and dark green leaves of the whinberry bushes competed for attention with their own indigo berries. The kitsch mauve of the heather laughed at all notions of subtlety. She turned to a fresh page and began to make quick notes, ideas for a future palette and thoughts about compositions. She jotted down plans for color mixes and drew the voluptuous curve of the hills and the soft shape of the whinberry leaves. Above the cacophonous colors rose the constant, sweet whirring of the skylarks. Laura had to shut her eyes for a moment to enjoy the birdsong without the distraction of the view.

"Look down there," said Dan. "That must be the nearest cottage to us."

She opened her eyes and squinted into the high end of the valley where Dan was pointing. Set close to a shallow stream, amid larch, silver birch, and rowan trees, sat a small stone croft. Even its roof was of stone, so that it looked almost as if it had been chiseled from the rock of the hill itself. Three black hens pecked about. A man stepped out of the cottage and into the sunlight. Even from so far away, Laura could see he was tall and lean. He picked up a hoe and began to work at the dry soil in the garden, moving with light, easy actions.

"And that must be our new neighbor," said Dan. "Wonder who he is? No sign of anybody else with him. And no road to the place. Must be a bit of an oddball, living all the way up here on his own."

As Laura watched, the man suddenly stopped and turned, looking in her direction, as if sensing that he was being observed. Although she knew the distance made it impossible, she felt as if he were looking straight into her eyes. Her pulse quickened and she became strangely disturbed by his gaze. Beside her, Dan waved. The man paused, then raised his hand slowly, the gesture somehow solemn, not the lighthearted greeting Dan had given.

"Right, let's press on. I want to get to the top of that ridge over there before you start fretting about your studio and nag me to go back." Dan leaned into the hill and walked on.

Laura lingered, finding it hard, for reasons she did not understand, to pull herself away from this curious connection with the solitary stranger.

⤞✦⤝

By six o'clock the next morning Dan was in his best suit and ready to leave. He stood in front of Laura.

"How do I look?"

"Like a supersharp businessman no cutting-edge charity could afford to do without." She brushed a speck of dust from his lapel as she spoke. She was not yet dressed and felt Dan's hand slipping beneath her kimono. "Now, now," she chided him with a smile. "This is not your usual commute. You've got the better part of three hours' driving ahead of you. Save your energy." She gave him an affectionate kiss.

He turned to leave and then hesitated.

"You will be all right here? On your own, I mean."

"I'll be fine."

"Sure?"

"Yes! I can't wait for a bit of peace so I can paint, so will you please bugger off?"

"I'll phone you when I get there."

"Fine. Good. See you Friday night. And don't go getting too used to your part-time bachelor existence—this is only temporary, remember?"

"I'm sure you won't let me forget." He kissed her again. "Bye then." He turned and hurried on his way.

Laura could tell by the set of his shoulders and his purposeful step as he walked to the car that already his mind was focusing on work. It would be good for him to get back to the office and be involved in doing what he did best. It would be good for both of them. All the same, it would be hard. They were not used to being apart, and although a part of her was thrilled at the prospect of peaceful painting time, uninterrupted by someone else's needs, she knew she would miss him. Still, it was, as she had reminded him, a temporary solution. A price worth paying in the long run.

She watched him go, then went to take a shower. They were still waiting for the telephone to be connected, but at least they now had electricity. The small en suite alongside the main bedroom was simply but prettily decorated with crisp white walls and powder blue woodwork. The rough, painted stonework and lathe and plaster did not allow for much in the way of tiles, but the shower itself was lined with an attractive mix of plain and patterned ones showing tiny harebells.

Laura turned on the water, slipped out of her robe, and stepped beneath the warm cascade, sighing as the water soaked her hair until it was heavy, then letting it course over her sleepy skin. She thought of how early residents of Penlan would have had to fetch water from the spring, and would no doubt have been horrified at such reckless use of it. She smoothed a light shower gel over her skin, breathing in the smell of neroli as she enjoyed the caress of the water. A sound, or rather, the *sense* of a sound, made her start. She looked around, but the room was empty, save for herself. She listened, waiting, but heard nothing more. Then, once again, she had a powerful impression that she was no longer alone. Her whole body tensed, alert, nervous, unsure of what might come next. Before she could move or react further, she felt again the overwhelming excitement she had experienced the day they arrived at the house. This time, Laura felt unnerved by the sensation. She switched off the shower, grabbed a towel, and walked quickly into the bedroom. Still the feeling persisted, as if some unseen lover were accessing the very core of her being, arousing her without her consent. She fought conflicting emotions— one telling her to run, the other wanting to stay and experience more. Then, as suddenly as it had started, the experience stopped, and Laura knew she was alone again. She stood waiting for her breathing to steady before slipping into a simple sundress. She let her wet hair hang loose about her shoulders and went barefoot downstairs.

"Laura Matthews," she told herself as she entered the living room, "you are letting your imagination run riot here. Get a grip." She allowed herself to consider the possibility that such an old house might be haunted but quickly dismissed the idea. She had

never been remotely sensitive to such things. A more likely explanation, she felt sure, was a mixture of erratic hormones and the
emotional disturbance involved in moving. Not to mention the
unspoken hope and expectation which she was still refusing to
allow herself to think about. Even so, a small part of her believed
it would not be unreasonable for such an old house, a house that
had been home to so many people, to have at least a memory of
those people still alive within it.

She set her mind to painting again and headed for her studio,
pulling open the heavy front door of the house. The sight of someone standing in the doorway was so unexpected she gave an involuntary shout.

"Oh! God, you startled me."

Laura recognized her visitor instantly as the man from the
croft. Up close he was indeed tall and lean. His hair was raven
black and fell almost to his shoulders. His face was strong and
angular with a naturally stern expression, but it was his eyes that
were the most remarkable thing about him. Laura had seen blue
eyes on a dark-haired person before, but not like these. She tried
to imagine how she would capture the color on canvas. Ultramarine with a dash of zinc white? Cerulean blue? She was so absorbed she barely noticed the lengthy silence between them. At
last she realized she was staring at him and looked away.

When he spoke his voice was softer than she had expected.

"Hi," he said with a sinfully attractive smile. "I'm Rhys, from
a little way up the hill. Just thought I'd come and introduce
myself, and welcome you to our magical valley," he said.

"Laura Matthews," she said. "Laura." She found herself smiling back. There was something catching about the casual confi-

dence this man exuded. "We are neighbors, then," she said. Now
she became aware of the fact that Rhys was staring at her, openly
appraising her. She felt a little vulnerable under his gaze, all
freshly showered and barefoot. "Would you like a cup of tea?" she
heard herself ask. It sounded a ridiculously polite and formal thing
to say. To cover her embarrassment, she turned and walked to the
kitchen, leaving the door open. The kitchen was comfortably
equipped but otherwise had changed little for centuries. The original flagstones provided an uneven but practical floor. The low
ceiling was supported by heavy beams and joists of oak cut from
the nearby woods generations ago. On the wooden lintel above
the window in the far wall, lovers' initials had been carved inside
a heart and worn into the wood over hundreds of years. The cen-
terpiece of the room was an antique wooden table, a proud find at
an auction shortly before the move to Wales. The green Aga stove
stood gleaming, waiting for winter, when it would be the warm
heart of the home.

Rhys followed her. "You've settled in quickly by the look of it.
Good for you. I'm sure you're going to love it here."

From the corner of her eye she watched him as she fixed the
tea. He looked around the room, taking in every detail. At first
she thought he was simply admiring the old place, then it dawned
on her that he was looking with the eyes of someone familiar with
his surroundings. Someone remembering. It made sense. After all,
he was a neighbor.

"Did you know the people who had the place before us?" she
asked.

He shook his head slowly. "No. But I do know this house. I
have been here before. Many times."

"We love it. Still can't believe it's ours."

"Do you believe a person can own a place? Have you never considered it might work the other way around?" he asked.

Laura was not sure how to respond. It seemed such a strange question. She wondered for a moment if he might be a Welsh Nationalist harboring resentment for yet another English home buyer. But somehow that didn't fit.

"Well," she said, holding out a mug. "We shall see, won't we?"

He stepped forward to take the tea, standing very close.

"The people who had the house before you only used it for holidays, you know? They never really fitted in. I've a feeling you will."

As Rhys took the teacup from her his fingers brushed her hand. She took a step backward and turned away, pretending to search for a spoon.

"Sugar?" she asked, feeling strangely unsettled.

When she turned back again Rhys had moved away and was leaning against the Aga.

"No, it's fine like this. Thank you," he said, sipping his tea. Then he met her gaze and smiled again, another irresistible smile which transformed his naturally rather stern features.

She relaxed a little, making a mental note to register with the local doctor so she could get her unpredictable hormones reined in. She had suffered from bouts of disturbing premenstrual tension for years, a fact every consultant had reminded her of during her quest for a child. It was quite probable that the change in her life circumstances now had knocked things out of kilter once more.

"So," she said, making a concerted attempt to behave sensibly. "Have you lived here long? You have a gorgeous little cottage up there. And a garden, too. Don't suppose we'll ever get around to planting much more than a few bulbs ourselves."

"This has been my home for a long time," said Rhys. "And I garden because I like to eat what I grow, and sometimes I sell stuff. I'll bring you some vegetables. Next time."

"Thank you. I'd like that."

"Has your husband gone to work? I saw the car leaving."

"Oh, yes. Back to London, I'm afraid." Even as the words left her mouth she wondered at the wisdom of telling this stranger that she would be alone in the house. She told herself this was not London. Rhys was a neighbor, someone she would be able to trust. "He works as an accountant in the fund-raising department of a charity," she told him. "Water Wings, it's called. Flies irrigation equipment and wells to all sorts of places."

"And you? What do you do, Laura?"

There was something about the way he spoke her name that made the skin at the top of her spine tingle.

"I paint."

He nodded, as if this was what he might have expected.

"You'll have an abundance of subjects here," he said. "The mountains have a hundred moods. I'm sure they will inspire you. I hope you will show me what you paint one day. I'm no expert, of course, but I think you can tell a great deal about a person from how they channel their creativity. Would you let me see them sometime?"

"Yes, if you like," she said with a nod, still finding it hard not to stare at him. A thought occurred to her. Rhys must have been the figure she saw the day they came to view the property. She wondered if he had seen her, too. She was about to ask him where his dog was when he abruptly downed his tea and handed her back the cup.

"Look, I've taken up enough of your time," he said. "I just wanted to say hello. Please feel free to call on me if you need help with that garden of yours. I'd be happy to lend a hand." He paused as he stepped past her. "I'm sure this is the right place for you," he told her. "You have come home." And then he was gone, leaving her wondering at his strange parting remark.

When Dan telephoned later that morning, Laura allowed him to tell her about his journey in some detail before she mentioned their visitor.

"Very neighborly of him," said Dan. Laura could hear office chatter behind him and was a little disappointed he hadn't sought some privacy for his call to her.

"He said he'd give us some of his homegrown veg next time," she went on.

"There you are, exactly the sort of thing you wanted to move out there for. Friendly locals and real food."

"Yes, I thought I'd walk down to the village later. Might meet a few more people on the way."

"What? Sorry, my love, didn't catch that. Someone bending my ear this end. What did you say?"

"Nothing important." She listened to him telling his PA to hold another call.

"There," he said. "Sorry about that. You know what it can be like here. You have my undivided attention now, promise."

She thought for a moment, then decided to speak, "I noticed something a bit odd upstairs today."

"Oh?"

"I can't say exactly what it was. It's hard to explain. For a minute I thought there was someone in the house."

"A burglar?"

"No, no. Just . . . a presence."

"A ghost, you mean?"

Laura shook her head, as much to emphasize the point to herself as anything else. "Good grief, no. Oh I don't know. It was nothing, forget it. It sounds silly now."

"Was it frightening?" Dan asked.

She was touched that his first thought was not to make fun of her, but to be sure that she was OK.

"No, it wasn't scary. Just overactive hormones and artistic imagination, I expect."

"OK. If you say so," he said. "You're not getting spooked by the place, out there on your own?"

"No, no. I told you, it wasn't scary. It was nothing. Forget it."

Laura wasn't sure what had made her share what she had felt with Dan. She didn't want him thinking she wasn't going to be able to cope by herself. Even so, a small part of her wished he hadn't been quite so quick to take the thing seriously. She was doing her best to dismiss the whole experience as fanciful nonsense; the last thing she needed was Dan suggesting ghosts as if he believed such an idea possible.

❧

ON THURSDAY LAURA collected her mother from the station for a short stay. Annabel prattled on about the journey and the heat and the revolting state of the toilets on the train while Laura drove. She had been dreading her mother's first visit, knowing she would be defending their new house and new lifestyle all weekend. As her mother rambled on, Laura found her mind wandering back to Rhys. She had seen no more of him and yet had found it hard to get him out of her head. It was only after he had left that she realized she knew nothing about him at all. She seemed to have talked about herself without a second thought, while he had given little away. She didn't even know how he earned his living. Or if he had a wife hidden away in that tiny cottage somewhere. She couldn't decide if he had been deliberately guarded, or if she had just been feeble about probing.

"Is it much farther?" her mother asked. "I can't tell you how much I need a proper cup of tea. And the opportunity to use a clean loo."

"Only another ten minutes, Mum. I want to call in at the village shop on the way."

"Oh, good. I shall buy some postcards."

"Postcards? Really, Mum, you'll be back in London in a couple of days."

"I know that. I just like to have some to show people. You know I'm no good with a camera."

Laura immediately felt guilty for poking fun when all her mother was trying to do was take an interest in the place. The fact she was even considering showing her friends the outpost where her daughter now lived was a good sign.

"You can see our mountain from here," she said, pointing into the distance. 'Look. It's the one with the wooded lower slopes."

"Very pretty, dear. Though I expect it will look a little different in November."

"Yes." Laura worked hard to keep the edge out of her voice. "I expect it will."

She parked outside the shop in the center of the village.

"Is this where you do your shopping? I can't imagine they have much of a selection of fresh vegetables in here. I've never seen a corner shop with a decent lettuce in it."

"There's a supermarket a few miles up the road. Besides, we're hoping to buy locally produced food, once we get to know people."

"From farm shops, you mean?"

"That sort of thing, yes. And neighbors. Come on, in we go."

The shop was clean and well stocked with essentials, along with a plentiful supply of pots of Welsh honey and jars of pickle. Laura made her way to a small shelf of books declaring themselves to be of local interest. She browsed through them. Mrs. Powell, who, despite being well beyond retirement age, held the dual roles of shopkeeper and postmistress, appeared at her elbow.

"Are you looking for anything in particular?" she asked.

"Oh, yes, I suppose I am. I wondered if you had anything on local ghost stories." Laura laughed as she spoke. "Not my sort of thing, really. Though it might make a nice present for Dan." She glanced over her shoulder and was pleased to see her mother fully occupied with the postcards.

"Oooh, I don't think we're going to be able to help you there." Mrs. Powell shook her snowy curls as she rifled through the books. "There's one here on local legends, myths, old stories, all that sort of thing. It's very popular with visitors to the area."

Laura took the book from her and studied its cover. It wasn't what she had hoped for, but it had not been a serious search in the first place. As she flicked through the pages one of the pictures caught her eye. It showed a tall man, powerful looking, in dark robes, a fearsome dog at his side. He carried a staff and was depicted standing in a wild forest.

"I'll take it," she said, trying to shake off the curious sense of unease that had descended upon her. On her way to the counter she passed her mother who gestured pointedly at the collection of sad looking vegetables.

As they arrived at Penlan Laura steeled herself for her mother's response to her new home. She was more than a little certain that Annabel would not be so instantly won over by it as she had been. Nevertheless she clung to the hope that, in time, she might come to see the charm and beauty of the place.

"Well, Mum," Laura began, unable to resist asking. "What do you think?"

"I think I shan't be visiting when there's ice on that lane." Annabel climbed out of the car and narrowed her eyes. "Not much of a garden to speak of, is there? Still, I suppose that could be remedied." She walked over to the nearest rambling rose and studied it closely. "No greenfly, at least. Too high up for them, I imagine."

Laura saw a possible chink in her mother's armor-plated resistance and made the most of it. "Some of the roses are nearly a hundred years old, according to the estate agent. It would be great to plant a proper garden. Not that I know anything about it. Would you help me sort it out? I'd be completely lost. You know what plants like which sort of soil and all that stuff. Please say you'll help, Mum."

"Well, it would be an enormous task, darling. I don't think

you've any idea how much work would be involved. There's quite a large area of garden here, and the weeds! Just look at all that ground elder and all those nettles, and brambles, for goodness sake."

"Oh come on, Mum, it'd be fun. We could do it together. Me and Dan can do the donkey work and you can be our expert adviser. Then you can enjoy telling us what a dog's breakfast we've made of it when you come and visit."

Annabel let slip a little smile. "I suppose I could help you draw up a list of suitable plants. Nothing too tender—the winds must be very cold up here."

"Brilliant! Thanks, Mum."

"Now, are you going to take me to a bathroom, or am I expected to squat behind a bush?"

The weather continued to be glorious, if a little humid. After a light supper, Laura put extra cushions on the garden furniture, and the two of them sat outside in the gentle warmth of the evening. The previous weekend Dan had arranged wooden chairs and a table on a reasonably level space of grassed yard just in front of the house. From here the view of the meadows and the woods sweeping to the valley below was enchanting. As they sipped cool Chablis and breathed in the perfume of the honeysuckle that climbed over the front door, Laura told herself even her mother could not resist such a seductive setting.

"This is the life," said Laura, stretching out her legs and leaning back in her chair. "Beats grimy old London any day, wouldn't you say, Mum?"

"I happen to like grimy old London, though I admit, this is all very pleasant." She sipped her drink. "In fact, I would say this could be the ideal place for holidays. Lovely to come here and enjoy the peace and quiet for a week or two. But to *live . . .*"

"Why not to live?"

"Well, darling, you know what I think. It's just so far from everybody and everything. I mean, you'll never see anyone up here."

"That's the idea," said Laura. "Besides, we'll have loads of visitors. You mark my words—our chums from the big smoke will be coming out here by the busload, bringing their high blood pressure and panic attacks with them. All desperate for a bit of clean air and real food and a pace of life that doesn't make you dizzy."

"Guests are all very well in the summer. Or the odd weekend. But what about the rest of the time? It's all right for Daniel, he'll be working and spending all week in London with his friends."

"I'll be working, too, Mum. I've got my studio sorted out here now. You know I'm happiest when I'm painting."

"Yes, but you will be on your own. All day, every day. Out here, with no one. What if something were to happen?"

"Like what?"

"I don't know. You could have a fall or something."

"You make me sound like a frail old woman, for goodness sake. And Dan's only at the other end of the phone if I need him."

"Now that it's finally connected!" Annabel wasn't going to be easily mollified. "And I'll bet that won't work if there's snow. Nor the electricity. Have you thought about power cuts?"

"Mum, people lived here for hundreds of years without electricity. I'm sure we could manage a few days if we had to."

"But why would you want to? I'm sorry, I know you think I'm just fussing, but I still worry you've rushed into this. Couldn't you have at least waited until Dan had found a job out here? That way you wouldn't have been here alone so much."

"I'll be fine. Please try to stop worrying about me."

"I must say I'm a bit surprised at Dan. That he agreed to all this, I mean."

"He wants me to be happy."

"Of course he does, but still, being apart . . . it puts a strain on a marriage. Any marriage."

Laura spotted the implication that theirs was a relationship already under plenty of stress, but she chose to ignore it. Part of her agreed with her mother. A small, nervous part.

"You had such a lovely house in Hackney," Annabel went on. "And your studio was so convenient, Laura. And close to all the galleries." She shook her head slowly, raised her hand and then let it fall again in a gesture of incomprehension. "I simply don't understand why you'd give it all up to be stuck in the middle of nowhere. A very pretty nowhere, I grant you, but is that so important?"

Laura leaned over and took her mother's hand in her own. "Listen to me, Mum. It's going to be OK. I've given this a lot of thought. Really, I have. We both have. True, it's not Dan's idea of perfect. Yet. But it's a decision we've made together. He'll find a job in Cardiff or somewhere else within striking distance soon enough. In the meantime you'll just have to keep visiting, won't you? Then you can check up on me and stop me ruining the new garden single-handedly."

"I have a life, too, you know." Annabel was trying to sound unmoved, but she held on tightly to Laura's hand as she spoke. "I can't keep hopping on and off trains."

Laura smiled at the picture in her head of her mother hitching rides on freight trains, like some American hobo. "Then you can come up with Dan on a Friday night sometimes. Won't take you long to hunt down the cleanest loos on the A40 between here and London."

Annabel took another sip of her wine. "I know you think I'm being a silly old woman. Of course you're an adult—you can look after yourself, Laura, I know that. It's just that I worry about you being on your own."

"Mum . . ." Laura withdrew her hand a little more abruptly than she had intended. "This is Wales, not the Australian outback. Really, I'll be just fine."

❧❦❧

LATER, LAURA FOUND it difficult to sleep. The bedroom was uncomfortably hot and the air thick with the threat of a thunderstorm that refused to come. She looked forward to her first thunderstorm at Penlan and wished for it now more than ever. Outside, a barn owl screeched. Laura switched on her bedside light and picked up the book she had bought at the village shop. She flicked through it to the picture that had so caught her attention and studied the strange figure again. He was standing in dense woodland, and the boughs of the trees gave the impression they were being disturbed by a great wind. The man's hair and robes seemed to be tangled with the branches. The man himself looked grim-faced, yet curiously handsome. She dipped into the chapter and began to read. The man shown was Merlin, who, so the local legend went, lived in the area in the time between his childhood and his going to serve at the court of King Arthur. Even at an early age, his powers as a seer were well developed, and he was both feared and revered in equal measure. The story told of how he fell in love with a local girl but also made an enemy of a powerful noble who set out to destroy the young couple. The legend said that Merlin kept as a companion not a dog, but a wolf. A wolf! No wonder it looked fierce. She turned back to the picture. Now she could see that the creature at Merlin's side was indeed no tame, domesticated animal.

At last she began to grow drowsy. She turned out the light and rolled over, her mind filled with images of wild men and wild wolflike creatures. Somewhere over the distant hills, muted kettledrums played an overture to the storm that was soon to break over Penlan.

3

BY THE WEEKEND the weather had still not changed, and the humidity levels had risen even further. Dan had arrived home tired and grumpy after a hectic week and a nightmare journey that had taken over four hours. He and Annabel had been on scratchy terms all the following day. In an attempt to build bridges Laura had persuaded everyone to go outside and do battle with the garden. This largely involved hacking back brambles, cutting down nettles, and pulling up rampant comfrey and wild mint. Even with gloves it was a prickly task, but Laura decided it was worth it, as she would rather Dan's temper and her mother's anxiety were focused on an unsuspecting plant instead of each other. By Sunday they had found some sort of rhythm, and small pockets of progress could be spotted here and there. With the roast in the oven they turned out for one more assault before Sunday lunch. Dan had found a rusting old scythe and was hacking through the jungle at the back of the house. Annabel took a fork to the mint outside the front door. Laura dug at the roots of the flattened nettles. She had never really done any gardening and had always been under the impression it was somehow soothing and therapeutic. Now, however, all she felt was tired, filthy, and covered in stings. The spade hit a rock with every second dig, causing a jarring clang, which reverberated through her already fuzzy head. After what seemed like hours of toil there was little to show for her efforts, save a mess of savaged plants and stony soil. She longed to be in her studio instead, preparing canvasses, sorting paints—anything other than what she was doing. She jabbed at the earth with all the determination she could muster, only to have her spade hit an old bottle, bending the handle shaft into a ludicrous angle.

"Shit!" she said. "In fact, shit and damn. Useless bloody thing."

"Swearing at your garden won't help it to grow."

Laura jumped at the unexpected voice. She turned to find Rhys standing close behind her, though she had not heard him approach.

"Actually, I was swearing at the spade," she told him, acutely aware of her grubby face, baggy shorts, and old, sweaty T-shirt. She had tied back her hair in a low ponytail, and most of it had wriggled free of its bonds, so that it hung in sticky clumps about her ears. Laura felt uncomfortable looking such a mess, though she knew she shouldn't. What did it matter?

Rhys held out a cardboard box. "I've brought you some eggs and a few things from my garden, though I can see you will have produce of your own soon."

"Oh, I think we might starve if we wait for that day. Thank you," she said, taking the vegetables from him. "Thank you very much." She noticed her mother stand up and peer at Rhys. "Mum, this is our neighbor, Rhys. Look, he's brought us some homegrown veg. This is my mother, Annabel Frey."

Annabel pulled off a glove and offered her hand, "Rhys? Is that a Welsh name?"

Rhys shook her hand and treated her to one of his smiles.

"That's right," he said.

"Ooh, look, Mum. How's that for a fresh lettuce?" Laura waved it under her mother's nose with some satisfaction. "And radishes and carrots, too. Lovely."

Annabel's expression did not soften. "I'm surprised any vegetables will grow all the way up here."

"Some will, others will not. There is a short growing season."

"And is that what you do for a living? Sell lettuces?"

"Mum!"

"What? It's a harmless question."

At that moment Dan appeared from behind the house, dragging his scythe.

"Good morning!" he said, sounding genuinely pleased to see their visitor. Laura knew he would have welcomed anyone to dilute the presence of his mother-in-law.

"This is my husband, Dan. This is Rhys. Look what he's brought us."

"It's nothing, really," Rhys insisted. "I can't eat it all myself. Besides, it gives me an excuse to come and investigate my new neighbors."

Dan laughed at this. "Wow, I bet those are good," he said, helping himself to an oversized radish and crunching into it enthusiastically. "Mmm, takes me back to my grandfather's allotment. Lord, they pack a punch, too."

"Rhys was just about to tell us what he does for a living." Annabel was determined to press her question.

"Mum, leave poor Rhys alone."

"The man hasn't even been offered a drink yet. That's not very neighborly of us, is it?" Dan pointed out, clearly happy to have an excuse to stop working. "Now, what can I get you?"

"Well, if I'm not intruding . . . I wouldn't want to hold up vital work on the garden."

"Nonsense!" Dan let his scythe fall to the ground. "Got to keep the workforce happy, and these girls look like they need a break. I'll admit I'm more than ready for a cold beer myself—what do you say?"

"Sounds good to me."

At that moment the peace was rudely broken by the screeching of a fighter jet. Laura flinched, and her mother threw her hands to her ears as it screamed through the sky above them. In a second it was skimming the far hill, barely clearing the craggy summit, and then it was gone, leaving only a dyspeptic echo.

"You see, Mum," Laura said. "We're not completely out of reach of the modern world after all."

"Afraid not," said Rhys.

Laura led the way toward the wooden chairs. "Come on, let's sit down. You must be as tired of battling with this garden as I am, Mum." She chose a seat opposite Rhys but behind the small table in an attempt to hide herself a little. She was surprised to find that her appearance bothered her. She remembered the last time she had seen Rhys. She had been freshly showered and wearing a pretty dress. Now she felt at a disadvantage, though she wasn't sure why. She chatted away about nothing, keeping the conversation going if only to stop her mother from asking embarrassing questions. All the time she was conscious of the fact that Rhys was looking at her. Watching her. Intently. And although she felt uncomfortable beneath his gaze she realized that she also liked the way he looked at her. She wanted him to look, even in her disheveled state. She wanted to return his gaze, but was inhibited by her mother's presence.

Dan emerged from the house with bottles of beer and a glass of white wine for Annabel.

"Here we are." He handed out the drinks and settled himself next to Laura. Soon he was chatting easily, enjoying being a host, apparently at ease with their mysterious neighbor. Even Annabel relaxed by the time she was halfway through her glass. Much to Laura's relief she gave up asking awkward questions, subdued by fatigue and alcohol. Laura found herself strangely on the outside, watching and listening as the other three talked of gardens and Wales and mountains and nothing in particular. In this way she was able to observe Rhys quite closely. His eyes were still the same unfathomable blue. His face stern, but relaxed now. His body lean. His hands long-fingered. His skin brown from days spent outside, but not from sunbathing, Laura was sure of that. Suddenly he looked directly at her. The others were talking, but between Rhys and Laura passed a shared moment of stillness. A connection. And a silent acknowledgment of something powerful in that connection. Through it all came Dan's voice.

"Laura? I was saying, Rhys should stay for lunch. Don't you think? It's the least we can do."

"No." Laura surprised herself with the sharpness of her own

response. Suddenly she could bear the strength of his presence no longer. Not here, like this, with her mother and Dan. "I mean, I'm sure Rhys has plans of his own," she said, trying to explain herself. 'We've taken up enough of his time."

Dan looked puzzled. Rhys stood up.

"Actually, I was on my way to the village. But thank you for the offer."

"Another time, then," Dan said.

After they had waved him off Dan went to the kitchen to see to the meal. Annabel put away the gardening tools. As she walked toward the barn she called back over her shoulder, "A strange sort of fellow. Quite unusual."

"Oh, really, Mum, a minute ago you were worrying about me being here with no one for miles around. Now you don't like it when the neighbors drop by. You can't have it both ways."

"I didn't say I didn't like him. I'm just saying you don't know anything about him," Annabel said without turning around. She came to the barn door and stopped. Now she pivoted on her heel to face her daughter, her tone serious. "Take care, darling," she said. "Take care."

Laura shook her head and gave a little laugh, but secretly she was in turmoil. Why had this man affected her so? Yes, he was good looking, but they had only exchanged a few words. And for once her mother was right, she knew absolutely nothing about him. Only that he invaded her thoughts. And that his presence disturbed her. And that now he had gone she felt something missing. She finished her beer and went into the house to help Dan.

❧❦❧

It was with some relief that Laura waved off her mother on Monday morning. Dan had talked her into staying the extra night so that she could travel back with him instead. It was an olive branch, and one Annabel had the good grace to accept. They had survived the weekend without major upsets, but the air was thick with things not said, and the effort of being upbeat about everything had been wearying for Laura. She knew she would feel guilty the moment her mother left, thinking of her going back to London to carry on her life alone. She promised herself to be gentler when Annabel next visited, to try harder, and to make her feel welcome whenever she wanted to come and stay. Perhaps, slowly, her mother would grow used to the idea of Penlan and come to see that the move was a positive thing for her daughter. For all of them. She was about to go to her studio when the telephone rang.

"Laura, Hi!" Penny's relentless enthusiasm bounced down the telephone line. "Got you at last! Beginning to think I'd lost you to the wilderness."

"I've only been here five minutes, give me a chance." She didn't feel like being nagged by her agent.

"Enough time to get things set up? I know how you can't stand to be without a painting on the go for more than a day or so."

"I was just on my way to the studio."

"A proper studio already? I'm impressed."

"You might not be if you saw it." She smiled at the thought of what her agent's reaction would be to the unfinished, dusty space that she had to work in.

"So long as you're painting, Laura. Time flies, and all that. How are things shaping up?"

"If by *things* you mean paintings, there aren't any yet. But I've got ideas. This place could give me subjects for the next twenty years. I just need a bit more time to find my rhythm again. You know, the move, new place, having had a break . . . Look, stop worrying—you know I always deliver."

"Of course you do. I have every faith, every confidence. *So* looking forward to seeing what you produce out there. Nearer the time I'll organize a van to pick it all up. We'll get everything framed down here, as per norm, yes? I'll get back to you once the gallery have confirmed the dates. A November opening is looking likely at the mo'."

"November? I thought you said Christmas."

"November *is* Christmas these days, Laura my love."

The phone call left her feeling rattled. Whatever she had said to Penny about ideas and inspiration she still found it difficult to settle into any proper work. Potching about was all very well, but it didn't put canvasses on walls. She still felt strangely restless and knew she wouldn't be able to concentrate until her state of mind settled. She had already had one failed attempt at painting the day before because she had not been able to focus. Her mood was in no small part due to the continued heavy, storm-laden weather. She had never known such humidity to last so long without breaking. She needed to shake the weekend from her head somehow and decided a little exercise and an hour or so of being on the open mountain might help. She took her sketching bag and headed up the path to the hill gate. The steep climb pulled at the back of her calves and made her knees ache. She forced herself to march on, breathing deeply, enjoying the physical effort. She followed the sheep track for a mile or so, then turned up across the whinberries and heather. She loved the vastness of the space, the distant mountains, the openness. It made her feel free and unburdened by life's petty problems. She walked for another half hour before sitting on the wiry grass for a short rest. The skylarks whirred and bobbed about her. High up a buzzard wheeled and soared. Nearby some sheep paused in their grazing to look at her, decided she was no threat, and put their heads down again. The view had a strangely muted quality because of the damp air. The sky was almost opaque, pregnant with rain that was still too high to descend. Laura thought how difficult it would be to paint the mountains when they were like this. How could she transfer all those nuances to canvas without rendering them dull and flat? Cobalt blue and Indian red for the clouds? French ultramarine and rose madder for the distant hills? She remembered Rhys had said the mountains had a hundred moods. She had thought it an exaggeration at the time, but perhaps he was right.

She pulled out her block and began to loosely sketch the view before her. She had not half covered the page when there was a sudden rumble almost directly overhead. The sky darkened as the thunderclouds lowered with tremendous speed. She barely had time to register what was happening when there was a sound like a hundred cracking whips and a fork of lightning struck the ground on the ridge below the highest point of the hill.

Her pulse raced at the unexpectedness of the storm. She had waited for it for days, and now it had caught her here, exposed on the open mountain, and she was truly frightened. She had never seen lightning strike the ground like that before. She looked around for somewhere to take shelter, but there was nothing. There were a few leaning rowan trees farther down the slope, but they were barely tall enough to sit under. And anyway, Laura remembered you were not supposed to get under a tree in a thunderstorm. But what *was* she supposed to do? If she stayed where she was she would be completely unprotected. She was at the tallest point for a mile around, and what little understanding she had of lightning was not reassuring. Logic told her that it would seek out the highest point of something.

That's why it strikes trees and chimneys, she thought, *and if I stay here, it will strike me.* There was nothing else to do but get off the mountain as fast as possible. Another clap of thunder galvanized her into action. She started to run. The springy grass of the path was dry and the earth beneath it firm, so she covered the ground quickly. Another flash of lightning, this time illuminating the whole sky, drove her on. By the third roar of thunder the storm was directly above her, and it was accompanied by simultaneous lightning, both sheet and forked. Laura had never been so terrified. She couldn't outrun the storm, and she felt only luck was keeping her alive. Luck that could run out at any moment. And then came the rain. Rain that had been pent up and longing for its release for days now hurled itself downward. Within seconds the path became impossibly slippery. She fell heavily, bruising her knee on a waiting rock. She picked herself up and ran on, limping, her injured leg slowing her down. She had reached the bracken now, but the path veered off around the side of the hill, not downward. She realized with mounting panic that she had missed the original track. This was not the way home. What was worse, this was not the way off the hill at all. In that moment, finding the house was not the most important thing anymore. Getting off the mountain and out of the storm was. The next crash of thunder was so loud it made Laura shriek and clutch at her ears. It was as if the storm had swallowed her up, and she might drown or be deafened before she was burned alive by the lightning. Her clothes were soaked, her hair heavy with rainwater, her bare legs mud-splattered, bruised, and scratched by the grasping bracken and thorns hidden amongst it. She tripped again and fell into the ferns, tumbling over and over down the steep hillside. At last she stopped and hauled herself, battered and sobbing, to her feet.

Get up! she told herself. *Get up and run, you stupid woman. Run!*

But she had lost the path altogether now and found herself battling through the near impenetrable bracken. At every step it caught her feet or wrapped itself around her ankles, so that she spent more time on the ground than walking. She dragged herself on. Such was her distress she failed to notice her sketching bag slip from her shoulder as she pressed on. Then, though the rain was coursing down her face with such speed she was half blinded by it, she spotted a building in the middle distance. She squinted at it, spitting out water and mud. It was Rhys's croft. She let out a cry of relief and pushed ahead with renewed hope. Another blaze of lightning forked into the ground terrifyingly close. She heard the crackle of the electric charge and a terrible sizzling noise as the wet earth hissed where it had been struck.

Laura reached a steep bank which was slippery with freshly watered mud, so that she quickly lost her footing at the top and slithered downward, coming to rest in an exhausted heap near the stream at the bottom of the slope. She felt herself unable to go on but knew she was not yet safe. Somehow she succeeded in staggering to her feet, and wiping water and mud from her mouth with the back of her hand. A sound close by made her jump. A sheep leaped from its hiding place behind a rock, all but knocking her over in its haste to get away. Another movement made her pause. A figure stepped out from the dense bracken. It was Rhys. Laura had never been so relieved to see anyone in her life before and was sure she never would again. Infuriating tears of relief spilled down her cheeks. Rhys hurried over to her, putting his hands on her shoulders.

"I was walking, on the mountain," she told him, her voice shaky and full of sobs. "The storm started so suddenly . . ."

"Shhh. You're safe now," said Rhys. He pushed her muddy hair out of her eyes.

In that instant, with that gesture, he transported her back to another time. Another place. There was something familiar, something Laura recognized in the feel of his fingers on her face. In that second all her fear was swept away and replaced with something else. Something equally strong, equally engulfing, yet completely different. Desire swept through Laura's body. Desire and excitement, real and raw and full of as much heat and fire as the lightning she had been trying to escape.

❧❧❧

WHEN MEGAN ARRIVED at Penlan the dew had barely dried on the grass, yet already the sun was hot. As she neared the farm she could hear Twm moving about in the barn, talking to his beloved horses. He'd grown so fond of each and every one that he'd bred and raised. Megan knew it was hard for him to part with them when the time came. She stepped into the shade of the barn entrance and let her eyes adjust to the change of light. Her father stood beside a beautiful white mare, speaking softly to her as he lifted the saddle onto her back.

"There we are, my pretty one, not so bad is it? No cause for you to be frightened."

Megan smiled, touched by her father's gentleness.

"She is beautiful, Father."

"Ah, Megan! You mustn't creep up on an old man like that," he said, laughing as he embraced her. "What brings you here twice in as many days?"

"Surely a daughter needs no reason to visit her father other than wanting to see him," she said lightly, but turned her face to the mare so he might not read her eyes. The animal bent its neck and sniffed at Megan with wide eyes. "I have not seen this one before, Father. She is very fine. And such a color. Whiter than a fresh fall of snow."

"It is unusual, in such a young horse. I bought her cheaply enough, though. Her owner had purchased her for his wife, but the mare proved too nervous. Not suitable at all, he said. She's too small for a man. She has to be a lady's mount."

"Do you think you can calm her?"

"We shall see. Of course," he said, looking pointedly at his daughter. "What would be of great assistance is a maid willing to ride her gently for me. Someone who will treat her kindly and whisper courage in her snowy ear."

Megan could not help her grin broadening into a smile. "But where would you find such a person?" she said with a laugh.

Twm unhitched the reins of the bridle and handed them to her. "Now don't go too far, mind. She's in no condition to gallop over the hills just yet."

Megan led the horse outside. "Does she have a name?"

"None that I know of. You name her for me," said Twm as he helped her spring into the saddle. She rode astride, hitching her skirts up to sit deeply in the saddle. As always she looked at home and at ease on a horse. Her earliest memories were of sitting on the saddle in front of her father. Now beneath her the mare fidgeted, taking small, nervous steps backward. Megan leaned forward and patted her sleek neck. She could feel the tension in the animal.

"Shhh, little one," she said. "I will look after you. There is nothing to fear. Come, let us explore the meadows, where the soft grass can cool your hooves."

The mare moved with short, anxious steps, as if afraid to leave a foot on the ground for a second longer than was necessary. She snorted at a pile of logs, arching her neck and moving her body as far from it as she could in the little yard. Where others might have tightened their grip or been concerned, Megan merely uttered soft words and urged her mount on quietly, through the gate and into the large, gently sloping fields. At the sight of the open space before her the mare began to jog and champ at the bit in her mouth. Megan instinctively dropped the reins, giving the animal its head, but sat deep and firm. She let the mare slip into a canter and as the horse gained courage its stride lengthened and loosened until it near floated over the ground. Gradually, Megan felt the horse begin to trust her. The mare flicked her ears backward to listen to Megan's words of encouragement. By the time they returned to the barn the mare was walking with a long, happy gait, her head low and her manner tranquil.

Twm grinned proudly up at Megan. "You and she are well suited, Daughter."

"She lacks courage, but she has a good nature." Megan slipped easily to the ground, rubbing the mare's ears fondly. "It will be a lucky lady who is given such a graceful and responsive mount."

"I may have to look far and wide to find a maid can get the best from the mare, as you have done."

"She will stay here some time then," she said with a smile as she led the animal back to its stall. "Good! Oh, I had almost forgotten, I brought this for your new colt. It will rid him of his scar." She took a small clay jar from her pocket and handed it to Twm. "Lavender oil. Enough for a full month, I think. That should be sufficient."

"You have been taking ingredients for your remedies from your mistress's garden again? Have a care—if she catches you, she will have a price from you, one way or another."

"Lady Rhiannon rarely visits the garden, and never after dark. Besides, she can spare a few heads of lavender. They are of more use to you."

They made their way to the stall where the young colt was eagerly eating his feed. He had not yet been weaned from his mother, who stood calmly beside him, but still he was hungry for extra sustenance. Growing so fast Megan could almost see him change before her eyes. He had a coat the color of the winter sun and with as great a brilliance, even in the dimness of the barn. He had not yet grown to fit his skinny limbs, and his whole frame was angular and stretched with the effort of transformation from babe to young horse. He was a bold animal and paid no heed to Twm as he rubbed the oil into his hind leg.

"He will make someone a fine destrier one day, mark my words," Twm said with pride. "Good enough for any lord or knight you care to name."

Megan watched him tend the horse for a moment, then forced herself to address the real reason for her visit.

"I hear you have a new neighbor. Someone has taken the croft."

"Ty Bychan, you mean? Yes, the castle gossips are well informed."

"Have you seen him?"

"From a distance. We have not yet met."

"You should introduce yourself, Father."

"I should?"

"Surely it is only neighborly," she said, searching for ways to probe further. "And it may be he has need of a mount. It is not like you to miss the chance of making a sale."

Twm straightened up and looked closely at Megan. "So, here it is, the true purpose of your visit. Did his Lordship send you to question me on this matter?"

Megan blushed, uncomfortable at having in any way deceived her father.

"No. It was Lady Rhiannon. She believes the stranger could be the prophet and magician Merlin. There has been talk. She wants to know the truth of it."

"It is as I have said: I have not yet met my new neighbor. But

take heed, Daughter. A man who chooses to live so far from others without apparent reason for doing so does not want to be trou-
bled. You would do well to leave such a person to himself. What
is more, I doubt your Ladyship's motives are of the purest nature."

"I am sorry, Father. I had no choice but to ask you. And I fear
Lady Rhiannon will not be content with such sparse information."

"Tell her I know little. Tell her the man seems ordinary. Of
no interest to her. She will send someone else to find out what
she wants to know. You are best off staying out of such matters,
if it can be done."

Megan nodded, biting her bottom lip. She wanted to be reassured by what her father said, but she knew her mistress too well
to think she would be so easily satisfied.

Twm put his arm around his daughter. "Now we have a far
more important matter to discuss," he said seriously.

"Oh?" Megan looked up at him.

"Yes. You still haven't named that white mare." He gave her
a hug and steered her toward the house. "And you can't consider
such a grave subject without a little food. Come, let me be a fussing father and feed you. You've no more meat on you than that
colt over there."

After a another hour in her father's company Megan knew
she could delay her return to the castle no longer. She said good-
bye to him fondly and set off on the route that would take her
through the woods on her way back. The heat of the day was
tiring, so that the shade of the leafy trees was very welcome.
She paused at the patch of garlic she had noticed the day before.
She knelt down and gently lifted one of the plants, carefully wriggling its bulb free of the dry soil. The strong, distinctive smell

filled her nose and stung her eyes as she packed her prize away in the pocket of her skirts. She was about to get to her feet when the sense of someone, or something, watching her made her freeze. Cautiously, she raised her head and peered into the woodland, searching for whatever was there. She felt frightened. Irrationally so, she thought, for she knew these woods better than the castle gardens and had never had cause to be afraid before. A low growl made her heart miss a beat. Into the glade, on stealthy paws, stepped a full-grown, dark grey wolf. The only time Megan had seen a wolf before was when her father's cousin, the wolf catcher from beyond the far valley, had brought a dead one through the town one market day. She had never encountered a live one, and the sight of it was terrifying, stirring in her her own animal instinct to keep motionless, or to run. The beast was too close to risk running, so she could think of nothing else that might save her skin other than to remain still as a stone and pray the pungent garlic would mask her own scent. The wolf raised his nose and sniffed the air, staring all the while straight at Megan with small, shiny eyes. A movement among the trees brought an involuntary gasp from her.

Could there be a pack of wolves? Here, in these woods she had known her whole life and where she had never seen a single one?

She waited, transfixed with fear, hardly daring to look and see what was going to emerge from the undergrowth. To her astonishment, it was a man. He was tall and lean, with a mane of black hair and a full beard. He looked to be young, but definitely a man rather than a boy. Somehow, though, his true age was hard to be sure of. He came to stand beside the wolf and let his hand drop onto the animal. A wordless command seemed to pass from him to the fearsome beast. The wolf lay down, still watching Megan closely, but no longer in an attitude of possible attack. Megan struggled to make sense of what she was seeing. First the shock of the wolf itself, and now this stranger who appeared to have tamed the animal. She rose unsteadily to her feet. The man nodded courteously.

"You were looking for me," he said. It was not a question but a statement of fact.

Megan was confused.

"I have been visiting my father. I am on my way back to Castle Craig," she told him.

"My name is Merlin," said the man, looking squarely at her.

She noticed now how uncommonly blue his eyes were, like rosemary flowers, or a noon sky in summer. They seemed to shine out of him with a light all their own. And when he locked his gaze onto hers she was as transfixed as she had been by the sight of the wolf.

Merlin stepped forward until he was standing not more than an arm's length from Megan. He gestured toward the wolf.

"Please, do not be afraid. He is harmless as any hunting dog. Only those who would threaten me need fear him."

The animal got up and loped to its master's side, where it nuzzled his hand. Megan watched in wonder.

"Can I . . . can I touch him?" she asked. When Merlin nodded she moved cautiously toward the animal, then reached out a trembling hand. The wolf sniffed her palm, then sneezed as the garlic burned his nostrils. Megan laughed, and looked up to see Merlin laughing silently, too, his face animated and softened by his smile. She reached forward once more and touched the wolf's dense coat.

"Oh," she said, "it is softer than a lamb's wool! Who would have believed such a thing?"

The wolf seemed to enjoy the attention and was happy to let her make a fuss of him. Megan found herself so fascinated by the creature she all but forgot Merlin until he spoke again.

"It is often true that being close to the object of our fears is not as terrifying as we had supposed it to be. It is the threat of terror that controls a man more than the terror itself."

Megan turned her attention away from the wolf and back to its master. He was softly spoken for such a powerful-looking man. There was a curious grace about his movements and a lightness to his footfall. Indeed, he seemed to have more in common with the wild animal at his side than with any man Megan could bring to mind. And yet, at the same time, there was nothing savage about him. She shook her head as if to clear it of such idle thoughts and bring her to the task she had been set.

"You have taken the croft above my father's house. You and he are neighbors now," she said, then added "I am certain he would welcome you, should you call on him." She was surprised to hear herself uttering such a suggestion, and was not at all sure it was true. Nonetheless, whatever her father's warnings, she felt this man could be trusted. "He is a breeder of fine horses, should you have need of one."

"I am looking for a mount. Something simple and hardy. I will call on your father one day soon." As he spoke he continued to regard Megan with interest, apparently searching her face, as if trying to read her every expression. "But it was not your father who sent you to seek me out. You were on an errand for your mistress."

Megan felt unnerved that he knew so much. She had heard

him called a prophet and a seer, but she had not, until this moment, stopped to think what that meant. Could it be he had somehow divined the details of her visit to her father's house? No, surely some of the gossip from the castle must have reached his ears. That was the more likely explanation.

"Lady Rhiannon expressed an interest in your being in the region. It is true she sent me to ask after you. She had heard of your reputation as a seer."

"But thought only sufficient of it to send a girl as her messenger?"

He was teasing her now, she was sure of it. Despite herself she heard her own temper in her voice.

"Is it such a reputation as only a man can value? Or does Merlin the Magician consider a woman unworthy of his conversation, perhaps?" Megan knew she had spoken sharply and was cross with herself for giving rein to her feelings.

Merlin's face showed he disliked her response, as if his gentle joke had been misconstrued.

"Forgive me," he said. "I had no wish to offend you."

"For you to offend me I would have to give weight to your opinion. It is of no matter to me how you regard me. I am merely carrying out the wishes of my Lady. Now that I have found you, I can inform her that her information was correct. What she chooses to do with that knowledge is not my concern."

She made as if to step past Merlin, but he moved to block her path. Now, close up, she could see that his apparently grim expression was born of trying to suppress a smile. That he should be laughing at her further fueled Megan's indignation.

"Be kind enough to let me pass, sir," she said, deliberately avoiding his hypnotic gaze.

"Tell your mistress I am her servant." He remained in her way for a moment longer, then stepped aside with a low bow in an exaggerated gesture of formality.

Megan swept passed, striding on without so much as a farewell. As she walked on she could feel his eyes still upon her. Only when she had marched some distance into the dense woodland did she allow herself to pause. Hesitantly, she turned, but he and his unnerving companion had melted back into the trees as silently as they had appeared.

THE FOLLOWING DAY Megan was summoned by her mistress. As she climbed the steep stairs, she felt strangely ill at ease at having to discuss her father's curious new neighbor with her mistress. She told herself he had been unconcerned at Lady Rhiannon's interest and had announced himself to be her servant. Nonetheless, he did not seem the sort of man who would, in truth, care to be associated with such a woman. Megan felt in her bones that no good could come of their meeting. And yet, why should she concern herself? Here is yet another man with no regard for women, save they can be of use to him in some way, she thought. Where then is the magic and wisdom?

She found her mistress reclining on soft bolsters and rugs on a low chair, her feet raised on a tapestry stool. She was dressed for day, but her left arm was exposed to the shoulder. Beside her stood a small man, late in years, stooped and slow. He wore a dark cap and the robes of a man of leechcraft. Megan felt her stomach turn as he took a needle-fine bodkin and pressed it to her mistress's exposed flesh. She had known, of course, that Lady Rhiannon favored the practice of bloodletting, but she had escaped witnessing the procedure until now. As the wine red stream trickled along the outstretched arm and flowed off her wrist in a narrow ribbon the lady's maid hurried forward with a pewter bowl. The sound of liquid pouring from a height onto metal signaled the collection of the noble blood. Lady Rhiannon appeared entirely at ease with what was being done. Indeed, her state of relaxation suggested she gained some pleasure from having her vein opened. Megan considered the habit the utmost stupidity. She had never even used the treatment on any horse she had tended, though she understood for some people in extreme sickness it could prove beneficial. But to use it as a cosmetic aid, to improve the whiteness of the skin, was, to her, pure folly.

The solar looked different in daylight, though it remained gloomy and dimly lit. The curtains around the bed were tied back, showing it neat, tidy, and empty. The floor had been swept clear but no fresh rushes or herbs thrown down. One small candle burned near Lady Rhiannon. The overall effect was of order. Gone was the warmth, the passion, the heavy air that had filled the room on Megan's last visit. In spite of the warm day, the space felt cold and unwelcoming. It was clear Lady Rhiannon was preparing for Lord Geraint's return.

"Well, Megan, what news have you for me?" Lady Rhiannon spoke with her eyes closed, her face languid. She signaled to her maid, who stepped forward to brush her lady's hair with long, soothing strokes, making it shine like the wing of a raven.

"Your information was correct, my Lady. The man now living at the croft is indeed the one they call Merlin the Magician."

"Good. Your father has met him?"

"No, my Lady. Though he has seen him from a distance."

"And this is all the proof you have of the man's identity? Is your father, too, in possession of powers of prophecy and foresight?" Lady Rhiannon opened her eyes now, but only to scowl, not to look in Megan's direction.

"No, my Lady. That is, I am certain he is the man you seek, as I myself have spoken to him."

"You?" Now she redirected her gaze, her interest aroused. She swatted away her maid with an impatient hand. "How did this come about?"

"I encountered him on my way back to the castle. He introduced himself to me."

"Indeed?" Lady Rhiannon studied Megan closely now. "It would seem I was wise to send a pretty maid to flush him out. He is a man like any other, after all. Tell me what he had to say for himself."

"Very little, my Lady," She decided not to mention the wolf. "I told him who had sent me and of your interest in his . . . work. He said to tell you that he is your servant."

"Well, well." Lady Rhiannon smiled at this, signaling for her maid to continue with her hair. "So, he is a man who knows it is wise to recognize his superiors, as well as a man who likes a pretty face. A worthwhile combination, I believe. We must arrange to meet."

"Indeed we must!" A gruff voice from the doorway made all three women start.

Megan swung round to see Lord Geraint, still in his traveling clothes, come striding into the room. Lady Rhiannon snapped her fingers and the old man finished his work. He pressed a cloth against the inside of the exposed elbow and bound it swiftly before collecting the pewter bowl and melting into the shadows with it. In his haste he moved the vessel too quickly and a splash of blood sloshed to the floor. Lady Rhiannon gave no sign of having noticed, but Megan and the maid exchanged glances, the significance of spilled blood being lost on neither of them. They curtsied as their master approached.

"My Lord." There was no warmth in Lady Rhiannon's voice at the sight of her husband. "You are returned early."

"As you see."

"Your business went well?"

"My business can wait. I am all ears to hear of our new neighbor. So clever of you, wife, to sow the seeds of an alliance with such a useful person. I know I can rely on you to have all our best interests in the forefront of your every thought and deed."

"Naturally, my Lord." Lady Rhiannon nodded slowly and risked a tight smile, but the tension in the room was evident to all.

"Good. Very good. We will invite this man to our home. Next week is Lammas Day. We will prepare a superior feast and bid him come as our guest. What say you?"

"An excellent idea, Husband."

"And you, Megan?" Lord Geraint turned to her. "You have met this marvel. What will he say to such an invitation?"

"I'm sure he will be honored, my Lord."

"Just so." He moved past Megan and took Lady Rhiannon's hand, leading her toward the low window seat. "Come, my Lady, sit with me awhile as I recover from my journey. Entertain me with details of how you passed the time in my absence."

Megan, knowing herself to be dismissed, slipped away.

❧ 4 ❧

A WEEK LATER Megan awoke to the sounds of workmen and servants busying themselves outside the castle. She slipped from her small bed and went to the glassless window on the far side of the little room. Below preparations were being made for the Lammas Day revelries. As always, Megan was reminded of the first such occasion she could remember attending—the last she had enjoyed with her mother. She could not have been more than four years old, and it had seemed to her that the whole world, rather than just the village, had turned out to enjoy the feast and the games. She remembered how the noise of so many people had shocked her. And the colors! So different from the normal muted greys and blues of everyday life. Here were people in their best clothes, and jesters and minstrels and troubadours and local dignitaries and Lords and Ladies in their finery. Even now, so many years later, Megan felt some of that excitement stirring within her. Everyone would be in a good mood today. Work and troubles would be forgotten. This was a time to celebrate the first harvest of the corn, the safe gathering in of the hay, and the promise of a winter free from hunger because of a healthy crop and a good yield. Everyone would be expected to join in the feast, from the lowliest farm worker to Lord Geraint himself. Of course Megan's father would be there, too, giving her another reason to feel happy about the day ahead. And Merlin. He had been invited expressly by Lord Geraint and Lady Rhiannon and was to sit at the head table with them. The idea of seeing him again caused a battle among Megan's emotions which she did not fully understand. She was still annoyed by the way he had belittled and teased her. But she saw now that it was meant in jest. Which made her reaction too strong, making her feel silly. And, somehow, it mattered to her how she might look in front of Merlin. As she admitted this to herself she felt a new nervousness and could not decide if the sensation was good or bad.

"Megan! Can we go outside? Please, let us go!" Huw burst in the through the heavy curtain that separated Megan's chamber from that of the boys. His face was already flushed with excitement. Brychan followed close behind.

"All in good time, Master Huw. You must first eat something, and we must dress you in your very best clothes."

"Must we? But I want to go apple bobbing, and Mama will complain if I get my best tabard wet. Can I not dress as I always do?"

"With the whole village coming to look at you? I think not. But you can wear something old for now, if you plan to go out and get dirtier than a hound pup before the day has even begun. You can change later. Come now, you, too, Brychan. Food first." She steered the boys back toward their room.

"I'm going to help take the cartwheel to the top of the hill," Brychan told her.

"So am I!" Huw cried.

"Are you now? Well, see that you don't get under people's feet. There is much to be done, and you will not help by getting in the way."

By mid-morning, all was ready, and people were beginning to arrive. Most came on foot; families with small children on their mother's hip or riding high on their father's shoulders; young maids giggling together in small, coy groups; young men, uncomfortably smart, watching the girls; the elder residents of the area, some riding on slow carts, nodding and smiling, having seen it all before so many times. Megan had fought to clothe the wriggling boys in the finery and now turned to getting herself ready. She unbraided her hair and let it hang loose while she pulled on her only smart gown. It was simple, made only from wool, but it was the color of crushed damsons, trimmed with a gold ribbon, and she loved it. The moment she put it on she felt just a little bit special. For once she was not a servant, but a maiden who knew herself to be pretty and was going to enjoy being so, at least for a few short hours. She twisted sections of her hair back from her face, allowing the rest of her russet waves to swing down her back. She finished the whole off with a neat headdress, which was small enough to show off most of her hair and matched her dress. She had no jewelry and briefly considered what it might be like to adorn her body with silver or beautiful stones. She smiled at her own silliness. She glanced toward the door, then stepped over to her bed and pulled a small pot from beneath the mattress. It had belonged to her mother and had a beautiful stopper that fitted snugly into the tapering neck. Megan removed the stopper and dabbed a few drops of the rose oil onto her throat. As her skin warmed, the concoction began to release its subtle, delicious scent. This was Megan's one small luxury, which she had made for herself with roses from the castle garden. She knew it was not really her place to wear perfume, but it lifted her spirits to do so, and it suited the joyful mood of the day.

Outside the sun continued to shine, though there was a humidity that had not been present the day before. There was no shade to be found on the sloping grass outside the castle, but most people wore caps or headdresses to fend off the strength of the midday sun. The castle servants had worked hard all morning with splendid results. Trestle tables had been put up in rows across the grass, with one longer table situated on a platform at the head of the others. Each was laid with tankards and trenchers freshly made from the first bread of the new grain. These hollowed-out bread plates were food for body and soul, a gift from the Lord of the castle, and a gift from the good Lord himself. The lower half of the loaf was for the villagers. Those on the top table would receive the upper crust. There was enough for every man, woman, and child in the locality, and they were provided with benches to sit on. At the top table there were cushions on the benches and two ornately carved chairs for the hosts. Stewards bustled about imploring everyone to be seated as his Lordship would be appearing at any moment. Megan hurried to her seat beside her father, who embraced her warmly. At last the excited crowd was persuaded to take their places on the low wooden seating, and all waited with eager anticipation.

A fanfare of trumpets announced the procession, led by the musicians themselves and a handful of guards in their finest livery. There followed Lord Geraint with Lady Rhiannon on his arm, both looking regal and confident in their position. Brychan and Huw came next. Megan felt a small pang of pride at how smart and grown-up they looked. After them came Lord Geraint's loyal knights and senior soldiers. Megan spotted Llewelyn among them and blushed at the memory of him in her mistress's bed. She craned her neck for a better view, but as yet there was no sign of Merlin. Surely he would not risk offending Lord Geraint by staying away after a personal invitation? As those at the top table took their places she noticed even Lord Geraint glance about him as if searching the crowd for his guest. In a moment he would have to decide whether or not to delay the feast or continue in Merlin's absence. Just as it seemed the issue would cause a cloud over the day there came the sound of hooves. All present turned to see the lone rider approaching. Megan was surprised to find herself so pleased to see him. She was not surprised, however, that he had seen fit to come without his tame wolf. There were many at the feast who would run screaming at the sight of him, and many others who would kill the animal without a second's hesitation. As Merlin slowed his mount to a halt a page ran forward to take the reins. Megan knew the horse to be one her father had been planning to take to market. It was a plain, unremarkable courser. A work horse. Hardly the mount she would have expected for someone so highly regarded. But then, Merlin had told her he needed only something hardy and simple.

Lord Geraint rose to greet his special guest and beckon him to the seat beside him. He made a great show welcoming the magician, knowing his identity would be common knowledge by now. It would not hurt any cause or plan he had in mind for it to be known that Merlin was his ally. Lord Geraint raised his hand for silence and addressed the assembled company.

"My friends, it is good to see you all here again, gathered to celebrate our first corn of the year. I bid you welcome. May you enjoy the day, and may the remainder of our harvest be as bountiful as the first. I give you Lammas Day! *Gwyl Awst!* Let the feast begin!"

The cheer that followed all but drowned out the fanfare that announced the arrival of the food. An army of servants scurried out from the castle bearing a bewildering amount of food. They hurried to the tables, where they placed a generous selection of roast meats, stews, and pies. The villagers wasted no time helping themselves. For some it would be the only beef or fish they would see until the next feast day some months hence. There was roast hog, of course, braised mutton, and casserole of the tenderest beef. Platters of trout and salmon gleamed like treasure, dressed with mint and parsley sauces. Dishes of glossy prunes and dates shipped from an unknowable country sat amid roasted apples, delicate custards, and jewel-colored jellies. Another heartfelt cheer went up as the last of the servants arrived with huge pitchers of ale, sufficient to give every reveler a merry glow and rosy cheeks that would have little to do with the August sunshine.

Megan felt her father nudge her arm.

"Go on, girl, eat! We'll put some meat on those bones of yours yet."

It was good to see him smiling and enjoying the company of others.

Later, as she selected a piece of fish she stole a glance at

Merlin. He was talking quietly to her master, who listened and then summoned a page. Megan watched the young boy trot away and was disconcerted to realize he was running straight to her.

"My Lord asks that you join him at the high table, Megan," he panted.

She turned to her father, who shooed her away with an impatient hand. "Go child, have no concern for me. I am more than content to be here with this splendid fare. Hurry now. Don't keep him waiting."

Megan followed the page back to Lord Geraint, uncomfortably aware that the eyes of the whole village were watching her progress. She straightened her back. Let them stare. What business was it of theirs?

"Ah, Megan." Lord Geraint wore one of his more diplomatic smiles. "Our guest has requested your company. It seems you made quite an impression. Come, be seated beside us." He clapped his hands and a place was laid in an instant. The food on this table was even more sumptuous and wonderful. There was a swan, roasted and dressed again in its feathers. And bowls of nuts from distant islands that Megan had only ever heard about in tales of Knights and their travels. Here, too, were silver goblets and bone-handled knives. And here the drink was not ale but the blackest of red wines.

The sound of Merlin's soft voice close to her ear made Megan start.

"I fear our first meeting left you thinking badly of me. I dearly wish to change that. I could not let the opportunity to speak with you pass. I am sorry if I have caused you any embarrassment."

"You are my Lord's honored guest. Of course you must have

what you request," she said, focusing on the food in front of her. "Besides," she added, "I do not so easily become embarrassed."

"No. I imagine that to be true."

Now she looked at him and felt her heart lurch at the directness of his gaze. Was that why they called him Magician? For those eyes could cast a spell all their own. She looked away and caught sight of Lady Rhiannon glaring at her. Her plans had clearly not included Megan, and her displeasure at Merlin's interest in her was obvious. Megan sighed. Now she would have to face the disapproval of her mistress, however unfair.

"So, sir, how should you be addressed?" Lord Geraint leaned across Megan the better to speak to his guest. "Magician? Seer? Some have even called you Prophet. What is the correct form of address for a person of so many talents?" He drank deeply as he waited for a response.

"My name is Merlin. Add to it what you will—it matters not." He spoke slowly, in the manner of one who knew he would be listened to.

"Ha! Such admirable modesty! Come now, speak to me of what you do. There is mystery surrounding you. I am a soldier, plain and simple, a man of hearth and war, come late in life to be Lord of this region and father to these wretches." He gestured toward the villagers. "Demonstrate, show us all, what wondrous things you can do."

"Forgive me, but the gifts I have been given are to be used for the greater good and are not tricks to be put on show."

"Laudable sentiments, my friend, but I would know more. Is it true you can foretell the future? Or that you can watch, unseen, the movements of a person in another place?"

"It is true."

"Ah-ha! By God, I could put such abilities to use in battle! Imagine the fate of my enemies were I to know their every step. Why, no man would dare set himself against me, I believe, with Merlin the Seer at my side."

"Naturally, my Lord, I will assist you when I can. But understand this: I am in the control of no man. My destiny will reveal itself, and until then I practice my arts only to aid those in peril. Not to wage war, nor to further the causes of avaricious men."

There was an audible intake of breath around the table. Lord Geraint's expression hardened.

"Why, sir, do you inhabit such a lofty pinnacle that you can look down and judge me?" He leaned in closer, his wine-fumed breath near Megan's face. "I have heard tell of how you battle with dragons. Are you dragon slayer, too? Shall you conjure one up so that we might see you wrestle it here and now?" He laughed heartily at the notion, his men joining in the joke enthusiastically.

Megan wondered that any man could keep his manners and his dignity under such brash ridicule. If Lord Geraint had truly hoped to make an ally of Merlin it seemed he was prepared to give up such an idea quickly if the stranger proved unwilling. He must fear the magician to treat him with such contempt. Was his purpose then to threaten him? To control him at any cost if he could not secure his friendship? If Merlin suspected any such thing he showed no outward sign.

"I see you have jesters and fools in your employ already, Lord Geraint. They would not thank me, I think, for acting in their place."

At this Lady Rhiannon could be heard laughing sharply. Lord Geraint frowned. Beside him his men at arms grew restless.

"Indeed, I know a fool when I see one," he said flatly. "Just as I know a man who would crush another beneath his foot to get to where he wants to be, and yet another who would smile as he pushed a dagger into your heart." He illustrated his observation by stabbing another piece of meat with his silver knife. "Which are you, I wonder?"

"I would not choose to be any such person, my Lord. But each man must do as his conscience bids him, surely?" Merlin held Lord Geraint's stare as he spoke.

"He must. And I aim to see that your conscience bids you assist me, Magician. I have these past seven years suffered unwanted intrusions and skirmishes from a neighbor who calls himself 'noble.' I plan to be rid of him once and for all. But the terrain that lies between us is dense with woodland and narrow valleys. It is a place for ambush and defeat for any army that ventures within, unless they had the advantage of surprise, perhaps. And of knowing the movements and actions of their adversary. Such a talented person as you yourself could, I understand, furnish me with this information at the precise time I require it. I can rely upon you to do this for me? Assure me of this."

All at the table fell silent now. While the feasting and merry-making continued among the villagers, and the minstrels played on, those within earshot of Lord Geraint's words waited for the stranger's response.

Merlin put down his knife slowly. He seemed on the point of speaking when a loud cry went up from the top of the hill.

"The wheel is ready!"

Everyone turned to look and the villagers scrambled to their feet. At the top of the hill a cartwheel had been daubed with tallow and was now set alight. Amidst much cheering and shouting it was moved into position. Children and young men raced from their places to take positions behind the wheel.

Brychan and Huw leaped from their seats.

"May we go, Father, may we?"

"Please!" they clamored.

Lord Geraint was in no mood for such frivolity, but Lady Rhiannon stepped forward, pushing the boys gently.

"Go, children, hurry up. Llewelyn, go with them. See they stay safe," she said.

Llewelyn narrowed his eyes at the indignity of the task, hesitating. Lord Geraint growled at him.

"Go, man! Do as she bids you."

The adults watched as the excited children took their places. The wheel was ready. The priest stood by muttering a harvest prayer, but his words were lost in the older, more basic exultations of the crowd. This was a ritual the church had seen fit to include in its celebrations, but it belonged to a time when gods were many and men made offerings and symbolic gestures to stave off starvation in the winter months to come. At last the wheel was heaved over the brow and began its descent. The faster it rolled the more fiercely it burned, until it was a fiery mass hurtling down the hill. Behind it ran the youngsters, screaming and shouting, caught up in the wake of the dancing flames. That the wheel kept to its given course and did not divert to plow through the villagers and their feast was nothing if not a small miracle in itself, and confirmed to all the blessing that was upon the occasion. At last the fireball came to a crashing stop at the bottom of the hill. The revelers danced around it, jeering and baying, in a moment that signified a mood shift in the day. The musicians struck up raucous tunes, their pipes and drums blaring and thumping into the hot air. Many people left their food and came to the wheel to dance, while others called for more ale, draining their tankards and banging them on the table to be replenished. As if some greater power watching the proceedings disapproved of these beginnings of bawdiness the sky darkened.

Megan's skin prickled in the damp heat, and something in the frenzy of the villagers' actions unsettled her. The awkward moment at the table had passed, though she knew it would not be forgotten. No doubt Lord Geraint had ways and means of getting most people to comply with his demands. Most people, but would that include Merlin?

"Ha!" Lord Geraint staggered to his feet, waving his goblet of wine above his head. "Enough talk of war. This is a day for celebration. Come, let us join in the fun. There will be battles enough to be waged tomorrow." He looked pointedly at his revered guest as he spoke. Merlin merely gave a small bow of acknowledgment and stood aside to let Lord Geraint pass.

Megan stood up, intending to slip back to her father if possible, but Merlin reached forward and took her hand. In that instant she felt something of the nearby fire coursing through her veins.

"Dance with me, Megan," he said.

It was the first time he had said her name, and she liked the way it sounded on his lips. She smiled at him and was about to let him lead her to the minstrels when Lady Rhiannon caught her eye. She pulled away her hand quickly.

"I am sorry," she muttered, studying the ground between them. "I am needed elsewhere."

Lady Rhiannon made her way to Merlin's side.

"They tell me that Magicians cannot dance," she said, her back to Megan. "I know you will prove this to be some wicked untruth."

She offered him her hand. Megan knew better than to stand in the way of her mistress's desires, and she stepped back, waiting for her moment to melt into the crowd. To her astonishment, she felt Merlin take her hand again.

"You will forgive me, Lady Rhiannon. I had already promised to dance with Megan."

So saying he led her, stumbling, away. Megan could hear her Lady's hiss of indignation and knew that Merlin had made not one but two powerful enemies that day.

Merlin took her not to join the restrained dancing of those from the upper table, but to the rowdy merrymakers nearer the burning wheel. Here was dancing that allowed him to hold her as they moved to the lively music. As they whirled and turned and spun across the short grass, Megan felt her fears for his safety and the rage of her employers lessen. Only the moment mattered. The moment and Merlin, his gaze locked with hers, his strong arms sending her spinning away and catching her again, his smile lighting up his dark face as he looked at her.

All about them the party grew ever wilder and more debauched. Mothers rounded up small children and dragged them back toward their homes. Men and women too old to join in such rowdiness began their stiff journey back to the village, their aching joints numbed by quantities of ale. Maids and their would-be suitors danced on. Couples embraced, some reclining on the turf, drinking more than was good for them.

At once there was a lowering of the clouds and the threatened rain threw itself down onto the celebrations. There were squeals and cries. Lord Geraint, Lady Rhiannon, and their entourage hurried to the castle, their servants scurrying after them. The stalwart merrymakers would not be put off, some crawling beneath the tables to continue their feasting, others slipping and falling in the fresh mud, too drunk to care or notice the filth and water. Some danced on, as the doughty musicians continued to play even as their instruments were waterlogged.

Merlin and Megan stopped dancing. They stood looking at one another, water coursing down their faces. She smiled, then laughed as the rain filled her mouth. She lifted her face to the sky, still laughing. Merlin held her hands, and they leaned back, bathing in the rain, letting the water wash away their cares, laughing as the party disintegrated into debauchery around them.

LAURA DID NOT protest when Rhys picked her up and carried her to his cottage. A mixture of fear, exhaustion, and relief had left her weak and tearful. Rhys kicked open the front door and set her down in front of the old, black range. The whole of the downstairs was a single space, with a kitchen area at one end and a sitting room at the other. The windows here were even smaller than those of Penlan, and it took a while for Laura's eyes to adjust to the low level of light. She found she was shivering and moved closer to the fire as Rhys prodded it into new life. He split some kindling with a chopper and threw a handful on the fire to produce more flame. There was a hiss as water dropped from his hair onto the range. He fetched a woolen blanket, draped it around her shoulders, and then set about lighting candles. Only at that point did Laura realize there was no electricity at the cottage. Now she could see candles on every surface, as well as oil lamps hanging from hooks in the beams. The ceilings were low, and Rhys had to keep ducking to avoid them. There was a wooden spiral staircase in the far corner of the kitchen. The furniture was simple and rustic, but beautiful, too. The top of the long kitchen table had been fashioned out of a single piece of wood, and the bench and chairs beside it were chunky and roughly hewn. There was a sink with a single tap and a collection of heavy pots and pans, blackened from hours of use on the range. In the sitting area were two low sofas, a wood-burning stove, and shelves sagging under an impressive book collection. Rhys poured hot water from the iron kettle into a large enamel bowl. He fetched a cloth and a towel and sat at Laura's feet. He dipped the cloth in the steaming water, wrung it out and, with the utmost gentleness, reached up and washed the mud from Laura's face. She sat motionless, letting him tend to her, enjoying the comfort of his care and the warm water, feeling her tired muscles begin to unknot at last. He dabbed her face dry with the towel before moving the blanket and bathing her arms and hands. He worked on wordlessly, changing the water before starting on her scratched and battered legs. Laura winced as he rinsed her stinging cuts. The smell of lavender replaced that of mud and mountain. When her legs were clean Rhys took the towel and dried them with light, tender movements. He looked up at her and smiled. She had never felt so cherished as she did at that moment. Nor had she experienced anything so utterly erotic. Neither of them had spoken, and yet she felt incredibly close to Rhys, as if she had known him a lifetime already.

He stood up, "I'll find you some dry clothes," he said, before springing lightly up the stairs to the room above.

His footsteps echoed through the wooden boards as he moved about upstairs. Laura turned to the small fire, gazing into the flames. She had thought Penlan to be a timeless place, a place capable of transporting a person back through centuries by the roughness of a beam, or the coolness of a flagstone. But here, in this cottage, she felt as if the modern world no longer existed. People must have lived in the croft just as Rhys did now for generations. Little had changed. The books, maybe. New glass in the windows. A windup radio on the windowsill. What must it be like to live in such a house alone, cut off from everyone? Laura remembered the dog she had seen with Rhys the day she and Dan viewed Penlan. There was no sign of it now, nor that a dog had been in the house recently.

Rhys returned with a shirt, jeans, and a belt. She took them, standing awkwardly. Should she strip off in front of him?

"We need some more wood. I'll be back in a minute," he said, saving her embarrassment. After he had gone out she changed quickly. Once in the dry garments she felt stronger and restored to some sort of normality, though with a frisson of excitement at the feel of his clothes against her freshly bathed skin. She undid her sodden hair and blotted it with the towel as she wandered around the room. Although the place was sparsely furnished and the facilities basic, it was anything but empty. In every niche and corner

Laura found an intricate wood carving or a beautiful piece of stained glass or a small cluster of pebbles. She picked up an egg-shaped stone and ran her fingers over it. It was smooth as fine china yet hard and heavy as lead. The one next to it was milk white with a hole through the center. She reached up and touched one of the wood carvings—a bird of prey. It occurred to her that though lovely to look at, most of these objects must have been chosen for their tactile qualities. They cried out to be touched, and through her fingertips they told of their individual origins. Of their own special beauty. Of their magic.

Rhys came back with the wood and built up the fire. The storm had moved off now, and with it the heat of the last few days. The rain had cooled the earth and left a dampness that Laura felt had got into her very bones while she was on the mountain. She shivered.

"Here," Rhys said as he beckoned her. "Stay by the fire. I'll fix you a hot drink."

She half expected some herbal concoction but was relieved to see him reach for a jar of good quality coffee. She settled back on a chair by the warmth of the range and watched Rhys. His movements were quiet and nimble for a tall man in such a small space. He took care in each task, fully concentrating on what he was doing. Laura admired that, having so often to rein in her own grasshopper mind in order to focus. Painting was the only thing that could absorb her so. And lately even that had failed to captivate her mind in the way it always used to.

Rhys pulled up a chair beside her, handing her a steaming mug.

"Thank you for everything," she said. "I was in such a state."

"More seasoned mountain walkers than you have got themselves lost up here when the weather changes."

"It happened so quickly. One minute a sunny day, the next . . . I'd never experienced a storm like that. I was terrified. So stupid of me."

"You were right to be scared. The open hill is not a place to share with lightning."

"Could it have killed me?"

"Of course."

Laura shivered again and sipped her drink, "It felt so powerful. And so eerie. It was as if the storm itself was a living thing. And it was angry. And it was after me. How ridiculous does that sound?" She laughed quietly at herself.

"The people who lived here long ago believed just that. Or later that the storms were sent by a god to show his rage."

"Didn't the ancient Greeks think thunder was the gods quarrelling?"

"I like your idea better," he said with a smile. "Though I shouldn't take it personally. Why would the storm single you out?"

"I don't know, perhaps it didn't want me up there on the mountain. Maybe I don't belong."

"Ah, so you do believe a person can belong to a place and not only the other way around after all."

Laura remembered now he had asked her that very question about her house. It had all seemed a bit New Age then. But now . . .

"I do think a place can change a person," she said. "And I do love living at Penlan. I have to say I think I'd struggle all the way up here, though. Especially on my own."

"Why is it that people are so afraid of their own company?" he asked.

His question threw her. She had been looking for confirmation that there was no one living at the croft with him. Instead he had turned her probing remark around and aimed it back at her.

"It's not that. At least, it wouldn't be with me. I like being alone a lot of the time. I just wouldn't choose to live on my own in such an isolated place. That's all. Anyway, I've got Dan, haven't I?"

Rhys nodded, drinking his coffee, giving nothing more away. Laura could stand his evasion no longer.

"So, no wife up here to help you with . . . all this?" She waved her arm at the range and the garden outside, and inwardly cringed at the crassness of her question.

"No. I'm not married. I choose to live here alone because this place suits me. This is where I feel I am able to be myself."

"But you're not local? I mean, you didn't grow up here, did you?"

"No. I have traveled a little, lived in other places, seen enough of the world to decide I don't want a great deal to do with it."

"Well, then, you're certainly in the right place. Is there even a road up here?"

"A track. I have an old Land Rover, but I don't use it very often."

"And you manage without electricity. I don't suppose there's a mobile signal up here either?"

"No electricity. No phone. That's the way I like it. And you?" he asked. "What made you decide to move to Penlan?"

"Oh, you know, had enough of the city, searching for a more relaxed way of life."

"You have no children?"

There was a tiny but eloquent pause before Laura answered.

"No. Not yet. That is, we'd like to have a family, but we've had no luck so far." She smiled in an attempt to keep her voice level. "Who knows, maybe all this fresh air . . ."

"I'm sorry."

She was about to ask what for, but his face told her that. He was not apologizing for raising what was clearly a difficult subject for her. It was as if he understood her suffering. As if her deepest pain was visible to him. She blinked away tears, cursing her own sensitivity.

"Some days I can be philosophical for a whole five minutes. You know, 'it wasn't meant to be' sort of stuff. Other days I feel so angry, and of course there's no one to be angry with. Except perhaps myself, given that it's my fault."

"Your fault?"

"I mean, the problem is with me. Dan could have children with someone else. But not with me, it seems." Laura fought to deflect the conversation from her own demons. "And you haven't any children yourself?"

"No. Maybe that is another thing not meant to be. Besides, I think I do best on my own," he said, a shadow passing over his face as he turned thoughtfully to the fire.

"Do you hate other people so much?"

"I don't waste my time hating."

Laura suspected she had touched a nerve. She heard her mother's voice in her ear and for once acted upon it.

"How on earth do you earn a living up here? You surely can't survive on selling your veg and eggs. Though it was all delicious, by the way."

Rhys frowned at this, and Laura feared she had been too nosy and asked one question too many. He leaned forward and picked up the small ax he had used earlier for chopping wood. He turned it around in his hand, staring at the blade. Laura stiffened in her chair. It came home to her now that she was alone, miles from anywhere, with a strangely solitary man whom she knew next to nothing about. Rhys nodded in the direction of the table.

"I make furniture. Things like that. Rustic, natural pieces. I sell them to a shop in Cardiff and another in Hereford. People with city lives like a little bit of the country in their homes, it seems."

Laura relaxed again, "I love that table. I might have known you'd do something creative."

"What about you—have you finished your studio yet?"

She was a little surprised he knew about that. She remembered telling him she painted, but couldn't recall mentioning she was setting up a studio. It was a reasonable assumption, but it made her feel as if he had been watching the house. She shook her head at her own silly notion.

"It's a long way off being finished, but I can paint in it as it is. Or rather, I will be able to once I've settled back into it. I think the move has upset my muse. Must have left her in one of the packing cases somewhere." She felt oddly uncomfortable discussing her problems with her painting with him. It was as if she ought to apologize for failing to be inspired by such a wonderful place. A place he clearly loved. She got up and walked over to his bookshelves. "Wow, this is quite a collection. I'm surprised you can read by candlelight. I think it would do my eyes in."

"You get used to it." He left his chair and followed her as she browsed.

"Hmm, let's see what you spend your winter evenings reading. Hemingway, Joyce, all the usual suspects. Oh, quite a lot of poetry. Some in Welsh, too. Do you speak the language?"

He nodded, "It is beautiful. Listen." He took down a well-thumbed book and selected a poem. He read quietly but confidently. Laura could not understand the meaning of the words, but the music in them was unmistakable. She had always thought Welsh to be made up of harsh, guttural, unmanageable sounds, but listening to Rhys now she heard nothing jarring or ugly, only rhythm and pattern and symmetry. He finished the poem and returned the book to the shelf. "I'll translate it for you one day. If you'd like me to," he said.

"Thank you, yes. I would like that very much."

She browsed on. There were books on gardening and horticulture and wood carving and herbal remedies and all manner of things that fitted with Rhys's obscure lifestyle. There were plenty of novels, too, and the poetry, and a section on philosophy and theology. Another shelf was given over to mathematics, and still another to psychology, dispelling at last any idea Laura had of Rhys being an aging hippy. Here was a voracious reader. A scholar, even. She was getting a clearer picture of him now, and it revealed a complex and ever more intriguing character. At last she came to a large number of books about legends and myths, most focusing on stories related to Wales and the Celts. "Oh, these are interesting."

"Do you like legends?"

"I've been trying to find out a bit about local ones. Actually, I started off looking for ghost stories. I don't know, something about Penlan got me thinking about ghosts. Ridiculous, I know, but with such old houses its easy to get daft ideas in your head."

"You shouldn't be so quick to consider your ideas ridiculous. You talk more sense than most, it seems to me."

"Really? You think? Anyway, I didn't find anything written about that sort of thing. I did get a good book on local myths though, stuff about Merlin. He lived around here for a while, so the story goes. Did you know that? Of course you did—look at all these books on him!"

"I do have a particular interest in him. And you're right about him having been here for a short time. Just one summer."

"You believe he was a real person, then? Not just a myth?"

"Of course. There is real evidence. He was someone who had an enormous influence, in more ways then most people realize."

"Looks like you've got every book ever written on him."

"There have been plenty written, not all of them worth reading. Some have references to his time here, which I find especially interesting, more so now that I live here, of course."

"It's quite a library."

"Borrow whatever you like," he said.

Laura became aware of how close he was standing to her. She could feel the warmth of his body and the movement of his chest as he breathed. She grabbed a book without even looking at it.

"Thank you. I'll return it as soon as I've read it."

"Take your time."

There was a pause—a highly charged moment. Laura knew

she must leave. Quickly, before she did something she might later regret. Something that would change her, and change her life, forever. She brushed past him with a light smile, though her pulse was racing.

"Well, thanks again, for rescuing me. And for the coffee. And the clothes."

"You are welcome. Come and visit me again, though perhaps not in a thunderstorm next time," he said with a smile.

Laura opened the front door, then hesitated. She turned and looked at him and allowed herself to acknowledge how much she wanted to stay. He returned her gaze steadily. In that moment she could so easily have given in, every particle in her body screamed at her to stay, to be with him. But a small voice in her head held sway.

A thought occurred to her as she was on the point of leaving.

"Where is your dog?" she asked. "Big, shaggy, grey thing?"

Rhys shook his head.

"No dog," he said. "I have never had a dog."

✣ 5 ✣

BY THE TIME Dan arrived home from work on the following Friday night Laura found herself reluctant to tell him about her visit to the croft.

"What have you been up to this week? I want all the details," he said, pulling off his tie and opening the fridge.

"Oh, I've been sorting out the studio, going for walks, making sketches, you know. Usual sort of stuff before getting started on a new lot of paintings."

"We had terrific thunderstorms in London, rattled the office windows. Did you get them up here, too?" He helped himself to a beer and passed one to her.

"Some, but not close up." She surprised herself with the first lie. She didn't want Dan to think her stupid for being on the mountain in the storm, but that was not her only reason for fibbing. "It did rain, though," she added.

"So I see. Freshened things up a bit, thank God." Dan perched on the edge of the table and drank.

Laura watched him. He was still the same old Dan, still the man she married. The man she loved. But she felt herself strangely distant from him. By not telling him about going to Rhys's cottage she was lying to him. She could not convince herself otherwise. And yet, how would it sound if she told him? She had behaved like an idiot in the storm, been rescued by Rhys, let him wash her, changed into his clothes, and spent time alone with him. But it had all been innocent, nothing had happened, so why was she hiding it? Deep inside she knew the real reason. She knew how close she had come to staying with Rhys. She knew how much she had wanted to. How much she still wanted to.

Later, as Dan snored lightly beside her, Laura read the book she had borrowed from Rhys. It had been a lucky choice, all about Welsh folklore. Six months earlier she could never have imagined herself interested in such a thing. Now it fascinated her. Particularly the section on fertility. She read that corn dollies had been thought vital to the success of a crop. Each year, after the summer solstice, dollies would be twisted from the ripe corn. They were often given as presents at weddings and for newborns— seedless for men, but with the grain inside for women. They had to be buried in the field the following spring to assure the farmer of a good harvest. Similarly, they were believed to help women conceive, and could be hung in the bedroom of a woman wishing for a baby. As Laura read on she learned that the birch tree was also reputed to have magic properties where baby making was concerned. She was just about to find out why and how when Dan stirred. He rolled over and smiled up at her sleepily.

"What's that you've got there?" He squinted at the cover.

"Welsh Folklore. Not your usual nighttime reading." Dan yawned and tugged the book from her hands.

"Hey!"

"Let's see, oh, 'Fertility Rites and Rituals'—sounds like a good chapter. Any tips for me? Should I be making wild love to you in the meadows under a full moon?"

Laura snatched back the book. "Very funny. I want to learn something about the history of our new home, even if you don't."

"All riveting stuff, no doubt." He shook his head and turned away again, making something of a show of getting comfortable.

Laura pretended to read until she was sure he was asleep again then put the book back on her nightstand. Why had Dan seen fit to make fun of something that had been a crucial part of people's lives for centuries? Who was to say what might or might not work? The whole business of conception was so mysterious, why not turn to magic? Could it be any less successful than anything else they had tried? She closed her eyes and tried to sleep, but now all she could think of was Rhys, and all she could see was his face close to hers. Outside a family of foxes called to one another in dry yaps and husky barks. Soon the young would leave the lair to make their own way in the world, but for now they played and hunted together. Laura thought of how everyone was driven to build a family around them, to be part of a pack. And of how Rhys had chosen to live alone, so far from anyone. What could have made him choose such a life? He was a man of intellect and of passion, yet he shunned company. Why? As she drifted into a fitful sleep a shadowy figure followed her into her dreams.

LAURA MADE A point of spending as much time as possible with Dan over the weekend. Whatever assurances she had given her mother, she knew she would have to work at maintaining the usual closeness the two of them shared, now that they were apart for so much of the time. And she so wanted him to fall for Penlan in the way that she herself had. She tried to think of aspects of their new home that would appeal to him, seeking out a wonderful local pub that sold good food and one of his favorite beers; introducing him to the delights of the one and only Indian takeaway ten miles away; renting a new DVD one evening and seducing him in front of it with a bottle of champagne. These were hardly rural pursuits, but they did help to reestablish a bond. The time passed swiftly, and she felt quite low watching him drive away through the pretty mist on Monday morning. She decided to redouble her efforts to paint. It was ridiculous to be so feeble about it. She had the time, the place, the subjects—what was stopping her? With amazement she realized she had not produced more than a few sketches in almost two months. She wondered why she had not gone mad.

As soon as Dan left for work she jammed her hair on top of her head with a wooden clip, slipped on a favorite painting shirt and jeans, and hurried to the studio. It was still basic and harbored a fair amount of dust, but it was a workable space. She had swept and scrubbed the cobbles of the floor so that they looked lovely yet they provided an unhelpfully knobbly surface on which to try and stand an easel. The original hay mangers were still attached to the walls, and served as useful places to store lengths of framing, old canvasses, and general materials. In time, there were improvements that could be made—more windows, more lights, heating—but such alterations could come later. For now, the old building, with its solid, ancient walls, and a sense of time passed embedded in every stone, gave Laura a sense of calm and of safety that was wonderfully conducive to producing good work. She felt certain of it.

She positioned her easel by the open door so that she had a clear view of the meadows sweeping down to the woods. The recent rain had washed grit and grime away and brightened the colors of the landscape. She selected her palette accordingly. Flake white, cadmium yellow, French ultramarine, alizarin crimson, burnt umber, and lamp black. The sight of the oils soothed her as she squeezed out generous splodges. She had already prepared a canvas, rubbing on a layer of burnt sienna mixed with a drop of turpentine. She always preferred to work on a somber background, traveling from dark to light as she built up the picture. She assembled her brushes—broad hog bristle filberts to give clear shapes with soft edges. As the smell of the materials filled her nostrils she felt a familiar excitement stirring within her. She had been away too long from what she did best, from her preferred way of relating to the world around her. It was good to be back in that creative space once more, and with such inspirational subjects for inspiration.

She gazed out at the landscape, looking with her painter's eye, truly seeing the shape of the trees, the depth of their shadows, the myriad tones and colors that offered themselves to her. She

paused, allowing time for the information to be processed somewhere behind her intellect, somewhere deep in her subconscious
where her artistic intuition dwelt. She picked a palette knife and
plunged it into the buttery paint, mixing ultramarine with a dash
of crimson, working at the blend until she had precisely the hue
she wanted. Selecting a brush, she took a breath, offered up a silent prayer as always to whatever god ruled her talent, and then
pitched in with bold strokes.

Three hours later Laura sat cross-legged on the cobbled floor,
her chin resting in her hands, staring at the disaster before her.
It had been a long time since a painting had gone so completely
wrong. There was no hope of saving it, despite her best efforts.
It was a failure. All that remained to be done was clean the canvas
with turpentine and begin again. Only she hadn't the heart. That
vital part of her psyche that made the difference between a mess
and a masterpiece was refusing to come out to play. She knew herself well enough to recognize a hopeless day when she had one.
To continue now would only frustrate her further. No good could
come of it. She hauled herself to her feet and set about cleaning
her brushes. Usually, when the work had gone well, there was
pleasure to be had in caring for her tools; in restoring the natural
luster to the bristles of the brushes; in watching the last of the
colors smudge from her palette; in tucking the tubes of oil paint
away in their snug wooden box. But that delight was fed by the
satisfaction of progress, of a measure of success, of a knowledge of
having set in motion a creation. Glancing now at the ugliness
standing on the easel Laura battled with despair and could not
even face tackling the canvas. She left it where it was and went outside, suddenly needing to be free of the pungent air of the studio.

The newly washed countryside was soft and calming. Though it was still warm, summer had had its finest moment and was winding down. Subtle changes were afoot, as the leaves began to lose their gloss, and colors started to fade with the waning of the year. Laura closed her eyes, choosing to experience her surroundings in any way other than as a painter. A zephyr rustled through the silver birch beside the house. Two jays quarreled somewhere in the branches. A laden bumblebee droned past her ear and away to its nest in the ground behind the house. She stood for a further calming moment, then strode down the hill toward the woods.

She found the proximity of the trees and the otherworldliness of the woodland helpful in dispelling the bleakness of her mood, if only a little. It was hard not to be comforted by the cheerfulness of the young birds darting and dipping, the glow of the sun through the leafy boughs, and the smell of wild honeysuckle and damp moss. The noise of her own footsteps seemed brutally loud as she snapped twigs and scrunched dust and small stones along the path. She tried to tread lightly, but still felt clumsy. As she rounded a bend she glimpsed someone up ahead, someone walking away from her farther along the same path. She hesitated, remembering her last encounter in these woods. The farmer, whom she had later learned was known as Glyn the Bryn, had warned her off walking here, and the last thing she needed right now was a dose of his surly rudeness. But as she squinted through the undergrowth she could see this was not the old man but someone younger, taller, and stronger looking. He had dark hair, was wearing dark clothes, and carried a heavy stick. A movement to his left caught Laura's eye. A dog, large and grey, was following the man. Now she realized this was the same figure she had seen that first day at Penlan. It hadn't been Rhys after all. Laura sped up, curious to see who this stranger was. A rambler, perhaps? He certainly did not look the type. Nor a farmer. Who then? Laura all but broke into a trot, stumbling on the uneven ground. The man seemed to glide over the forest floor with his surefooted, long stride. Try as she might she could not gain on him, and he kept vanishing behind the trees. She thought of calling out, but what would she say? Then, as suddenly as they had appeared, the man and his dog merged with the trees and were gone. Laura stood, peering into the woods, but she had lost him. She had come to a part of the forest she had not visited before and had reached a field. Looking across it she could see a small farm. There was a scruffy stone house and a collection of equally dilapidated barns and sheds forming a muddy yard. An engine roared and Glyn the Bryn pulled out of one of the buildings, his dog barking beside him. He swore at the animal, and it leaped onto the back of the quad bike. The farmer revved up the machine and tore out of the yard and off down the lane, away from the woods, much to Laura's relief. She waited until he was well out of sight and then climbed the fence and headed for the farm.

Close up everything was just as unkempt and shabby. The yard was covered in a layer of mud and sheep dung and must have been a mire in the winter. The barn roof was of rusty corrugated iron, as were some of the stable doors. Skeletons of ancient farm machinery lay about the place. A pigsty housed nothing but an elder tree, which had long ago forced off any roof there might have been. Laura was about to explore the barn when a tinkling laugh from behind her made her jump. She wheeled around to find an old woman watching her. If this was Glyn's wife, then she was his physical opposite in every way. She was round and plump with a smiley face and bright, sparkling eyes. Her skin was not so much lined as creased and dimpled, and her abundant silver hair was tied back in a low, loose bun. Her ample body shook as she laughed. She wore a spotless white blouse and a long, heavy skirt over which was an ample apron, the strings of which tied her all together like a butcher's parcel. On her feet were heavy boots that looked almost as aged as the woman herself.

"Oh," said Laura. "I'm sorry, I . . ."

". . . thought there was no one here." The woman laughed some more. "Don't fret, Glyn won't be back before his stomach tells him it's time for tea. Anyway, his bark is worse than his bite. Not that you can say the same about that dog of his!" She laughed again.

"Thanks for the warning." Laura smiled and stepped forward, holding out her hand. "I'm Laura, from Penlan."

"Of course you are," said the old woman, her accent swooping and soaring like one of the woodland birds. She took Laura's hand in her own pudgy one and squeezed it warmly, "You can call me Anwen."

"I'm sorry. I was snooping. That was really rude of me."

"Oh, don't you worry about that, now, *cariad*. No harm done. You come and sit down with me, 'ave something to drink. I was just going to open a bottle of my elderflower cordial. Such a fine crop of blooms this year. Nothing like it on a dusty day. Come along."

She led the way on painful legs to a warped, wooden seat at the front of the house. She gestured for Laura to sit and went inside. Laura wondered how such a mean-spirited dry stick of a man could have such a warm woman for his wife. Anwen reappeared moments later with two tall glasses. She handed one to Laura.

"Here you are. You try that and tell me if it's not the best elderflower you've ever tasted."

Laura sipped thoughtfully, deciding not to let on it was the only elderflower she had ever tasted.

"Delicious," she declared, meaning it. "Absolutely delicious."

Anwen shook with more gleeful laughter. "There we are, then. You want to try making some yourself. You're still young. You might get it right by the time you're an old crone like me."

"I'm sorry, but I've never met anyone less cronelike in my life."

They both laughed at that, then sat enjoying their drinks for a moment. Laura felt wonderfully at ease with this cheerful neighbor, and a little of the morning's disappointment began to lift. It occurred to her that Anwen must know everyone local, including, perhaps, the man she had seen in the woods.

"I saw someone, as I was walking from Penlan. A man. Tall, dark, with a grey dog. Does he live around here?"

Anwen's face altered minutely. She still wore her habitual smile, but a shadow of seriousness fell over her eyes.

"Oh, you've seen him, then, have you?" She looked at Laura differently now, as if studying her, trying to get the measure of her. After a moment's silent consideration she nodded, to herself it seemed, and then sipped her drink. She leaned back on the seat, causing it to creak alarmingly, and stretched out her legs stiffly, letting out a deep sigh before speaking.

"You don't wear a watch, Laura," she said, looking ahead into the middle distance now.

"No. As a matter of fact, I never have."

"And do you have to look at a calendar to know which day it is?"

"Pretty much, yes."

"You see, there are some people who live their lives by time. A time to get up. A time to go to bed. A clock on every wall. A date for this and a day for that. Those people wouldn't know how to go on without an hour chiming or a watch watching them. Other people, people like you, Laura, well, they live their lives to the rhythm inside themselves, not the ticking of a clock."

As the old woman paused Laura struggled to find the relevance of what she was saying. It was observant of her to notice Laura wasn't wearing a watch, and it was an accurate description of the way Laura lived, inasmuch as she didn't follow a nine-to-five workday. But what had any of that to do with the stranger in the woods?

"Such people have a way of looking at the world," Anwen went on. "A way of seeing things that is sometimes a little bit different to the rest." She turned to face Laura again, her expression gentle but earnest. "There is plenty in this world to be seen by those who are able to look, *cariad*. You are one of the lucky ones."

Laura felt her scalp begin to tingle. Was the old woman talking about ghosts? Surely not. Laura had never been even remotely susceptible to such things. She was the only girl at a séance at school to get a hopeless fit of the giggles and had never found ghost stories the smallest bit scary. There were those strange, unexplained experiences in the house. Those sensations, and the thought that she wasn't alone somehow, but she had already dismissed the idea of ghosts. It just wasn't her. An echo of past inhabitants of the house, maybe. She could accept that. As if their voices and deeds might be somehow held in the walls of the ancient place. Recorded, in some way. But dead people wandering about in broad daylight? No, definitely not. Laura fidgeted on the wooden slats of the bench. She did not want to offend Anwen, but there had to be a more mundane explanation as to the identity of the unknown walker.

"I know the air is pretty thin up here, but I really don't think I've started seeing ghosts," she said with a smile.

"Ghosts! Did I say they were ghosts?" There was an edge to Anwen's voice now. "That man you saw was as real as you or I. As real as you or I. Not dead. Not imagined. Not a will-o'-the-wisp. All I'm saying is not everyone would have seen him. And you did. Was this the first time?"

"No. No, I saw him when we first came to the house. He was in the distance, so I didn't get a good look. But I'm sure it was the same person. Actually, at first I thought it must have been our neighbor, Rhys, but it wasn't. You know, from the croft up the hill?"

"Ty Bychan, you mean?" Anwen looked away again. "There are those who can not be seen clearly, even when you are standing toe to toe. Look closely, girl. Look with that artist's eye of yours."

Laura's mouth dried. She stared at the old woman.

"How did you know I was an artist?"

Now Anwen laughed again. "Well, it could have been village gossip, but let's say your clothes gave you away this time."

Laura looked down at her paint-splattered shirt. "Oh, of course." She felt Anwen was trying to change the subject, but she couldn't really make sense of what she had told her. She tried a different tack. "I've started doing some reading about the area. It's another world, isn't it, out here?"

"You're used to city life. It will take time for you to slow down to the rhythm of the countryside, but you will. Eventually. Let the seasons be your calendar."

"I so want to paint the landscape, but I don't seem able to settle. So far all I've produced is a mess. So much for my artist's eye." She waited, hoping Anwen might offer something more about ghosts that weren't ghosts and the mysterious walker, but nothing came. The old woman seemed tired now, distracted, and barely aware of her visitor anymore. Laura felt she had overstayed her welcome. She stood up. "I'd better get back. Thank you so much for the drink. Please, call in if you find yourself up near Penlan."

"Oh, I don't go far from the farm anymore." She rose with difficulty, puffing as her legs took her weight.

Laura thought now she looked very, very old.

Anwen turned to her with a tired little smile. "Penlan has been waiting for you for a long time. Don't be surprised if there are those who are eager to show themselves to you once more."

So saying, she gave a little wave and shuffled back inside the house, leaving Laura more baffled than before.

The sun was beginning to dip toward the horizon, and long shadows fringed the field as she made her way back to the woods. The low light flashed between the trunks of the trees now, rather than fighting its way down through the woodland canopy. Laura squinted against the glare as she walked, her mind busy with muddled thoughts. She had never met anyone quite like Anwen before. She could not imagine her getting many visitors in so remote a place, and yet she had been very welcoming and friendly. What could she have meant about people wanting to show themselves to her? "Once more," she had said, as if they were people Laura had already met. And as for Penlan waiting for her, it reminded her of something Rhys had said, the first time he came to the house. Something about her being where she belonged. Again. The thought of Rhys made her feel even more confused. She had hoped to lose herself in a new painting and forget the intensity of the time she had spent with him up at the croft. So much for that idea. And what was it Anwen had said about him? That some people *couldn't* be seen? Maybe she was a barmy old woman after all, and nothing she said should be taken too seriously.

A snapping twig behind her made Laura pivot on her heel. There was nothing visible. She craned her neck, searching the undergrowth, half hoping and half fearing to see the man with the dog again. Her breath quickened a little, whether in fear or excitement she could not be sure. She waited, but there was no sign of movement. She hurried back toward Penlan. When she reached the gate from the meadows into her own yard she was surprised to see the studio door open. Had she left it like that? She couldn't recall doing so. Cautiously she pushed it and stepped inside. At first the room seemed empty, then she heard a sound from behind some of the unpacked crates.

"Who's there?" she demanded. There was a second's pause, then a tall, dark figure stepped out from the shadows.

"Rhys! Oh, my God, you startled me. I thought . . ." She left the sentence unfinished, not knowing how to explain. She barely had time to register the oddness of finding him wandering about in her studio without invitation before he had moved to stand close to her. Close enough for her to feel his breath on her cheek. His eyes were serious and his expression intense.

"I had to come and see you," he said, quietly reaching up to stroke her hair.

Laura thought how strange it was to stand so physically close to someone and yet to not get a proper sense of them. She truly had no idea what was going on in his mind, beyond his obvious desire for her. Anwen's voice came into her head. *Some people cannot be seen, even when you are standing toe to toe.* She felt him staring at her and raised her eyes to meet his. The strength of his gaze sent a thrill through her entire body.

"You are beautiful, Laura," he said quietly. "But of course you already know that. What you don't know is how incredibly special you are. You are different from other women, different in such very important ways," he told her. As he spoke he wound her hair around his hand at the back of her neck, holding her with a firm grip now, pulling her head back ever so slightly. "I knew from the first moment I saw you that we were meant to be together. *Shhh!*" He held a finger to her lips to silence her protest. "I know this is not easy for you. Don't worry. I will take care of you. I will take care of everything, Laura. Trust me."

"Rhys, I . . ."

With a suddenness that surprised her he pulled Laura to him and kissed her hard on the mouth. For an instant she thought to resist. She knew that she should. That this was wrong. That people she loved could be badly hurt. But her hesitation was fleeting. Rhys held her tight and close, and Laura began to return his urgent kisses. The next moment he drew back and ripped open her shirt. He yanked her head back farther as he plunged his hand inside her bra and leaned down to take her breast in his mouth. Laura cried out, half of her panicked by the roughness of his actions, half of her inflamed by it. She took his own hair in her hands and pulled him up, kissing him hungrily again. His response was to push her backward onto the workbench behind her. Jars of turpentine and medium and tubes of paint and boxes of charcoal and pots of brushes were scattered and thrown in all directions as Rhys tore at her clothes.

She looked up at him, breathing hard, half naked beneath him, trapped on the hard bench, wanting him with a desire she had not felt in many, many years.

Suddenly, she knew she had to stop. She could not give in to this, however much she wanted it.

"No! Rhys, stop!" She turned her head from him. "I'm sorry," she whispered as he leaned over her, panting. "I can't. I just can't."

THE NEXT FEW days passed in a blur. Laura was horrified to find she had bruises on her wrists and back after her encounter with Rhys. She was relieved to see them fade quickly, particularly as Dan announced he would be home a day early that week. She locked herself in her studio and immersed herself in her work, struggling to shut out vivid flashbacks of Rhys kissing her. They had come so close to making love. She had never behaved like that before and was shocked, not just at the fact that she had so nearly been unfaithful to Dan, but the nature of that act. The wildness of it. By Thursday evening she had pulled herself together a little but still found herself wracked with guilt at the sight of Dan. In the kitchen, she cracked an egg on the side of a pan and watched the yolk split and spread into the oil. Cursing silently she tapped another and watched the same thing happen again. She was not in a fit state to cook, but Dan was upstairs having a shower after a long day at work and a long journey home from London, and she had to throw something together for supper. Her hair was still wet from the shower she herself had taken after coming in from the studio. She remembered the shower she had had a few days earlier. After Rhys. She had stood under the water for a long time, trying to wash away the guilt along with the sweat—his as well as hers. She had put on fresh clothes and even some perfume. She had stopped him—she kept reminding herself of this crucial fact. She had not, technically, been unfaithful to Dan. But still she felt she stank of lust, of betrayal. Her abandoned thrashing about with Rhys had made a terrible mess of the studio, and it had taken an age to clear it all up. It was as if, with him, she was a different person.

She wriggled a spatula beneath the eggs and did her best to work them into an appealing shape. They refused to cooperate, as if even the simplest things around her were now in chaos. The fat spat spitefully.

"Ow!" she blurted out in pain, then quickly sucking her finger and whipping the pan off the heat.

"Steady on," Dan said as he entered the kitchen. "What have those eggs ever done to you?"

Laura was rendered momentarily speechless by the sight of what Dan was holding in his hand. It was a loose cotton shirt. The one Rhys had given her at his house after the thunderstorm. She might have been imagining things, but she fancied Dan was watching her reaction to seeing the shirt very closely.

"This isn't mine," he said.

Laura turned back to the stove and fiddled with the eggs in an effort to cover her panic.

"Oh, I did a bit of shopping. Got it in a secondhand shop. In Abergavenny. You'll need some more casual stuff out here, and I know how you hate shopping for clothes."

"I found it in the ironing pile."

"Thought I'd wash it before I gave it to you." She tried to keep her voice casual, but her mouth was uncomfortably dry. She felt hysteria rising at the thought that her lies were already tripping her up.

"How sweet." He came over and kissed the back of her neck. "Hmm, you smell delicious. I think I fancy you more than I do those poor eggs."

Laura wriggled free, busying herself with laying the table.

"Sit down. It'll be ready in a minute. Do you want mushrooms? Or tomatoes?"

"No, just murdered eggs." He steered her toward a chair. "You sit down. I'll finish this off. You are obviously too away with the fairies to be left in charge of a frying pan. How has the painting gone this week?"

Laura leaned her elbows on the table and rubbed her temples. Was she going to have to lie about that, too? She took a steadying breath.

"Oh, it wouldn't go right. Too keen after such a long break, I suppose. I went for a few walks. Found Glyn the Bryn's farm. It's a bit of a shambles."

"Now, why doesn't that surprise me?"

"I met his wife, Anwen. She's lovely. Not a bit like the old man."

"Was he there?"

"No, thank God."

"Here you go." Dan set platefuls of food on the table. As he sat he gave Laura's hand an affectionate squeeze. She had to fight her impulse to pull it away.

"Let's have some wine," she said, getting quickly to her feet. With her back to him she bit her lip and rolled her eyes, wondering if life would ever feel within her control again.

Later, after more pinot grigio than was good for her, Laura fell into a fitful sleep. As she slept she dreamed. She dreamed of Rhys, of his strong arms, his powerful gaze, and his warm, passionate kisses. She dreamed she was lying beneath him, waiting, wanting, looking up at those exquisitely blue eyes. Then, as he lowered himself to her, his face changed subtly. The mouth that descended to cover hers was not Rhys's, but belonged to the dark stranger in the woods. Laura tried to cry out as the stern-looking man loomed over her. She let out a silent scream and woke up gasping. And as she awoke she realized that she knew who the stranger was. She glanced at Dan, who had slept through her shriek, and then rifled through the books beside the bed. At last she found the one she was looking for. She flicked quickly through the pages, searching anxiously. She stared at the picture as she located the right page. The man stood with his hair and clothes seemingly entwined with the branches and briars of the windswept woodland around him. In his hand was a stout walking stick. At his side was his tame wolf. This was Merlin, magician of myth, seer and prophet, hero of legend. And this was, beyond any doubt, the man Laura had seen in the woods.

MEGAN WALKED BRISKLY along the road to the village. Dafydd had taken the boys out riding, and she had seized the chance to go to the market on her own. The boys would no doubt sulk when they learned they had missed an outing but Megan would be quicker about her errands without them. She needed thread and more woolen cloth to repair some of Huw's shirts and fashion new ones for both children. She would have help with the sewing from other servants at the castle, but the duty of seeing that the children were properly clothed fell to her, and she trusted no one else to go to the mercer's stall.

Penybont was a large village when judged by others in the district but the weekly market was still a modest occasion. This was not a fair, nor a wake day, but a practical gathering of sellers and buyers. A day for peddling produce and replenishing stores and bargaining for snippets of this and snatches of that for a dress or a blanket or a necessary tool for a tradesman. There would be poultry and some livestock, as well as vegetables from growers with surplus, and a good bakery stall, as well as the mercer, a candle maker, a knife sharpener, and doubtless the odd fortune-teller and fool. The village was a little over a mile from Castle Craig, and by the time Megan arrived the stalls were set out and much noise and bustle announced that brisk business was already being done. Chickens sat in baskets peering balefully out between wicker bars, or lay feet-bound on the sticky ground. The recent rain had changed the streets from dust to mud, so that with every footfall the going became heavier. Pigs squealed, a don-key brayed, men shouted the quality of their wares, and every-where children darted between the stalls. Megan hitched up her skirts to avoid the soupy earth. She pushed her way through the throng, nodding greetings to those she knew, pausing to inquire after the health of an elderly friend of her father's, and to tickle the bare toes of a new baby. The smell of freshly baked bread made her mouth run. She stood awhile looking at the display of loaves and cobs and homity pies, before deciding to buy a treat to take back for the boys. She could picture their hungry little faces after their ride and knew a warm pie might go some way to mol-lifying their irritation at not having attended the market them-selves. As she waited for her purchases to be placed in her basket she became aware of someone standing close beside her. In the general hubbub this was not noteworthy, but she knew at once whose presence she felt so strongly.

She smiled, without looking around, and said, "So, a magi-cian has a weakness for pies like any other man, I see."

"If you believe it is the pastry that brings me to stand here, you do yourself a disservice," Merlin answered.

Megan turned to face him, her spirits lifting further at the sight of him.

"Am I to think then that you came to market all the way from Ty Bychan to find me?"

Merlin smiled, his naturally serious expression softening. "Where else would I look for a maid on market day?"

"I am on errands for my young masters. I am here to buy cloth from the mercer."

"Then I should tell you, you have just handed your money to a baker!"

Megan laughed, taking her basket and walking on. Merlin followed, slipping into step beside her to take her arm. She raised her eyebrows at this familiar gesture.

"The mud is uncommonly deep in places," he explained. "Would you have me let you fall into the mire?"

Before she could answer a cry went up and the frantic squealing of a hog grew louder as the animal broke free of its owner and plunged through the crowd. Men, women, and children were scattered, some clambering onto stalls and wagons for safety, others pitching headlong into the mud. Those who were able joined in the chase, doing their best to corner the bolting creature, but mud made it slipperier than an eel, and panic made it quicker than a deer. It darted this way and that, upturning a table of vegetables and trampling a tray of eggs. Fists were waved and oaths sworn, but still the animal could not be contained. A boy with a wagon of turnips pulled by a young courser chose that very moment to turn into the main thoroughfare of the village. The pig barreled into the hind legs of the horse, which gave way to its natural fear of swine and galloped forward. The boy was unseated from his perch, leaving the wagon to career through the marketplace unmanned. Angry shouts at the hog turned to anxious cries and shrieks of terror as the runaway cart plowed through the market, straight toward where Megan stood. She held her ground, reaching out a hand to steady the terrified horse, but Merlin wrenched her from its path. The courser attempted to turn suddenly, causing the wagon to pitch at a dangerous angle. The heavy load made the outfit unstable at such speeds and as the horse strained against its harness one cartwheel rose up. There was a second of silence, then a bone-crunching crash as the wagon fell onto its side. Megan and Merlin dashed forward, as did others who could hear the desperate cries of those pinned beneath the cart. The horse lay still and lifeless, trapped between the shafts, an unlucky combination of weight and angle having snapped its neck. People were pulled from under the wreckage, some bloodied, some bruised, some with broken limbs.

A cry went up.

"Mair the Cwm is stuck fast beneath the wheel!"

Men struggled to right the cart, but the dead horse and collapsed load made it a near impossible object to lift.

"Fetch poles!" shouted a stallholder.

"Cut loose that horse!" yelled another.

Megan knelt in the mud, sinking up to her thighs. She could see Mair, eyes wide and frightened, pain distorting the young woman's gentle features. Megan crawled under as far as she could, reaching out to take hold of Mair's hand.

"Do not fear, Mair. Help is here," she said. But even as she spoke she could see the light fading from her neighbor's eyes. She peered out, meeting Merlin's questioning look. "We must free her. The breath is being crushed from her body."

"They are dragging away the horse," Merlin told her. "And bringing poles to use as levers."

Megan shook her head. "It will be too late."

Merlin took in what she said, then moved back a short way. Megan watched, knowing he was about to do something, but having no idea what. She noticed sounds diminish. She could still see the mouths of the people around her open and shut and knew them to be shouting, but her own ears were cloaked with an unnatural silence. She felt a cool breeze against her skin, although the clouds sat steady in the sky. Then, as if some mighty unseen hand were lifting it, the underneath of the cart began to move. While Merlin remained unblinking, his eyes glazed, his breath shallow, the wagon raised itself up until it was hovering a hand's breadth above Mair's chest.

"Take her out!" Megan screamed, coming to her senses. "Pull her free!"

A dozen hands grasped the girl and slid her free of the cart. An instant later it crashed to the floor once more, its own weight splintering the wheel and splitting the framework of the underside of the wagon.

Megan scrambled to her feet. Merlin had fallen forward, shoulders slumped, and was struggling for breath. She put her arm about his shoulders.

"Merlin? Merlin, are you well?"

Slowly he straightened up, his labored breathing returning to a more normal rhythm. He put his hand over hers and nodded. About them people fussed and hurried to tend to Mair. In all the muddle and noise no one save Megan seemed to have noticed how the wagon came to move. She looked at the man she still held on to, wondering what manner of being could possess such a gift, and fearing that what could today be a blessing, could tomorrow prove a curse.

6

LESS THAN ONE week later Megan stood uncomfortably beside the long table in the great hall. She did not know exactly why she had been summoned to Lord Geraint's presence, but she was certain it would have something to do with Merlin. The Lammas Day feast had left matters unresolved between the two men, and Megan knew her master well enough. He would not give up so easily. If he had his mind set on gaining Merlin's help, one way or another he would get it.

Lord Geraint sat at the end of the table, leaning back in his grand wooden chair, eyeing Megan in a way that made her feel naked before him. Two of his favorite hunting dogs lay at his feet.

"Why is it you are always so stiff in my presence, Megan? Do you fear me?"

"No, my Lord."

"You know I wish only the best for you," he said, getting to his feet and coming to stand behind her. His speech was made unclear by wine and his breath smelled strongly. He put a hand on Megan's shoulder. "You looked most beguiling in your pretty clothes at the festival. You would wear finery well, I think. I could give you everything your heart desires." He leaned forward to whisper in her ear. "Imagine, Megan, the softest spun wool, cool cotton, and silk from distant shores. Silver at your throat. Shoes of the supplest leather. Splendid food. The very best of everything. All that I would ask in return would be your favor."

His breath was hot on her neck now. It took a great effort of will for Megan not to pull away, to push him from her.

"You are too kind, my Lord. But I am a simple maid. I have no desire for luxury. Only that I be permitted to follow my own heart."

She waited, expecting his rage, or at the very least his displeasure. Instead he produced a small leather bag.

"I have something for you," he told her. "A token of my affection, if you will." He took from the bag an exquisite ring of silver set with the biggest amethyst Megan had ever seen. She could not help but gasp.

"Does it please you?" he asked, for once sounding as if her opinion truly mattered to him.

"It is most beautiful, my Lord. But I could not possibly take it."

"But I insist. I shall be most offended if you refuse." He took her hand and slid the ring onto her finger. "There, a perfect fit. No, do not object. I want you to wear it and to think of me each time the sun's rays gleam from it. Remember, this is the way things could be for you, Megan, in return for your own affection. And your loyalty, of course."

"I hope I am always loyal to both my master and my mistress."

"Lady Rhiannon's interests need not concern you. Have no fear of reprisal from your mistress. She is herself well versed in the ways of the world. No, you can show your loyalty, to both of us, and to our boys, whom I know you care for greatly."

"I do, sir."

"Just so. And you would see them stay safe?"

"Though my life depended on it."

"I do not ask so high a price. Only that you keep us all in your mind when next you visit your magician."

"My Lord?"

"Come now, let us not play games. It was clear to the oldest man with the poorest sight that Merlin was charmed by you and that he will seek you out. Well, good. We can use such interest to best advantage. I make no secret of the fact I wish him to assist me against Lord Idris. I have not yet pressed the issue, but I already sense his resistance. You, my dear, could persuade him. Of that I have no doubt."

"Merlin is his own man, my Lord. I could not make him act against his will."

"Could not, or would not?"

Lord Geraint began to pace the long room, not looking at Megan now, his eyes cold, his face stern as he spoke.

"Let me speak plainly. I have found, in my many years of soldiering, that there are two effective strategies which can be employed before so much as a sword has been raised in anger. The first, and my preferred method in this instance, is that of persuasion, of negotiation, if you will. This can provide the best outcome for all concerned." He paused to ruffle the coat of one of his hounds. "The second can be used with equal success, though at the expense of those weakest in the suit." He looked up at her now, a tight smile belying the force of his words. "Just as every foe has

his weakness, so has every potential ally. Merlin, it seems, is a solitary figure, and though he shows an interest in you, that is a
new affection, and may indeed not be enough on its own. Unless
you were to press matters, to cajole, to influence . . . You have
voiced your own reluctance. You suggest you cannot be persuaded
by gentle means to do as I ask and use your charms to bring Merlin to my heel. Take care, Megan, for there is someone else who
has a claim on your heart. Should you fail me, things might not
go well with him."

"My father?"

"Let us simply say that his continued good health is in your
delicate hands, my dear."

After being dismissed by her master Megan was too dis-
tressed to go straight to her chamber. Instead she walked the
gardens. The moon was full and the sky cloudless, so that her own
moon shadow followed her as she paced and fretted. She could feel
herself being pulled deeper and deeper into the muddy waters of
Lord Geraint's ambitions. To deceive Merlin, to press him to ally
himself to such a man as her master was unthinkable. But if she
refused, what fate awaited her poor, dear father? Should she leave
now, warn her father, persuade him to quit the farm and flee?
He would never do that. Perhaps she could simply stay away from
Merlin. If she had no contact with him, Lord Geraint could surely
not hold her to blame for her lack of influence. She could tell him
he had placed too much value on the magician's interest in her.
That it was a passing fancy. That she could bring no influence to
bear in any case.

Megan stopped by the pond and gazed down into the glossy
water. Frogs belched and growled. An owl hooted nearby. She

contemplated her reflection, her face tense and frowning. As she watched the water rippled, though she had not seen a creature break the surface. Then, suddenly, her mirrored image faded before her eyes and was replaced by another face. Merlin's face. Megan gasped, as much from wonder as from fear. She looked closer, assuring herself this was no trick of the moonlight. He was there. Watching her. The thought of his presence made her feel calmer. Stronger. It also made her realize that keeping from him was not a course she could make herself choose.

A noise behind her made her start. She wheeled round.

"Who is it? Who is there?"

"Forgive me." Dafydd stepped into view. "I did not mean to startle you, Megan."

"Dafydd. Were you looking for me?"

"It is Midnight. He is ailing." Dafydd looked deeply concerned.

"What ails him?"

"I cannot be sure."

"Is his condition grave?"

"I fear we may lose him before morning. Will you come?"

"You had only to ask." In an instant all other thoughts were banished from her mind. "Take me to him."

In his stall, Midnight stood with his head hanging low. The horse's eyes bulged and rolled in pain. His flanks were slick with sweat, and his chest heaved with labored breath. Megan ran a hand over his proud neck. It moved her near to tears to see him suffering so. She gently pulled back his lips to reveal gums the color of rotting carrots. She sniffed his breath and recoiled at the putrid stench.

"There, fellow, you are a sorry sight. How long has he been like this, Dafydd?"

"Since dusk."

"You should have fetched me sooner."

"At first I thought 'twas just the colic. He's had it before. I dosed him as usual, but the pain became worse." Dafydd shook his head. "Can you save him, Megan?"

It was a question of importance not only for the sake of the poor beast. If Dafydd let his master's favorite mount die he would, at best, be stripped of employment and home. At worst, Lord Geraint's temper might not be restrained.

Megan was all too well aware of what was at stake.

"Bring me an armful of fresh-cut bracken—the greenest ferns you can find. And warm water, plenty of it. And a large piece of calico. Salt, too. Go to the kitchen—you will have to wake the cook for the key."

"You do not think it is simple colic then?"

Megan shook her head.

"He is not rolling, nor kicking his belly. There is a sickness poisoning him. Something he has eaten or a disease. I cannot tell which. Either way, we must purge him."

"That could work."

"It could, if the sickness has not yet spread to his blood and taken hold. I won't lie to you, Dafydd, we may lose him yet."

The two exchanged worried looks before Dafydd hurried away to fetch what was needed. Megan took the animal's head in her hands and kissed it fondly.

"There, there, my handsome one. You must be strong now. Show me what a brave heart you have, and we will see the sun rise together."

A short time later when Dafydd returned he was not alone.

"Huw! Why are you not in your bed?" Megan was too concerned for her patient to keep the harshness out of her voice. She regretted sounding so sharp at the sight of the boy's hurt expression.

"I could not sleep, Megan. I came to look for you and found Dafydd instead. Please let me stay. I can help you."

"Your mother would not allow it."

"She need not know. Please, Megan, let me see what it is you do."

Megan saw in the child a memory of herself at a young age. She recalled sitting silently in the straw watching her mother tend an ailing animal. Watching and learning.

"Very well. But stay quiet, young master, and keep out of the way. We have work to do here."

"He looks very sick. Is he going to die, Megan?"

"Is that your notion of quiet, Huw?"

Chastened, the boy settled himself down and said no more.

Megan took the bracken from Dafydd and broke it into small handfuls. She pressed the bruised ferns into a large pail before pouring warm water over them. She used her hands to stir the concoction, kneading the greenery until the water was stained and pungent. Her sparkling ring was soon dulled and dirtied by the soupy liquid. She took the cloth and strained the mixture into another bucket.

"Dafydd, fetch the drenching horn."

"Is it ready?"

"If we had time I would let it steep for an hour or more. But Midnight cannot wait even that long. Help me hold his head up."

She kissed the animal's cheek and spoke softly to him. "Let me help you, my gentle giant. All will be well."

While Dafydd raised the horse's head, tipping its nose uppermost, Megan clambered onto the manger. She leaned forward and placed the drenching horn in Midnight's mouth.

"Drink, Midnight. Drink," she told him.

The horse flicked his ears and rolled his eyes, but put up no resistance until at last all the bitter liquid had been given.

"Good boy." Megan stroked his damp nose as he lowered his head once more. She took the precious salt from its wrapping and held out a handful. Midnight showed no interest. Megan rubbed a little onto his mouth. He licked slowly at first, then with more vigor, until he had cleaned her palm of every grain. "There, that's a better taste. And it will strengthen you, you'll see."

Megan went to sit with Huw.

"What will happen now?" he asked.

"We hope the medicine will wash out the poison from poor Midnight."

"Can it really do that?"

"It can, but it is a strong remedy, Huw. If he is too weakened by the sickness, it could prove too much for him."

"You mean, it could kill him?" Huw was terrified at the prospect.

Megan and Dafydd exchanged concerned glances, for the boy had voiced a new fear—that Megan would now also be held to account if the cure did not succeed.

An hour later, after the drench had done its work, the creature that stood before them was a trembling shadow of the noble animal it had once been. Dafydd worked to clear away the stinking straw and replace it with fresh. Midnight groaned and snorted, then sank heavily to the ground.

Huw leaped to his feet, tears in his eyes.

"Oh, Megan. He is dying!"

Megan took his hand and squeezed it but could find no words of comfort or reassurance to give. She knew the boy might be right. Only time would tell. She stepped forward and tried to tempt the suffering horse with more salt but he was too weak to so much as lick her hand. Megan closed her eyes as she stroked him. He had trusted her to help him; had she merely hastened his end?

"Dafydd! Dafydd, where are you, man?" Lord Geraint's shouts could be heard before he even reached the barn. He strode through the door, his rage palpable. "What is this? I hear word that Midnight is grievous ill, and I find a maid and a boy attending him!"

"My Lord, my own remedies were having no effect," Dafydd said as he stepped forward. "I asked Megan to help. She has saved mares and colts here before today."

"So you let her practice her arts on my finest destrier?" Lord Geraint picked up a handful of the discarded bracken. "And she feeds him this poison!"

"I sought only to save the animal, my Lord," said Megan.

"Perhaps. Or perhaps you found an opportunity to vent your own anger by killing a favorite of mine."

"No! No, my Lord."

"Father, she was trying to help poor Midnight."

"Hold your tongue, child! I have no interest in your view of the matter. Go back to your bedchamber where you belong!"

The boy shrank back as if his father had struck him.

"You would let Brychan stay," he shouted, his voice shaking. "But not me. Never me!"

"Go, I tell you!"

The child ran from the stall. Megan wanted to chase after him, to take him in her arms and comfort him, but she was not free to leave. And Midnight still needed her.

Lord Geraint stared at the horse for a moment, then hissed at Megan.

"He had better live, d'you hear me? I will not be taken for a fool."

So saying he left, his anger lingering in the stable after he had gone.

Megan shut his threats from her mind and turned back to her fading patient. His eyes were glazed now, and he lay flat in an attitude of hopelessness.

"Do not give up, my brave friend. Stay and fight, though this is the fiercest of all the many battles you have seen." Megan did her best to sound calm, but tears coursed down her face. It would take nothing short of magic to give the horse the strength he must have to survive his ordeal now. As the thought formed in her head a new possibility came to her. She stole a look at Dafydd. He was busying himself with yet more bedding. Megan closed her eyes again and summoned up Merlin's face behind her closed lids.

"Merlin," she whispered his name. "Help us. Help us now."

The stable fell unnaturally still. Megan waited. The horse lay motionless and touching the hem of death. A thin wind blew as if from inside the barn itself, whining around the stall, stirring up the straw. Dafydd stopped his futile work. Megan stood up, more than a little afraid, not knowing what could come next. The force of the wind increased, blowing Megan's hair wildly about her, flinging bedding and hay in a whirlwind. Dafydd threw his arm over his eyes. Megan fought for breath as the dust was churned and hurled around the stall. Then, in a heartbeat, the tempest stopped. An eerie stillness filled the place once more. Neither Megan nor Dafydd moved. Midnight lay lifeless, until his great chest heaved in a giant, rasping breath. The animal coughed, raising his head, then hauled himself back onto his feet.

"By all that's holy!" muttered Dafydd.

Megan rushed forward, steadying the stumbling horse.

"There! There, my brave warrior." She patted his neck and rubbed his clammy ears. "You see? Your story has not yet ended." As she calmed the animal she offered silent thanks to the unseen power who had answered her call for help.

❧

WITH DAN HOME the weekend passed in an exhausting series of emotional swoops and highs for Laura. She would be doing her best to focus on her husband, enjoying some simple task in the garden with him or sharing a bottle of wine, when she would catch her mind straying to think of Rhys. And the thought of him made the hours crawl by. By the time Dan left for London two days later, Laura was desperate to see Rhys again. She waited until Dan's car disappeared out of sight and then hurried upstairs. Despite the fact that an autumn coolness was in the air, she chose a floaty, button-down summer dress. She wanted to look pretty for him, to look feminine. His touch, the way he looked at her, had made her feel womanly in a way she had never thought she could. It was as if the shortcomings of her body, her barrenness, her lack, were made to matter less. Not because Rhys could take away her longing for a child, but because with him at least her body was desirable, nubile, ripe, willing, and joyous. At least when she was near him she felt as if she was a complete woman, a woman who could give him all that he wanted. It was many painful years since Dan had been able to make her feel that. Laura brushed out her hair, leaving it loose and glossy, slipped on a pair of flat, leather sandals, and spritzed herself with perfume. She had her hand on the front door when the phone rang. She hesitated, moved toward it, then decided to let the answering machine click on. Penny's voice was chipper as ever.

"Hi, Laura. Just to let you know, I've had the dates confirmed. We open the last week in November. Private view on the twenty-fifth. Give me a ring when you get this. Ciao!"

Laura frowned. She should pick up and speak to Penny, but her mind was focused elsewhere. She set off for the croft.

Summer was losing its glow. The landscape looked a little tired and scruffy as plants finished unburdening their seeds and fruits, flowers faded, and the sun's rays weakened. Laura walked briskly along the shortest route she knew to Rhys's cottage. She felt exhilarated. She knew she was being reckless. A part of her was appalled at what she was doing. But still she found herself unable to turn back. If she stopped to think about how her actions might affect Dan, or about what the possible consequences of such an affair might be, she would be paralyzed with guilt and fear. As it was she pushed such thoughts to the darkest recesses of her mind, determined to allow herself this experience, this pleasure.

As she neared the croft she could see Rhys, shirt off, working in the garden. She felt a thrill at the sight of him and at the memory of how his body felt pressed against hers. How it smelled. How it tasted. She raised an arm to wave at him. The movement must have caught his eye, for he straightened up and waved back slowly, watching her as she climbed the last few yards of the hill.

She stood in front of him, a little out of breath. She found it difficult to speak, to put what she was feeling into words. "I wanted to see you again," she said, holding his gaze.

He propped his hoe against the garden wall and brushed dirt from his hands. He moved close to her, sliding his arms around her waist and pulling her gently to him.

"My beautiful, beautiful Laura," he whispered into her hair. He kissed her neck softly, then found her mouth. Laura was surprised by the urgency and force of his kisses now, and surprised at herself. She kissed him back eagerly, running her fingers through his hair, pulling him tighter to her, meeting his body with her own. Rhys grabbed her wrists, holding her hands firmly by her sides, laughing at her enthusiasm, teasing her, taking control.

"My beautiful, impatient Laura," he said, before swiftly lifting her up and carrying her into the house. She liked the fact that he took her straight to his unmade bed. It didn't matter that he had been working in the garden—she delighted in the saltiness of his skin. When he pinned her down and quickly bound her hands with his leather belt before tying them to the bedpost it only increased her excitement and desire for him. With Rhys she wasn't the Laura anyone else who knew her would recognize. With Rhys she was reckless, hungry, completely shameless. She lay watching as he kicked off his sandals and removed his jeans. His body was toned and muscular and tanned from spending hours out of doors, naked, apparently. He was glorious. Laura felt deliciously vulnerable as he began to undo the buttons of her flimsy dress. He kissed her shoulders, and her arms, and her belly, until she was inflamed to the point of madness. Sensing her intense arousal Rhys smiled at her.

"I know what you want," he growled into her ear. "I know you, Laura. I know you."

In an instant his mood and behavior changed. He became rough, wild, almost animalistic in the way that he made love to her. She was at first shocked, and then fiercely aroused. She submitted to Rhys for a moment, almost passively. But soon she found herself responding in kind. She had never experienced such abandoned, uninhibited, satisfying sex before. If Dan had treated her the same way she would have been appalled. With Rhys it was different. *She* was different.

After prolonged and athletic lovemaking, Laura slept in Rhys's arms, astonished at how happy she could feel when she knew she was behaving unforgivably. By the time she woke up the September sun had already dropped toward the horizon.

"What time is it?" she asked.

Rhys stretched lazily. "Don't worry," he said. "It's early yet. Stay there. I'll make us some coffee."

Laura watched as he crossed the room naked, completely at ease with his body, and with her. He disappeared down the spiral staircase and she could hear him whistling as he filled the kettle. Only now did Laura begin to take in what Rhys's bedroom was like. There was something uniquely intimate about being there on her own, in his private space. The bedroom was built into the roof of the cottage, so that the ceilings sloped steeply, making it impossible to stand up unless you kept to the center. The large, low bed filled most of the available space. There were candles and lamps and a chest of drawers, as well as a clothes rail by the small dormer window. The end wall was covered by a large wall hanging. There was little space for anything else. Even so, there were books stacked in every spare corner. Laura leaned over to rummage through a pile on the floor beside the bed and as she did so she glimpsed a small plastic box in the shelf of the bedside cabinet. She peered at it. It was a case for contact lenses. She was mildly surprised. For one thing, it was hard to imagine Rhys's body being anything but perfect in every way. For another, if he did have poor eyesight, she would have thought him much more the type to wear glasses, not lenses. It seemed somehow too vain and too self-conscious. She turned her attention back to the books. Most were on myths and legends and local folklore. They all looked well thumbed, with turned-down pages or makeshift bookmarks. One was devoted entirely to the subject of Merlin. Laura sat up in bed to study it but found the limited light made reading difficult. She was still squinting at the pictures when Rhys returned with the coffee.

"This looks interesting," she said. "Or at least it would if I could see it properly. How do you manage to read anything in here?"

Rhys grinned. "Your eyes are accustomed to brighter light-

ing. It's all a matter of what you're used to. You're right, though—
it's a wonderful book. I read it again and again."

"Is Merlin a hero of yours?"

"Something like that. I do have an interest in him, you
could say."

"I admit I know very little about him," said Laura, sitting up
more to take her drink from him. "Actually, I'd never really
thought about him before I came to live here."

"And now?" Rhys settled himself on the bed next to her not
bothering to cover up his nakedness. He smelled of clean sweat
and dirty sex. Laura decided that on him this was the perfect combination of aromas.

"And now I find he is part of a local legend. Feels like I should
read up on him a bit. Besides," she hesitated, wondering how she
could explain what she had seen. What she had felt. Would Rhys
understand? She was puzzled to realize that the reason she was
reluctant to discuss her sighting of Merlin with him was because
she thought he might be jealous. The ridiculousness of the notion
made her give a little laugh.

"Besides?" Rhys was waiting for her to finish her sentence.

"Oh, nothing. Like I said, if he's part of a local story I feel I
should find out a bit more. This is my home now—I want to understand as much about it as I can."

"Well, if you want to know about Merlin you've come to the
right man," Rhys told her, flipping shut the book on her lap. "You
don't even need to strain your eyes to read about him—just ask
me anything you want to know."

"Great, thanks." Laura sipped her drink, annoyed that she had missed the chance to ask to borrow the book. She did want to find out more about the mysterious figure who she seemed to connect with in some inexplicable way. True, she could quiz Rhys. He obviously enjoyed the subject and clearly had done a lot of research. But no, this was something Laura wanted to keep separate from Rhys. As to why she was baffled, instinct told her not to confide in him about her experiences. She decided to shift the focus of the conversation. She leaned down and pulled another book from the pile. It was a heavy tome, the size of a good dictionary or a city telephone directory. It was bound in leather of faded crimson with flowing titles tooled in gold.

"This one is quite beautiful," she said.

"Have you ever seen one of those before?" Rhys asked.

"What is it?"

"A *grimoire*."

"Sorry?"

"A *grimoire*, a book of spells."

Laura's first reaction was a small laugh, but she could see from his face that Rhys was in earnest. She settled the book onto her lap and opened the cover. The pages were gossamer thin, hundreds of them, each with detailed descriptions of spells, incantations, curses, hexes, and other things Laura had only ever heard of in fairy tales.

"I never knew such a thing really existed," she said.

"Of course. Just as a cook needs her recipe book, so every witch needs her *grimoire*. There are spells here collected from magic practices from the far ends of Earth. And some a little nearer to home. Look here, for instance," he said, turning the pages. Laura read the heading.

"'Spells for Fertility and Conception.' Look how many there are!"

"You're not the first woman to need a little help. It's a well-trodden path. Look, this one is a Celtic spell. It originated in Wales, centuries ago. I'll copy it out for you if you like."

Laura smiled. Hadn't she tried everything else? Was this any sillier or more far-fetched than some of the cranky diets or crystal healing or divination she had endured?

"OK," she said. "Do that. I'll give it a go. What harm can it do?"

Rhys smiled back at her.

"What harm indeed?"

LATER, AN HOUR or so after she arrived home, Dan telephoned. He was not given to calling during his working day and Laura could sense the concern in his voice. Could he possibly suspect something? She told herself she was being ridiculous.

"So you're OK, then?" Dan asked for the second time.

"Why wouldn't I be? Stop worrying about me, Dan."

"I know, I'm fussing. You just looked so small, standing there all alone when I drove off this morning. And this weekend you seemed, I don't know, distant, I suppose."

"Did I? I'm sorry." She paused, relieved he was not able to see her face. All at once the enormity of what she had done, of the measure of her betrayal, took hold of her. *I can't do this*, her voice screamed inside her head, *I cannot do this*. She took a steadying breath, then said "You know how distracted I get when I'm painting sometimes. Especially when I'm working on something new."

"Of course. I guess I'm just feeling a bit guilty, about not being there with you, I mean."

Laura closed her eyes, her own guilt swamping her. "Don't be daft. It's only for a little while, remember?"

"Yes. I know. Look, I've got to go. I'll call you again tonight."

Laura clicked off the phone and took a moment to steady herself. "Laura Mathews, what on earth do you think you are doing?" she said aloud.

7

THE MORNING AFTER Midnight's illness, when Lord Geraint learned that his steed had survived, he did not see fit to apologize to Megan, nor to thank her for her efforts. She had not expected anything of the kind. Instead he sent word she was to be excused from her duties with the children for the day. This might have been to allow her to recover from a lost night's sleep, but when the page completed his message saying she could have use of a horse, Lord Geraint's intentions were clear. He would expect her to go to Merlin. Megan found herself battling with conflicting emotions. She dreaded the prospect of running her avaricious master's errands, yet feared for her father if she did not do as she was bid. However weighted with another's purpose her visit was to be, though, she was also conscious of a lifting of her spirits. Of a lightness in her step as she walked to the stables. The truth was she was eager to see Merlin again and was glad of the chance to thank him for his magical intervention the night before. But for his help, Midnight would have died, Megan was certain of it. The thought of a mortal being having such power both frightened and thrilled her. Such gifts could be used for great good, for healing, for helping those in need. Or they could be misused for personal gain and base desires. The idea of Lord Geraint forcing Merlin to act for him had now taken on a more terrifying aspect.

Megan paused to spend a moment with Midnight. He was still weak, but his condition was improving by the hour. She instructed Dafydd to continue to add salt and ground garlic to the horse feed and made him promise to find a plentiful supply of honey to speed Midnight's recovery. She saddled Hazel and set off toward Ty Bychan. She rode slowly up the hill, enjoying the rhythm of the little palfrey's stride and the peaceful beauty of the landscape. The hot and heavy weather had been washed away by the storm of Lammas Day, and now summer was subsiding into a gentle, fruitful autumn. She felt stiff and weary from lack of sleep, but was in part revived by the freshness of the morning. As she climbed higher up the mountain, beyond her father's farmhouse, the air was cool beneath high, white clouds. Megan dismounted to pick a palmful of whinberries and ate them as she continued her journey. At last she could see Ty Bychan, sturdy and humble, built low into the lee of a slope against the weather. She glimpsed Merlin and her stomach tightened with a mixture of delight and foreboding.

By the time she reached the little stone wall of the garden Merlin was standing at the gate to meet her. As she slid from her saddle the wolf padded out on silent paws. Hazel snorted and began to pull back on the reins. Megan stood her ground. For an instant she was afraid, but the wolf greeted her gently, wagging his tail and licking her hand.

"He remembers you," Merlin told her. "How could he not?"

"He is certainly something I will remember all my life," said Megan, loosening Hazel's cinch and looping the reins over the gatepost. The horse at once rested a hind foot and settled to doze.

Merlin took Megan's hand then stopped, surprised by the amethyst.

"A present from Lord Geraint," Megan told him, her tone making her feelings plain. "He insists I wear it."

"It is very pretty."

"It makes a pretty shackle."

"Come, sit with me beneath this benevolent sun."

He led her to a low bench beside the front door. Megan sat as he went inside the tiny house. A moment later he returned with wooden cups of spring water and a small loaf.

They sat in silence, drinking the peaty water and breaking the bread. The mountain was singing with life. Well-grown lambs bleated in the meadows far below, their bold voices carried up on the breeze. Robins and finches pipped and cheeped as they hopped about the garden, competing for worms and beetles. Crickets whirred in the wiry grass. Bees mumbled into foxgloves. Above it all rang the *pee-wit* of the ponderous curlew. There was not a house nor a sign of man's hand on the land to be seen and it was, for a brief moment, possible to believe that nothing could reach such a place to threaten its peace. Megan watched Merlin as he ate and knew she had never felt so at ease. Never felt such a sense of freedom, and yet of belonging to someone else. How different was Merlin's hold over her from that she had known all her life— the grip of ownership, of control, of noble birthright. She saw now that love meant giving your freedom willingly, and to take that freedom by threat or force was the very opposite of all that was loving. She knew she had to speak plainly.

"Lord Geraint hopes I will be able to convince you to help him defeat Lord Idris," she said.

"And do you think I should?"

"No. That is, you should do what you think is right."

"Do you know why your master is so set on routing his neighbor?"

"Well, Lord Idris has designs on land beyond his own."

"You know this?"

"There have been skirmishes. Battles even. I have seen Lord Geraint's men return from the fray. I have treated some of the wounded horses."

"Yes, there has been fighting. I have heard of it. But I do not believe these battles were of Lord Idris's making. I think it is Lord Geraint who wishes to increase his holding in the region. It is he who causes men to be cut down and slain to further his own purposes. And there is another reason he despises his neighbor so."

"Oh?"

"At one time they were allies. They banded together against their common enemies."

"I do remember such times, but that was many years ago."

"Seven years, to be exact. Tell me, Megan, how old is Master Huw?"

"This is his seventh summer."

"And has it never puzzled you that he has neither the black hair of his mother nor the brown of Lord Geraint?"

"I have always thought his blond curls an endearing quirk."

"But you must certainly have witnessed the way in which Lord Geraint favors Brychan."

"It is natural. He is his first born, his eldest son."

"His eldest, or his only?" Merlin looked at her levelly now.

Megan gasped as she took in the implications of what she was being told.

"Huw is the child of Lord Idris? Why, yes, it could be true. It would explain Lord Geraint's hatred of the man, as well as his coldness toward Lady Rhiannon. In truth, he barely tolerates Huw. Poor Huw." She played with the ring on her finger, pondering life's twists and turns. She met Merlin's gaze. "What will you do?"

"For the present, nothing. Lord Geraint is an impatient man, but even he will wait awhile for my response. I bide here only until I am called to service elsewhere, Megan. My gifts are not for the use of people such as your master, and my destiny does not lie in these hills."

Megan studied his face, trying to be clear about what he was saying. Was he telling her he would be gone soon? That she could not be a part of his life? That there was something more important that would take him from her? She opened her mouth to tell him of Lord Geraint's threats, of the danger both she and her father faced if he did not agree to her master's demands. But she could not make herself say the words. She knew that to do so would place Merlin in an impossible position. And she would not be the one to force such a man to bend to Lord Geraint's will. She would have to find her own way to ensure her father's safety.

Instead she placed her hand over his. The warmth of his flesh made her heart ache for him.

"I wanted to thank you," she said quietly, searching for the right way to explain herself. "To thank you for your help. Last night. With Midnight. It was you, wasn't it?"

Merlin smiled at her.

"Such a brave animal, and with such a fine doctor in attendance. Do you really think you needed my help?"

"I know he would have died without it, and that this morning he is instead enjoying honeyed hay. I know also that I was not the only healer by his side last night," she said with a smile.

Merlin nodded but said no more. Leaning forward he lifted his hand and, with the tenderest of touches, stroked Megan's cheek.

LAURA STOOD AT the newly fitted window of her studio and watched the rain beating down outside. A warm September had quickly given way to a wet October, and for weeks the view had been obscured by low clouds. Her visible world had shrunk to a few hundred yards. Feeling hemmed in and mildly claustrophobic was not something Laura had expected when she moved to Penlan. The weather made walking on the hills both treacherous and unpleasant, and painting outdoors was impossible. She turned to contemplate the canvas on her easel. At last she had found her stride once more and was painting again. But it was not solely the landscape of her new home that had inspired her. There was something else. Or someone else. What or who exactly was still a muddle in her mind. At first she thought it was Rhys. Or, more accurately, the lustful sex she had shared with him, the wild side of her own nature he had unleashed. But she had come to realize that wasn't it either. That lust, that passion, had been all but obliterated by guilt. Acrid, sour, corrosive guilt.

She walked over to inspect her morning's work. The impasto paint was still sticky and wet. It would be several hours before she could continue with the picture. To be impatient and touch it now would produce a muddied mess. Laura had produced, at first glance, a strongly atmospheric painting of the oak woods. Gone were the summer colors of clear greens and bright blues. Now her palette was made up of ochers and umbers and siennas. In the picture a tempest disturbed the branches of the trees and whipped up the fallen leaves, creating a maelstrom of color and texture as the woodland twisted and tangled in the fierce wind. The old Laura would have been content with such a scene, happy to depict nature in its wildness, in its struggle. But the new, obsessive Laura had included aspects of her own passion and turmoil in the painting. A girl could be glimpsed among the trees. It was not a self-portrait as such, more a notion of that wild and young part of herself that was attracted to Rhys. The girl's hair was long and loose, her dress floor-length and flowing, her attitude ambiguous. Was she lost or free? Laura was undecided.

Later, when she had packed up for the day and returned to the house, she was about to pour herself a glass of wine when Rhys appeared in the doorway. She started at the sight of him, her emotions flipping. Desire leaping up to be quelled quickly by guilt, shame, and a fresh resolve to pull herself together.

"Rhys, I wasn't expecting you." She put the bottle down on the kitchen table, not wanting to offer him a glass.

He stepped forward and scooped her into his arms.

"My lovely Laura," he murmured into her hair. "I had to come. I've been hoping you would come to me, at the croft."

"Oh, it's been difficult. You know . . ."

He nodded. "I understand. Don't worry. I can be patient. I've waited for you for so long, a few more weeks . . . I always knew you existed out there, somewhere, and that I would find you. Or that you would find your way to me. Laura, who was meant for me. Returned to me."

Laura frowned. "I'm sorry, Rhys. I don't know what you mean."

"It's a lot to take in. I know that. All will become clear."

She pulled away from him, smiling, but not meeting his eyes. She had to play for time. To put some distance between herself and Rhys. To let him slowly realize that what had happened could not happen again. She wouldn't let it. She busied herself putting away plates that had been draining by the sink.

"I'm a bit distracted at the moment. We've got guests coming this weekend."

"Friends or family?"

"Friends. My oldest and dearest, her husband, and their two delicious little boys. Though actually they feel more like family. Her parents are elderly and live in Spain. Angus has a dipsomaniac father roaming the Scottish highlands somewhere. We're all they've got, I suppose. We've spent Christmases together for as long as I can remember."

"How old are the children?"

"Let me think, William is just seven. Hamish is five. He's adorable, all soft and puppyish. William is fascinating, such a grown-up little chap. I so enjoy spending time with them. They call me Auntie, which makes me feel about ninety, but I don't mind. I'm lucky to have them in my life."

"Sounds to me like you love those little boys."

"Of course I do. I'll always be there for them, no doubt doling out unwanted advice when they're older. In fact, Dan and I are down as their guardians, should something ghastly happen to Steph and Angus, heaven forbid."

"Really? Their parents must think a great deal of you."

"Like I said, they're very dear friends."

Rhys reached out and took Laura's hand, squeezing it gently as he caressed her palm with his thumb.

"You'd give anything to have a family like that, wouldn't you, Laura?"

"Yes. I suppose I would," she said. There was a pause, a moment's silence. Laura began to feel increasingly uncomfortable. "I'm sorry, I really must get on. I have beds to make. Food to organize. You know the kind of thing." She looked at him. "Or maybe you don't. Anyway, this is the way things are, Rhys. I have my life. You have yours. D'you see?" she asked, hoping against hope he might just pick up on what she was implying, work out for himself that she regretted what she had done, and behave like a true friend and leave her alone. It was a faint hope, and a futile one.

Still he held her hand. "Things could be different. You know that, don't you?" he said. "We could be together."

She shook her head. "Rhys, I . . ."

"We're good together, Laura. We are meant to be together, all the time, not just like this. I know you feel the same way."

"You don't know what I feel. Good grief, *I* don't know what I feel. But I do know that I can't see you at the moment. Not here.

Not like this. I'm sorry, Rhys." Why couldn't he see that what they had shared was sex, nothing more.

She was still trying to find the words to make her feelings clear to him when he suddenly asked "Are you still in love with Dan?"

"What? Yes! Yes, of course I am."

"Are you sure about that?"

"Yes."

"Only it didn't feel that way when you were with me. When you were in my bed. When you were . . ."

"I can't give up on my marriage just like that," she said, moving away from him again and clattering plates into cupboards. "Things aren't that simple, Dan and I . . ." Suddenly she gasped, clutching at her belly.

"Laura? What's wrong?"

"Oh!" she cried out as she bent forward, unexpected pain almost bringing her to her knees.

Rhys put his arm around her shoulders.

"What's the matter?"

"Please, help me get to the bathroom." Even as she spoke, Laura could feel blood beginning to run down her thigh. Her fickle menstrual cycle had chosen this precise moment to throw up a heavy and brutal period. She let out a sob as Rhys helped her to the small downstairs toilet. The physical pain and the embarrassment she was experiencing were increased by another all too familiar feeling. The perpetual disappointment of another failed conception descended on her like a grey mountain cloud. She realized now, as she sat weeping, waiting for the flow to steady, that some small part of her had been harboring a new hope.

Somewhere, deep in her desperate psyche, she had been nurturing the notion that Rhys might, just *might* be able to make her pregnant. She knew it was ridiculous. It had already been established that there was nothing wrong with Dan. That their childlessness was her own fault. Her own failing. And yet . . .

By the time she returned to the kitchen, Rhys had already poured two glasses of wine.

"Are you OK?" he asked.

She nodded, not trusting herself to speak. She felt like weeping all over him, but knew she had to stay in control of her emotions. Sharing her grief with him now would somehow be far more intimate than anything that had happened between them before.

He pulled out a chair and sat her down, handing her a drink.

"Here," he said. "Drink some of this. You'll feel better."

She did as she was told, one or two unstoppable salty tears splashing into the wine. "I'm sorry," she sniffed.

"Don't be silly. There's nothing for you to be sorry about. My poor little Laura. I hate to see you so sad." He stroked her hair. "Don't give up hope," he said. "I have brought you something. It was one of the reasons I came." He pulled a small packet and a piece of paper from his pocket. "Two things, in fact. Some henna for your hair—I think you'd look even more beautiful with it red. Why not give it a try? And I wanted to give you this."

Laura looked down at the envelope he was handing her. "What is it?"

"It's the spell you wanted, from my *grimoire*. I copied it out for you."

Despite herself, Laura was touched. The idea seemed ridiculous now, amid the reality of their deceit and her obvious lack of fertility. Even so, it mattered to her that he cared. And she knew, later, when she was alone again, she would look at the spell. What did she have to lose?

"Thank you," she said, taking the henna and the envelope from him. "That was kind of you. Now, if you don't mind, I need to be on my own."

To her relief, he left without a fuss. She went upstairs and took a shower, on impulse applying the powder he had given her to her hair. Maybe a bit of color would give her a little lift. She needed to find some way to improve her mood before Steph and Angus came. Not more than an hour later there was a sharp rapping on the door. She opened it to find Anwen's bulky shape filling the porch. The rain had eased, but a heavy mist still swirled about the yard, wrapping itself around the old woman like a billowing shroud.

Laura blinked away the unsettling image. "Hello," she said as brightly as she could manage. "This is a nice surprise. Not a very good day for a walk, though." She was surprised at how little mud Anwen seemed to have met on her way. The path through the woods would have been sticky and even bogging in places in such weather.

"Have you seen him again?" Anwen demanded.

The boldness of the question took Laura completely by surprise. Did the old woman know Rhys had been at the house? Could she know what had happened between the two of them? Could village gossip know something about her even her own husband had failed to notice?

"I'm sorry, Anwen, seen who?"

"The man you call the dark stranger. The one you saw in the woods."

Now Laura understood. It was not Rhys Anwen was questioning her about. It was Merlin.

"Oh, no. No, I haven't." She could not meet the old woman's fierce gaze. The realization that she had been glimpsing a mythological figure had unsettled her so much she had pushed it from her mind. She had reasoned it out. The move. Hormones. Too much reading about the subject. Her emotions in turmoil over Rhys. Her lust. Her guilt. Anyone might start imagining things with all that going on. She had simply refused to let herself think about it further. She forced a bright smile. "Look, it's very damp out here. Why don't you come in? I'll put the kettle on."

Anwen's face remained inscrutable. "No use trying to hide from him, Laura. If he wants to find you, he will. You shouldn't fight it. He means you no harm. He is the reason you came here."

Suddenly Laura felt very weary. She had neither the patience nor energy for Anwen's riddles. She was tired, and her cramping stomach was crying out for aspirin.

"Look, I'm afraid I'm not feeling very well. I've been working all day, and . . ."

"Oh, I know what you've been doing." Anwen looked openly cross now. She fumbled in her deep coat pocket and brought out what looked at first glance to be a handful of twigs. She thrust them into Laura's hand. "This is for you," she said. "Hang it over your bed. Don't forget, mind."

Laura examined the gift. It appeared to be some sort of corn dolly, but rougher and spikier than any she had ever seen. Rather than corn it was made of plaited sticks and grasses and moss. Laura remembered what she had read about women wanting babies hanging such things up in their bedrooms. Could the old woman really know so much about her? She looked up to thank her—and to question her—but was amazed to see her neighbor already padding across the yard. How could someone so old, with such swollen legs and stiff joints, move so swiftly and silently?

"Thank you!" she called after her, watching her go. "Goodbye!" She raised her hand to wave, but the old woman did not so much as glance back in her direction.

As Laura settled into her chores, preparing for her visitors, she tried to make sense of Anwen's visit. It could not have been easy for the lame old woman to walk all the way from her farm. She clearly had to have a strong reason for her visit, but what exactly that reason had been was not so obvious. She had questioned her about Merlin, yet her brusqueness seemed to be concerned with her seeing Rhys. Could she really know of their affair? And the curious corn dolly—Laura could not remember discussing her childlessness with Anwen, though it was possible talk had gotten around the village by now. It was a pity she had not stayed for a cup of tea. There were beginning to be questions Laura wanted to ask her. Somehow she sensed her neighbor held answers to some of the things that had been confusing her since her arrival at Penlan. If only she could sit down and have a proper talk with the old woman things might start to piece together. She promised herself she would take a walk to the farm at the next opportunity. The sound of an approaching engine shook her from her thoughts. The low clouds had been blown away by a fresh wind and the rain had stopped, so that looking out of the bedroom window she could see Steph's minivan winding its way up the lane. She ran downstairs, excited at the prospect of seeing her friend after what felt like a very long time.

Angus stopped the car at the top of the yard and the children spilled excitedly out of the back.

"Auntie Laura!" they cried, running to her.

Laura bent down and hugged them, nuzzling into the downy neck of little Hamish. At five he was no longer a baby, yet still had that newness and softness about him that toddlers often did. His light brown hair and pale eyes gave him an endearing vulnerability. William looked every inch the big brother, already tall for his seven years and with his father's rusty coloring.

"Look at you two!" She kissed them as she squeezed them. "I swear you've grown an inch a day since I saw you. Such big boys now."

"You really do live on a mountain!" said Hamish.

"Can we go up it? I want to go hiking. Look, I've got proper boots." William showed her his impressive footwear.

"He's been practically sleeping in the things," said Steph, her voice sleepy from the journey.

Laura hurried over to greet her.

"I can't believe you're really here at last."

After a hug Steph held her friend at arm's length. "Wow," she said. "Love the new look, darling. You never used to wear your hair loose. And you've colored it. A secret redhead all along. Who knew?"

"It's just henna. A friend gave it to me."

"Did someone say redhead? Stand aside!" Angus heaved himself out of the driver's seat and grabbed hold of Laura. "What is this vision I see before me? Can it be our city girl, now a wild mountain woman?" He pulled her to him in a bear hug. As always, Laura felt tiny in the arms of this enormous man. He was well over six foot and broad shouldered and carried a little more weight than was good for him. His unruly hair and bushy beard were beginning to show grey hairs among the auburn, but there was still a youthful strength and vigor about him. "The air up here suits you, lassie. You look fabulous."

She smiled but said nothing. Steph narrowed her eyes.

"You do, damn it. Too bloody fabulous, if you ask me."

"Come inside. I'll make some tea."

"Tea!" Steph was scandalized. "Two hours on the M4 with Roald Dahl story tapes on a loop and the car stinking of cheese and onion crisps and you offer me tea? You've been away too long, girl. Angus, fetch the provisions."

The next hour passed with much excited running around on the part of the children while the adults inspected the house, champagne glasses in hand. Angus declared the upstairs a place of unprecedented hazard due to the low-flying beams. Steph was relieved to find comfortable bathrooms and said so repeatedly.

"I don't know what you expected," Laura said. "A plank over an ash pit, perhaps?"

"If not something worse. No, seriously, I'm impressed. A little rustic for my taste. A smidge folksy, if you'll forgive my saying so, but no, it's clean, it's tidy, it has pretensions of chicness here and there. I see the hand of Laura the artist and the mark of Dan the hedonist and the results are pleasingly comfortable."

"Will I phone up and cancel the local B and B, then?" asked Angus.

"Scoff all you like, you poor town mice," Laura said with a laugh. "I love it here."

"Yes," Steph said, looking at her friend closely, "I can see that you do."

Laura felt uncomfortable under such close scrutiny. Her friend knew her so well. Right now it felt as if she were looking inside her, hunting around for all her little secrets. Laura knew her affair with Rhys had changed her. She also knew that Steph would be sensitive to those changes.

"Let's go back downstairs," she said. "Dan will be home soon."

"Ugh! What is that?" Steph had spotted the corn dolly which Laura had suspended above the bed.

"Oh that. A neighbor gave it to me. It's traditional around here, I think. Supposed to bring good luck in a new home, dozens of babies. That sort of thing."

"I couldn't sleep under it. It'd give me the creeps. Far too Wicker Man for my liking."

Angus raised his bushy brows. "D'you have virgins dancing round maypoles, too, m'be? No wonder Dan finally agreed to move out here. Hey! Boys, watch the soft furnishings with those sticky fingers."

The children had found their way upstairs and flung themselves onto Laura's four-poster.

"You've got the best bed, Auntie Laura," said William.

"Can we sleep in it?" asked Hamish.

"No, you can't," Steph told them.

Their disappointed wails were only silenced by Laura promising to read them a story in it before they went to sleep in their own beds, and by tempting them downstairs with the offer of chocolate biscuits.

In the kitchen, Laura and Steph put away the treats brought from London while Angus and the boys explored outside. Laura was aware of her friend's eyes upon her the whole time.

"So," Steph began, leaning against the Aga with her second glass of champagne, "you are clearly thriving on life in the wilderness. Must be all the fresher-than-fresh air. How's Dan finding it?"

"Oh, you know Dan. He's takes a while to get used to new things. But he's coming around to the idea. Slowly."

"No regrets, then?"

"No regrets."

"Are the natives friendly?"

"Most of them. Although we do have a grouchy farmer living up the road."

"Any local talent?"

"Steph, how should I know?"

"There must be a social scene of some sort. Can't believe it's all barn dances and Women's Institute."

Laura shrugged. "We haven't been here long enough to make proper friends yet."

"I suppose not," said Steph. "I suppose not."

Laura was surprised to find herself longing for Dan to come home. If she were honest, she didn't know how long she could avoid telling Steph about Rhys. They had known each other too long. With Dan home things would be easier. The evening would slip into friendly drunkenness and banter once the men got together, and the focus would move away from her.

In fact, Dan arrived back from work early, so that by the time Laura snuggled in her big bed to read the boys their story, raucous laughter could be heard from the adults downstairs. She cuddled the children tightly as she read to them from an old book of fairy tales. They listened enthralled, Hamish sucking his thumb, William following the words on the page as she read. Moments like these were still exquisitely painful for Laura. She had always loved Steph's boys and had been close to them from the day they were born, but naturally they reminded her acutely of her own childlessness. Steph and Angus had always been very sensitive and thoughtful, but a certain amount of hurt was inevitable. Laura remembered Steph telling her almost apologetically when she had become pregnant each time. Of course Laura was happy for her friend and adored spending time with the children, but still there was the envy that would never go away, irritating and impossible to ignore like a stone in your shoe.

"There you are. Time for bed," she said as she shut the book.

"One more story, Auntie Laura," pleaded little Hamish.

"You've already had two."

"Look at this." William had picked up a book from beside the bed. It was the one Laura had borrowed from Rhys. "This is the same as your one, Auntie Laura," he said, pointing up at the corn dolly hanging above the bed.

Laura squinted over his shoulder at the picture he had found. He was right. The drawing was very detailed and, aside from small variations in the materials, it was indeed identical to what Anwen had given her. The note beneath the picture caught her eye. She had expected to read of the powers the dolly had to help a woman conceive, something about increasing fertility perhaps.

Instead she found what she had dangling above her head was a powerful talisman for protecting whoever slept beneath it. It was used when there was a close and imminent danger from an unseen evil. Why on earth would Anwen give her such a thing? Who did she think she needed protecting from? Laura shivered and slammed the book shut.

"Come on, lads," she said, pulling them gently from the bed. "Teeth, faces, and sleep for you."

That evening, with Dan home and in top form, it was a pleasant change to be in the company of old friends. Laura had not been conscious of missing such small social gatherings, but now she felt a pang of nostalgia for her old city life and the closeness she had felt with those who knew her well. As the four of them worked their way through their first bottle of good claret, Laura allowed herself to relax properly for the first time in a long while. The first time, if she was being honest with herself, since she had been with Rhys. She glanced at Steph, wondering what she would say if she knew. Laura was certain she would be shocked, and would tell her she was mad to risk losing Dan. She could be trusted with such a secret, of course, but Laura was reluctant to face her friend's disapproval.

"Glad to see young Daniel still keeps a fine cellar," said Angus, returning from the kitchen to join the women in the sitting room.

"How's it going in there?" Laura asked.

"Chef says dinner will be served in fifteen minutes."

"It'd better be good and plenty of it," said Steph. "I'm ravenous."

"Another glass of this and I won't care what it's like." Laura picked up the bottle and topped off everyone.

"I've always admired Dan's culinary expertise." Angus lowered himself heavily onto the squishy leather sofa beside Laura. "Sadly, I am a man who could burn water."

"Or so you would have us believe," said Steph. "Don't think you're fooling anyone with this klutz-in-the-kitchen routine, Angus. You're just happy to let someone else do all the work."

"And happy to eat the results," said Laura with a laugh as she prodded at his ample tummy.

"Och, Laura, I am wounded. Wounded!"

Laura let Angus pull her into an affectionate embrace. She had always had a soft spot for this gentle mountain of a man, with his good humor and kind heart. It was a comfort to have him with her now, but also a sharp reminder of what she risked by seeing Rhys. Deceiving Dan, should she have been found out, would have affected more than just the three of them.

"Never mind," she told Angus. "You can walk it all off tomorrow. Dan's determined to get you up that mountain."

"I'm up for it. And the boys will love it."

"Smart move, taking the boys," said Steph. "Even you can keep up with a five-year-old."

"Just mind you don't get lost," Laura warned him. "The weather can change in minutes up there. We've had a lot of mist and fog lately. And Dan is frankly hopeless at map reading."

"Did someone mention my name?" Dan appeared in the doorway, tea towel over his shoulder, spatula in hand. "Grub up, people!"

The four ate hungrily, enjoying Dan's excellent cooking and washing it down with more wine. By the time they reached the pudding, Laura was feeling deliciously mellow and more than a little drunk. Looking at the others she could see she was not the only one.

"So," Dan said, leaning back in his chair. "What do you two city slickers think of our humble dwelling?"

"I'll admit it's nothing like as bad as I thought it would be," said Steph.

"That's her way of saying she loves it," Laura pointed out.

"Steph could never love anything outside zone two," said Angus, helping himself to more apple and whinberry pie.

"I didn't say I'd want to *live* here. Someone pass me that pud before Angus eats the lot. All I meant was, it does have a certain charm. All this"—she waved her hands about—"old stuff. Very atmospheric. If a smidge spooky."

"Spooky? How so?" asked Angus, spooning more cream onto his second helping of pie.

"Oh, I don't know. Just the thought of generations of people dying in their beds here, probably of some ghastly disease."

Angus rolled his eyes.

"Stephanie, you've a fascination with all things morbid, woman. How will I dare close my eyes tonight after what you've just said?"

"Hasn't bothered you enough to put you off your food I notice," said Steph.

"This might be my last meal!" he said with a laugh.

"Actually," Dan said, sitting up and adopting a ridiculously somber voice. "Laura has noticed the odd . . . *presence* here and there."

"Dan . . ." Laura shot him a look.

"Ghosts, d'you mean?" asked Angus.

"Great!" Steph tossed her napkin onto the table. "Now I won't be able to sleep either."

"Not ghosts." Laura shook her head.

Angus raised his brows. "No manacled peasants wandering the house, head tucked under arm?"

"Sorry to disappoint you, Angus. Dan was exaggerating, as usual." Laura really did not want to be drawn into the discussion.. She wished she had never mentioned anything to Dan.

"Well," said Angus, pushing his plate away at last, "the only kind of spirits I want to find way up here are the ones young Daniel's going to offer me with my coffee."

Laura stood up and began to clear the table, relieved the conversation had turned away from such a sensitive topic.

Steph got up to help her.

"Doesn't it give you the heebie-jeebies, Laura? You spend so much time here on your own. Have you really noticed something?"

Laura stacked plates and spoke without looking up, "No, of course not. It was nothing, just getting used to a new place. Like I said, Dan was exaggerating. I'll put on the coffee."

❧ 8 ❧

MEGAN HAD GAINED an unexpected day of freedom when Lady Rhiannon decided on a whim to take the children to visit her sister on the far side of the valley. She had pointedly stated that Megan would not be required to accompany them, though she must be ready to attend to the children's needs when they returned that night. Megan took the chance to pay a visit to her father, only half admitting to herself that she might go on to see Merlin later in the day. She did ponder the thought that Lord Geraint may have instructed his wife to leave Megan behind. If she were to do as he commanded and persuade Merlin to aid him she would need the opportunity to spend time in his company.

She enjoyed the walk through the woods to Penlan but this time did not dally to collect plants. In truth, her feelings for Merlin were distracting her so that it was often hard to focus on any given task. As she approached her father's house she saw four horses tied to the meadow gate. Three were workaday coursers, but the fourth was a fine white destrier with legs the color of polished silver. Four men stood in the yard talking to her father. Her unexpected appearance clearly startled them. Megan noticed two of the men reach for their swords. Their hands were stayed by a small signal from the tallest member of the party. He was dressed in simple clothes but had a commanding presence.

"Megan! Come here, Daughter," Twm said as he beckoned her. "I have customers, as you see, searching for new horses."

Megan stepped forward and bobbed a polite curtsey.

The tall man glanced about him, looking disconcerted.

"Why do you bow your head to me, girl? I am a merchant, like your father."

"Forgive me, sir." Megan blushed, confused. "A destrier of such quality ordinarily signifies an owner of noble birth." She saw the four exchange glances. Whatever they had told her father, Megan was quite certain these were not merely men of trade. The tall man had a handsome face and a shock of blond hair. As she studied him Megan realized she knew that face. She opened her mouth to speak, but another voice made everyone present wheel about.

"It seems Megan has more wit than any of you." Merlin strode into the yard, his face clouded with anger.

"Well, well," said Twm. "My house is a popular place for chance meetings today."

"It is not chance that brings Lord Idris to your door, Twm," Merlin told him.

"Lord Idris!" Twm looked afresh at the man he had taken for a horse buyer.

Now Megan knew why his face was familiar. She knew also beyond a doubt that Merlin had been right in his suggestion of Huw's true parentage.

Lord Idris stepped forward.

"Forgive me, Twm, for this deceit. I came to seek out Merlin. Word had reached me he was to be found near your house. I cannot travel safely in the district of Lord Geraint without disguise."

"A disguise not well enough done to fool a maid," Merlin said. "Your business is with me. You have put this family in danger by coming here."

"Had my spies kept me better informed I would have come straight to your own dwelling, Prophet. I accept the fault is my own."

To Megan's amazement, Lord Idris sank to his knees and bowed his head. She had never before seen a man of noble birth behave in such a fashion. What reputation Merlin must possess to have powerful people fall at his feet. It was Twm who found his tongue first.

"Let us go inside," he said. "Please, my Lord. We cannot know who may be watching us even now."

Merlin placed a hand on the young noble's shoulder.

"Come," he said. "Twm is right. We must talk inside."

Megan hesitated, uncertain of her place in such company. Merlin saw her hanging back.

"Come with us, Megan. If I cannot keep you separate from these affairs then I must keep you close." He held out his hand and she took it, and together they went into the house where Twm was already spooning *cawl* into bowls.

❧

ON SATURDAY MORNING Laura got up early after a restless night. She slipped out of the house while everyone else was still asleep, leaving a note explaining she had gone to the village for milk and papers. In truth, she wanted to see Anwen. She reasoned that farming families always started their day at dawn, and that the old woman wouldn't mind her dropping in. Laura had questions she wanted answered. She could only hope Glyn would be out tending his flock, or whatever it was he did on his wretched quad bike. As she drove up the bumpy track to the farm there was no sign of life, save for a few moribund cows and a solitary hen. Laura paused to look for the dog before stepping out of her car, but it was nowhere to be seen. The rain had turned the yard that she remembered as dusty into a sea of ankle-deep sludge. Cursing herself for not wearing her Wellington boots, Laura picked her way to the front door, her leather trainers unrecognizable by the time she reached the garden gate. She got no farther. The door was snatched open and the bad-tempered sheepdog ran out. It circled Laura, growling as it did so. Laura froze, fearing that to move might result in her first-ever dog bite. Glyn appeared in the doorway. He wore his usual raggedy collection of clothes, but without the all-encompassing coat. This time his trousers were accessorized with baler twine. His grubby flat cap was still firmly stuck to his head.

"Oh, good morning." Laura did her best to sound cheerful, despite the dog. "So sorry to call unannounced." She knew she was being ridiculously formal, but the old man unnerved her. "I was hoping to have a word with Anwen."

"What's that?"

Laura wondered if long hours riding the noisy quad had damaged his hearing. She tried again, a little louder this time.

"Your wife. Is she at home?"

Glyn's already grim face set into a harsh scowl now, his thin lips almost disappearing altogether.

"Why don't you go back where you came from!" It was more an instruction than a question. "Leave me be," he added. He gave a silent signal to the dog, which shot back inside as if stung by a bee. The old man paused to clear his throat and spit onto the path before turning his back on Laura and slamming the front door behind him.

Laura stood open mouthed for a moment. What had she ever done to this weasel of a man to make him hate her so much and be so consistently rude to her? How Anwen could stand living with such a creature was beyond her. Seething silently, she trudged through the mire, back to her car and sped away, vowing to approach the farm from the woods next time. And only to knock on the door when she was certain Glyn was well out of the way.

By the time she arrived back at Penlan the children were playing football in the yard. The murky cloud and rain of the previous day had lifted, leaving no bad weather to speak of, although the mountains themselves were still veiled in mist. Laura was pleased that the boys were able to enjoy being outside, but was secretly disappointed there was no sunshine to show off the house at its best. She was proud of her new home, and it was important to her that Steph and Angus like it, too.

She carried the heavy newspapers and milk into the house.

"I'm back," she called out. "Wake up, you lazy lie-abeds. There are hills to be walked out there."

She stopped short with a sharp intake of breath at the sight of Rhys standing next to Steph in the kitchen.

"We have a visitor," Steph said unnecessarily.

"I brought you some more veg and some eggs," said Rhys with an innocent smile.

"Oh, that's great. Thank you." Laura put down her shopping and made a show of looking in the box Rhys had left on the table.

"It'll be the last this year, I'm afraid. Just a few carrots and sprouts and onions."

"I'm impressed," said Steph, handing round mugs of coffee. "Organic veg and free-range eggs delivered to your door. And at the weekend, too." She smiled as she spoke, but Laura could see her scrutinizing Rhys, weighing him up. Laura knew she could easily give herself away. What had made Rhys come? She had told him they were expecting visitors. He must have known this could be awkward. She was glad Dan and Angus were still asleep. She was determined to have Rhys gone before they came downstairs.

"I told you we had some nice neighbors," she said lightly.

"You didn't tell me about this one." Steph raised a questioning eyebrow.

Laura felt horribly trapped. She wanted Rhys to leave, but could hardly tell him to do so. Mercifully, at that moment there came a wail from outside.

"That'll be Hamish," Steph said as she headed for the door. "Trying to play football with two left feet, poor lamb."

The second they were alone Laura rounded on Rhys.

"What on earth are you doing here? I told you we had people coming. Steph is my oldest friend. Have you any idea how difficult this is for me?" she hissed.

"I'm sorry, I had to see you." He stepped toward her, but she turned to the sink, plunging cups into soapy water. He put his hand on her shoulder. "Please, don't be angry with me. It's OK. Don't worry so much. I wanted to meet the boys and bring you the eggs, that's all."

She was spared the trouble of responding by the sound of voices as Dan and Angus came down the stone spiral staircase.

"Hi." Rhys stepped forward to greet the men.

"Rhys brought us some more veg, Dan," she said. "Wasn't that kind? I'll just put them away."

"You see, Angus? Top neighbors up here. You won't get people dropping in with your homegrown carrots in Islington now, will you?"

Laura left the men talking and took the vegetables into the little pantry. She found having Rhys and Dan standing together in her kitchen, making small talk, deeply unsettling. She realized she simply did not know Rhys well enough to trust him. He could say anything, do anything, at any moment. She had to steel herself to return to the kitchen. She was dismayed to see Dan making a fresh pot of coffee. The children had come inside demanding drinks. Laura was surprised to see Rhys taking such an interest in them. He squatted down to their level, looking directly into their eager little faces as he listened to them.

"We're going on a mountain walk," Hamish told him. "Right up there." He gestured toward the sky.

"Are you now? That sounds great."

"Ah, Hamish." Angus ruffled the boy's hair. "Slight change of plan, laddie. It's misty today so we thought we'd try our walk tomorrow, give the weather a chance to clear, eh?"

"Aw, Dad!" both boys protested.

"I want to go today!" William whined. He turned to Rhys for support. "I've got proper hiking boots, look," he said. "And a back-pack with things in case of emergencies."

"We want to go on the mountain today, Daddy." Hamish was pink with indignation. "You said we could. You *promised*!"

Dan stepped in. "But you haven't heard the good news yet, guys. Today we're going to Llangorse Lake to do some sailing. How about that? And your mum will come with us—you know you can't keep her out of a boat."

Hamish was just about convinced this was a fair deal, but William was on the verge of tears of disappointment.

"I want to go on the mountain," he said in a very small voice. "I've got everything all ready."

Rhys put a hand on his shoulder and spoke softly to him.

"You sound like a true mountaineer, my little friend. I bet you're strong walkers, too, the pair of you."

"I am! I am!" cried Hamish.

"Not as good as me," said his brother. "I can walk for miles and miles and miles."

"I'd like to see that," said Rhys.

"You can come with us if you like," William told him.

"Oh, well, you know I'd be happy to be your guide, but it would have to be tomorrow. I'm busy today."

Laura saw him shoot her a glance and prayed no one else had noticed.

"That's a brilliant idea," said Dan. "With you along there's a good chance we won't spend all our time getting lost."

"As long as I'm not gatecrashing."

Dan put his arm around Laura's shoulders. "What do you reckon, Laura? Do you think we should let him tag along?"

"Are you sure, Rhys? The children have to go quite slowly. It won't be the sort of walk you're used to."

"It'll be a pleasure," he said, smiling brightly. "I'd be pleased to help. I can't wait to see these budding mountaineers in action." He stood up, winking at William as he spoke.

"That's settled then," Dan said smiling. "Tomorrow morning you girls can sit about and gossip. We men are going to climb a mountain! How perfect is that?"

"Perfect," said Laura. "Just perfect."

Once the others had set off for their trip to the lake Laura decided to take the chance to look at the spell Rhys had given her. She sat at the kitchen table with a fresh mug of coffee and smoothed out the crumpled piece of paper which she had kept hidden. She had glanced at it only once, there being little time alone with the house so full. She sipped her coffee and began to read the spell written out so beautifully in Rhys's elaborate hand. As she read it she wondered how many women longing for children had scanned these same words hoping for a little magic. Rhys had written a note at the top of the page.

This is an ancient Celtic fertility spell, my love, so you have to say the incantation in Welsh. You can use one of the eggs I brought you, as my hens are the right type. Ideally it is supposed to be cast in a waxing moon, though it doesn't have to be done at night. You've got a couple of days before the full moon, then it'll be wan-

ing. Choose a place that means something to you, and make sure you are alone. Good luck, my lovely Laura, R. xxx

Laura glanced down at the incantation and read it aloud, struggling with the unfamiliar sounds: *"Boed i'r rhai hynny sydd â'u henwau'n ysgrifenedig yma gael eu gwahanu a'u cadw oddi wrth ei gilydd am byth bythoedd."* She had no way of knowing what the words meant, but that only added to the mystery and strangeness of the spell. She turned back to the instructions, which were in English:

Take an egg from a black hen and boil it in urine. [Yuck!] *Let it grow cold, then cut through with a clean blade. In black ink inscribe the names of both the man and the woman for whom the spell is designed. Dig a hole no more than one hand's depth and plant the egg, keeping the halves separate. Cover with earth and a stone, then walk around the spot chanting the given words for six circles clockwise and six circles counterclockwise.*

"Wow," Laura said to herself. She stared at the piece of paper in her hand. It occurred to her that giving her the spell had been a generous gesture on Rhys's part, as it would be helping Dan as well as herself. Unless, of course, he had intended her to use his name in the spell and not Dan's. No, she couldn't do that. As she realized this, she recognized that she was actually taking the thing seriously. How desperate would she have to be to give it a try? The idea began to thrill her. She had all the ingredients. The moon was waxing, and the others wouldn't be home for a while.

She should be painting, painting, painting, but the thought of Penny's incredulity at someone being too busy to work because they were casting a spell made her laugh aloud for the first time in ages. That decided it. She got up and rattled through the cupboard for an old saucepan. She dropped her jeans and quickly peed in it—feeling more than a little ridiculous—then set it on the stove. She plopped in one of Rhys's eggs, her hand over her mouth as the vile smell of boiling urine began to fill the kitchen. She opened a window, and found a black marker. Fifteen minutes later she had severed the egg and carefully written her name on one half and Dan's on the other. She put the pieces in a tub, snatched up the paper with the spell on it, and hurried down to the woods. She already knew where she was going to cast the spell. "Choose somewhere that means something to you," Rhys had written. She made straight for the glade by the sloping oak. Once there she glanced over her shoulder to make sure she was not observed, then chose a patch of ground without too many roots. The earth was soft after the recent drizzle, and she did not have to dig very deep, so she was able to scoop out a hole with a stone and her hands. She settled the eggs into the soil, packing it gently between them so that they did not touch. She covered them as instructed and found a smooth, flat stone to go on top. She stood up, brushing mud from her hands, and took the spell from her pocket. She frowned at the incantation, wishing she had paid more attention to Rhys's reading of Welsh poetry and made more of an effort with local place names. Slowly she began to walk in clockwise circles, chanting self-consciously as she went. By the sixth circuit, she had grown more confident and spoke the words a little louder. She paused, then started on her counterclockwise circles. She had only two more to do when a shout from the trees startled her so much she dropped the piece of paper as she wheeled round. Anwen came striding toward her, her face thunderous with fury.

"What is this madness?!" she demanded, her features almost unrecognizable they were so distorted by rage. "What wickedness! What treachery!"

"Anwen, you made me jump. I was just . . ." Laura let the sentence trail off, unnerved by the state of her normally friendly neighbor, and at a loss to understand why she should be so angry. "It's just a harmless fertility spell. I don't see why you're so upset."

"Harmless! Harmless, you say!" Anwen snatched up the paper, reading quickly through narrowed eyes. "Who gave you this . . . this *evil* thing?"

"Does it matter?" Laura was beginning to feel irritated by Anwen's reaction. She felt foolish enough being caught doing something so bizarre as casting a spell in the first place. She really did not need to have such a fuss made.

Anwen glared at her. "It was Rhys, wasn't it? I warned you," she said, hurling the piece of paper to the ground.

"He was only trying to help. Hey! Stop that!" she cried, as the old woman used her walking stick to knock away the flat stone. But Anwen was intent on what she was doing. She dug her stick into the disturbed ground again and again, eventually exposing and crushing the egg halves.

She turned to Laura now, a stubby finger wagging in her face. "You never, never, *never* cast a spell if you do not know exactly what the words mean. You are playing with the very fires of the underworld, my girl, and its heat will consume all those you love if you persist along this path."

Before Laura could think of how to respond Anwen spun on a heavy heel and stomped away through the woods. She watched her go, shaken by her reaction, and disturbed by what she had said. She picked up the piece of paper and all but ran back to the house, determined to find out just exactly what it was she had been chanting over that damned egg.

MEGAN HURRIED INTO the boys' bedchamber, the sound of Huw's tearful cries unmistakable even over the noise of the tempest outside. The flame of the candle she carried spluttered and shrank as thin winds snatched at it through the shuttered windows. Megan cupped her hand around the wick and continued on. She found Huw trembling on his bed. He stretched his arms out when he saw her.

"Oh, Megan, I heard dragons fighting on the roof of the castle, I swear it!"

"Hush now, Huw," she said as she sat beside him, her arm around his slender shoulders. "It is only the wind."

"I never heard such a noise before. It will surely blow the castle down!"

"No, it will not," she said, though she could well understand his fears. The evening had begun with a wet wind moaning through the castle walls like a restless spirit, but now the storm had gathered strength and force. It was as if it chased around the high mountains until even they could contain it no longer, so that it came crashing down the valley, breaking on the castle like a giant wave at sea. The heavy rain of the preceding week had been swept away by the gales, the clouds dispersed like the seeds of a dandelion clock. Another blast flung open the shutters of the bedroom window. Huw shrieked as Megan struggled to close them again. It took all her might to shut the little wooden doors against the tumultuous air and refasten the latch.

"There," she said, returning to Huw. "The wind belongs outside—let him stay there."

The noise had awoken Brychan, whose own fear had finally conquered his pride. He trotted across the room and climbed into bed with his brother.

"Please, Megan, tell us a story. I can't bear to listen to that fearsome noise any longer."

"Oh, yes." Huw brightened at the thought. "A story Megan!"

"Very well. Which one shall we have?"

"Pwll in the Underworld!" cried Brychan.

"You always choose that one," Huw complained. "I want the one about the people turned into harvest mice."

The boys began to clamor and argue.

"Hush now, children—you will frighten away any story that might be waiting to be told."

They became quiet at once and sat attentive, ready to listen.

"I will tell you the story of Gelert, the noble hound whose loyalty knew no bounds." Megan set down her candle in a small nook in the wall, tucked the boys under the covers, and curled her feet up on the bed beneath her. As she told the tale she watched the boys' faces, seeing in them the lives of the heroes played out in the widening of a young eye or the pursing of incredulous lips.

"Once, in a land very like our own," she began, "save for the bigger mountains and the deeper rivers, of course, there lived a fine young prince named Llewelyn ap Iorweth. He was loved and held in high regard by all those who knew him, for he was brave and honest, a man to be relied upon in times of trouble, a man to be trusted. He had fought many battles to protect his village and his people, and when he was not fighting he enjoyed his sport, in the main hunting with his beloved hounds. These were fine animals, descended from a line of dogs known for their keen noses, swift legs, and fearless hearts. And the best of these was called Gelert. Gelert was the prince's favorite. He was a hand taller than any of the others, with strong shoulders, grizzled grey fur, and a kind eye. He had fought wolves and bears and brought down the greatest boar in the forest, even when its tusks ripped into his side.

"Prince Llewelyn loved this hound more than any other and even took him to battle with him. More than once he saved his master's life, though the arrows and swords whistled about his ears. Some years passed, and Gelert became slower and his legs a little stiff. Still the prince kept the animal by him, though he was too old to hunt now.

"It happened that Prince Llewelyn took a wife, and very soon they had a child. The baby was all the world to the prince now, and whenever he could he would spend time with the boy, playing with him, even taking him riding with him on occasion. His wife joked that Gelert would be jealous, but Prince Llewelyn laughed at this. 'The old hound knows I am forever in his debt,' he told her.

"A few weeks later the village was attacked. In the battle the prince's wife was slain. Soon after, the attackers fled. Near mad with grief, he swore to avenge his bride. He placed the baby in its crib and set Gelert to stand beside it. 'Guard him well, faithful hound, for he is all and everything to me now.' So saying he rode away.

"That night, with the village all disturbed and the men away, wolves came to see what was to be had. They even stole into the room where the baby slept. Gelert stood his ground. Though old he would not let the wolves approach. He fought them all, though they inflicted grievous wounds upon him. At last he chased them away. Fearing they might return, he went to the crib, and took the blankets between his teeth. With great care he lifted the infant out and carried it to a safer place where he could hide it. Then he took his position once more.

"Hours later Prince Llewelyn returned. He hurried to see his child and was horrified to find only an empty, bloodstained crib. In a fit of panic and rage he turned to Gelert, and seeing the animal covered in blood and thinking it to be that of his child, he raised his sword and cut down the poor animal. 'You evil hound! Your jealously has made you murder my son!' But even as Gelert lay dying a servant came running forward with the babe in his arms. 'Master, look, the child is safe! Gelert drove off the wolves.' Realizing too late that he had wrongly accused the faithful dog the prince fell to his knees. 'Gelert, my most loyal friend, forgive me!' Gelert stretched his neck out and tenderly licked his beloved master's hand before death carried him away to the other world."

As Megan finished her story the wind dropped momentarily, so that the end of the tale lingered in the silent space. The boys were spellbound and had quite forgotten their fear of the storm.

"Poor Gelert," Huw whispered.

"If I had such a hound I would never doubt him for a second," said Brychan, leaping up to stand on the bed. "I would take my sword and kill those wolves. Like this! And this! And this!" he said, slashing at imaginary beasts with a swordless hand.

"Hush now. The story was to help you sleep, not set you jumping about. Get into bed and I will fetch warm milk."

On her way down to the kitchen Megan passed the great hall. The door was ajar, and as she walked on she heard voices. She would not have hesitated but the mention of a name made her stop dead in her tracks. Merlin's name. Carefully, she crept over to the door and peered in. She could clearly see Lord Geraint sitting near the fire, a silver goblet of wine in his hand. His hounds lay at his feet, and beyond them stood Llewelyn. Megan turned her head the better to listen to their conversation.

"You think he could prove a threat, my Lord?" Llewelyn was asking.

"I cannot know. In truth, I had hoped to use him. To that end, I had set young Megan to win him over to our cause. But time has passed. He shows no sign of yielding. And now this news that he has met with Lord Idris. What may they be plotting? Why would my enemy risk journeying onto my land to see the magician without some purpose?"

"My spy was unable to listen to their conversation," Llewelyn explained. "He told me Idris spoke of his plan to ride to the house of Twm under guise of being a merchant looking for a new horse, and so he put himself forward as escort. He was not, however, privy to the meeting itself but had to remain outside. What was said was out of his hearing."

"It is enough that they met."

"Do you wish me to question the girl?"

Megan shuddered at the idea of what Llewelyn's notion of questioning might be. She thought how different this man was from the prince in her story.

"There is little point. If she has simply failed, she will be too afraid to admit to it. If, as I suspect, she has instead colluded with him and refused to do my bidding, we will only alert her to our plans. And I do not wish to have Merlin forewarned."

"We could lock her in the castle. That way she could not reach him."

"Remember the nature of our adversary, Llewelyn. Were the maid to learn of our plans she might have only to cast her words on the wind or talk to the sparrows to inform her lover, for all that we can know." He tipped more wine down his throat before continuing. "No, we must be certain Merlin is not given reason to flee. It sits badly with me that he will not fight for us. How much worse would it be should he choose to ally himself with Lord Idris? I will not afford him that opportunity."

"You want me to kill him, my Lord?"

"Yes. Tonight. And do it yourself, I trust no one else."

"Of course, my Lord."

"And the girl's father must be dealt with."

Megan stifled a cry at these words. One of the hounds raised its head, looking in the direction of the doorway. It let out a low rumble.

Lord Geraint kicked the dog impatiently.

"Be silent, foolish creature," he said, standing up and moving toward the table. "Twm showed where his allegiance lies by permitting my enemy to cross his threshold. Further, I will not be made a fool of by a maid. She will see, as will all others, that I do not make threats of no consequence. Come, Llewelyn, eat with me before you set about your errands on this wild night."

Megan flattened herself against the wall as the men crossed the room to the long table. She waited until they were seated and engrossed in their food before creeping on to the kitchen. She fetched the jug of milk, pausing to plunge a hot poker in it for a moment. As it steamed her mind ran in a dozen directions. She had to warn Merlin. And her father. And it was clearly not safe for her to remain in the castle. While she might reach Merlin through her thoughts there was too much at stake to risk failure. And besides, she and her father would have to leave the valley. She must go at once. But she must not alarm the boys. If she did not return with their milk they would come looking for her. She sped back to their room, doing her best to appear untroubled and calm.

"Here, children, drink this down quickly." She waited until they were in their beds before handing them the milk. She felt a sudden stab of sadness at the thought that she would never again kiss them goodnight, nor watch them ride their ponies, nor tell them a tale to calm them. She had been closer to the children than their own mother all these years and now she must vanish from their lives forever. She knew Brychan would survive without her. He was old for his years and had a confidence built on his father's obvious love for him. But she feared for little Huw. He was so gentle and earnest, and so lacking in affection from either of his parents. Megan stroked his hair as he settled back on his pillow and wished with all her heart that she could scoop him up and take him with her. He still had a young child's ability to slip into sleep in a second, and his breathing was steady and soft by the time Megan crept from the bedchamber.

She shut the door and went to her own room. She had time enough only to snatch up a few treasured possessions. She took her good dress and her comb and wrapped them in a wool blanket, tying the bundle together with the soft rope she sometimes used as a belt. She threw her heavy cloak around her shoulders and stole out along the hallway. She was about to descend the spiral stairs when she remembered her mother's perfume flask. It was the only thing of her mother's she still kept, she could not leave without it. She ran back to her room and retrieved it from under her mattress. She had gotten as far as the top stair for a second time when the sound of a heavy door opening made her freeze.

"Megan?" Lady Rhiannon's voice was unmistakable. "Where are you going?"

Megan hardly dared move. What possible explanation could she give for running about the castle in the middle of the night clutching her belongings? If she did not leave now she would not reach Merlin or her father before Lord Geraint's men. She let her bundle slip quietly from her hand down the steps in front of her, then turned to face her mistress.

"I wanted to tend to Midnight, my Lord's destrier. He is not yet completely recovered from his illness."

"You thought to go to the stables at this hour?"

"The wind woke me. I have attended Master Brychan and Master Huw. They are both sleeping."

"Very well, go to the wretched animal. But see you are about your duties in the morning."

"Thank you, my Lady." Without waiting to be questioned further she turned and fled down the stairs, grasping her package as she passed.

She crossed the garden to the stables without need of torch or candle, as the clear sky boasted a full and luminous moon. The wind still blew with great strength, so that every tree strained at its roots as if it had somewhere else it would rather be. Inside the stall the animals dozed or chewed their hay peacefully, unbothered by the fierce weather. Megan entered the barn with such haste that she was inside before she realized there was a light still burning. Dafydd stood beside a grey mare, a lamp raised.

"Megan?"

"Oh, Dafydd." She was thrown. She needed a horse and had planned to slip a bridle on Hazel, but she could not now do so without Dafydd's agreement. Could she trust him? She had no choice. She stood close to him and kept her voice low, fearing others may have been kept awake by the noisy night. "I have to leave this very minute, Dafydd. And I need a horse, or I shall be too late."

"Too late for what?"

"That I cannot tell you, for to do so would condemn you as well as myself. Only believe me that I have no choice, and that great harm with befall innocent people if I do not go now." She watched his face, searching for some sign that he would help her. "I had thought to take Hazel," she told him.

There was a moment of quiet between them filled only with the wailing of the wind and the creaking of the barn timbers as the weather pressed down upon them. Dafydd shook his head.

"I cannot let you do that, Megan," he said slowly.

Megan felt despair beginning to descend.

"Hazel is no match for such a night," Dafydd went on. "We must find you a more suitable mount. Come," he said, leading her to another stall.

"You mean me to take Midnight?" Megan was astounded.

"He has the speed and the sureness of foot you will need in the dark and through such weather. He will go well for you—of that I have no doubt." As he spoke Dafydd deftly saddled the horse. He took Megan's small bundle of possessions and tied it to the pommel, then held the fidgeting animal as she sprang onto its back.

Megan looked down at her kind friend. "This will mean trouble for you," she said.

"If time is scarce, Megan, do not waste it on fretting for me."

For a second they looked at one another, connected in a way that every serf or slave had always been and would always be, and then Dafydd flung open the great door at the front of the building.

The wind rushed into the barn and seemed to lift horse and rider up with it as Midnight plunged forward out of the shelter of the stables and into the wild darkness outside. Megan was unprepared for the terror she felt at hurtling through the countryside at such speed with so little light. The moon's beams showed outlines, shapes, notions of objects, but not their detail, nor a clear picture of the path on which they galloped. For all she could see she might as well be blindfolded. She had no option but to give Midnight his head, urge him forward, rely upon his superior night vision, and trust him completely. She grasped a handful of mane and sat deep in the saddle, knowing that to fall would be disastrous. She felt the power of the great horse as he flew across the uneven ground. Not for the first time she marveled at how something so strong, something possessed of such force and courage, would allow itself to bend to the will of a flimsy girl. With each stride she found a little of her usual confidence in the saddle returning. Within moments they were out of sight of the castle and heading for the woods. Megan considered the paths she could take and chose to skirt the forest, rather than enter it. It was a longer route, certainly, but she judged it a faster one. And a safer one. Midnight charged on, never slowing his pace nor questioning her instructions for a second. On they galloped, Megan's heart pounding to the urgent rhythm of the horse's hooves. She knew she could only be minutes ahead of Llewelyn and his men. At last the path turned upward, running along the side of the hill, climbing, climbing all the while until finally the dim shadow of the croft could be seen up ahead. Her heart quickened at the sight of the now familiar building. The recent weeks had seen her slipping away to be with her lover on every available occasion. He had come to mean so much to her in such a short time. The thought that she might be too late to keep him safe filled her with renewed terror. But by the time she reached the door of the dwelling Merlin was standing outside it as if he had sensed Megan's approach. His wolf stood beside him.

"Merlin!" She hauled on the reins, causing Midnight to slide to a stop. She slipped from the saddle as Merlin ran to her. Her breath came in ragged gasps as she tried to explain why she had come, and she had to raise her voice to be heard above the howling of the wind and the heavy blowing of the fidgeting horse beside her. "You must leave! At once."

"Megan? What has happened?"

"Lord Geraint has tired of waiting for your answer. He has ordered your murder."

"When did you learn of this?"

"This night. I left the castle as soon as I could. There is no time to lose." She placed a hand on his arm. "If we do not reach

my father before Lord Geraint's men get there they will kill
him, too."

Merlin covered her hand with his own for a brief moment.
"Stay here," he said. "I will fetch my horse."

He returned in minutes, but the wait had seemed an eternity
to Megan as she sat on her restless horse. She noticed he carried
no possessions at all.

"We may never return," she reminded him. "Is there nothing
you wish to take with you?"

"All that I hold dear is riding beside me," he said.

Megan opened her mouth to respond but Merlin held up his
hand. The wolf let out a menacing growl.

"Riders!" he said.

Megan strained her ears against the noise of the night but
could hear nothing. She peered into the gloom of the valley and
at last could make out spluttering torches moving swiftly up the
valley.

"They will catch us!" she cried.

"No, listen to me, Megan. Ride to your father, go with him
away from this place. Lord Geraint's men will follow me."

"Then give me your courser. You will need Midnight's
speed."

"No, better you keep him. Do not fear for me. I have my own
ways of eluding my pursuers," he told her, Then, seeing uncertainty on her face, he added, "We will be together again, my love.
When you are clear of this place call me and I will come to
you. Remember, call, and I will find you. Now go!" So saying he
brought his staff down on Midnight's rump, sending the animal
leaping forward.

Megan snatched up the reins and rode on without time for so much as a backward glance. As she charged across the hillside she heard shouts from the soldiers and knew they had seen Merlin and gone after him. It took all her strength of will not to turn and help him, but she knew there was little she could do. Just as she knew her father needed her more. And just as she believed Merlin when he said they would be together again.

As she neared her father's house clouds began to cover the moon, so that a deeper darkness surrounded her. Heavy rain fell now, quickly changing the firm ground to sticky mud. She felt Midnight adjust his stride the better to run across the slippery earth. At last she could see the light from the window of the long-house. She had just started to descend the field to the side of the house when the front door was thrown open and her father flung out into the rain. As he struggled to his feet five strangers followed him out of the house. Megan gasped and heaved on one rein, swinging Midnight about in an effort to stop him plunging farther down the hill. As he spun around she saw horses tied to the wall. She recognized them as being from Lord Geraint's stable, and as the men raised their guttering torches, she could see they were his soldiers. Before she had time to think what to do one of the men struck her father brutally with the hilt of his sword. As she watched a second soldier roughly forced him to kneel. Megan's breath was taken from her body as she realized what was about to be done. She opened her mouth to scream, but at that moment her father looked up. Although the light was poor and the rain beating down, she looked into his face and knew he had seen her. She froze, rendered powerless by the horror of what was

unfolding, knowing she had arrived too late to save her beloved
father. He seemed to look directly at her, and she was certain she
saw him mouth the word *ride* before his features fell into a gentle
smile. Megan saw torchlight flash on a raised blade. She let out a
silent scream of anguish as the sword was swung down, slicing
noiselessly through her father's neck.

Megan fought for breath, all the while struggling to restrain
her wheeling mount. At that moment, one of the soldier's horses
became aware of his stable companion and let out a shrill whinny.
The soldiers looked up. She had been seen. Even as she turned
and raced away, she knew the men were coming after her. Despite
Midnight's speed, Megan would be caught if she tried to cross
the open mountain. Her only hope of escape was to ride through
the woods. She turned toward the trees. Feeling Midnight hesitate
at the edge of the tangle of forest and undergrowth she used her
heels and voice to send him on.

"Fly, Midnight, fly as if the wind itself were carrying you, my
brave friend," she said, tears for her lost father mingling with the
rain that coursed down her face. The shock of what she had witnessed had left her breathless, weakened, and bewildered, but her
instinct for survival told her to keep moving, at all costs. As Midnight plunged through the woodland she had to cling flat to his
neck or risk being knocked from his back by low branches. Brambles and vines whipped at her as she rode, and mud flew up from
the horse's pounding hooves as he slithered through streams and
ditches and soared over fallen trees. The sweat on the animal's
neck was making the reins slippery and difficult to hold. Specks
of blood flecked the foam from his mouth as he bit down on

his pelham. Megan could hear the shouts of the soldiers now and knew they, too, had entered the woods. She kicked at Midnight's flanks, making the horse race on with even more reckless speed. They rounded a bend in the path and crossed a leaf-strewn glade past a sloping oak. Just as Megan thought they might lose their pursuers Midnight let out a bone-chilling scream, dropped his shoulder, and came crashing to the ground. Megan was sent hurtling through the air. She landed heavily, her head meeting an ivy-covered stump, so that she barely knew what was happening. With tremendous effort she dragged herself to her feet and staggered back toward the stricken horse.

"Midnight!" she called, then stopped when she saw what it was that had caused the horse to fall with such violence. The beautiful animal flailed on the ground, unable to right itself, a vicious iron trap clamped to its leg. The metal teeth of the cruel device had bitten deep just below the knee, all but severing the limb. Megan sank to the ground beside the poor horse, laying a hand on its head, its eyes rolling as it fought to free itself.

"Forgive me," she whispered, even as she heard the soldiers come thundering into the clearing behind them. "Forgive me."

She tasted bile rising into her mouth and had the sensation she was falling from a great height. Then, to the unforgettable roar of the dying horse, blackness claimed her.

9

ON SUNDAY MORNING the children had dragged everyone out of bed early for the promised walk. The mist had lifted just enough to make it a viable option, though the skies were anything but clear. Angus had already been to the shop for the papers and breakfast had been eaten at record speed. Laura washed up as Steph tried to organize the boys.

"Hamish!" Steph grabbed the boy as he sprinted past her. "You haven't cleaned your teeth this morning. Go on, quickly now, everyone else is ready to go."

"Mum, do I have to?"

"Did you ever see a mountaineer with bad teeth? Course not. You want to go hill walking, you gotta have clean teeth, OK?"

"OK," he grumbled, heading for the stairs.

Laura watched the way William stepped forward to make the most of his brother's temporary absence.

"Look, Auntie Laura, I've got everything we might need in my backpack, in case of emergencies."

"Wow, you do look well equipped. Let's see, bandages, a compass, packets of dried food. How long are you planning on being up there?"

"You have to be prepared. Look, this is so cool. It's a survival blanket."

Steph peered over Laura's shoulder. "Looks like something to wrap the Sunday roast in."

"Mum! It's made of the same stuff astronauts use in space. It's to stop you dying of exposure."

Laura laughed with the others, but she could not shake off the feeling of unease that had dogged her since casting the spell the day before. After Anwen's extreme reaction Laura had spent a difficult hour on the Internet trying to translate the words of the incantation. If she had only bothered to acquire a Welsh dictionary when they had moved to Penlan the task might have been a simple one. As it was, she could only find translations for a few of the words by picking through place names and snippets of quotations and poems given in parallel texts. Despite gaps, though, she discovered enough to make her feel ill at the thought of what she had been doing. It was clear Rhys had lied to her. This was not a spell to increase fertility or the chances of conception. This was a hex, a curse, and a very specific one at that. No wonder he had been keen for her to use Dan's name in it. It had not been a generous act at all. He must have known her conscience would not allow her to put Rhys's name on the egg, so he had rightly assumed he would not be the one cursed. From what Laura had gleaned the incantation implored whatever powers where listening to separate the two people named and see that they were kept apart forever. She found the wickedness of this deceit breathtaking, and did not wonder, now, at Anwen's fury. She also marveled at Rhys's cleverness. Had he had her sticking pins in dolls or setting fire to a few stolen hairs from Dan's comb she might have been suspicious. But an egg, somehow it was such a universal symbol of fertility that she never questioned it. At first she had wanted to confront Rhys, to tell him what she knew. How dare he trick her like that? How could he lead her into doing something so vile? But, after a restless night spent turning the thing over and over in her mind, she decided to say nothing. At least, not yet. She would wait until Steph and Angus had gone home. It was too complicated to deal with Rhys while they were still at the house, and there was the wretched walk to get past first.

Dan came into the kitchen, clapping his hands together, full of purpose and enthusiasm.

"Right! Are we all ready?"

Laura pointed to William's pack and said, "Ready for anything, I'd say."

"It's stuff in case of emergencies, Uncle Dan."

"Splendid. Be prepared for anything, William, absolutely right. I was a boy scout myself, you know. In fact, I got my whittling badge when I was only . . ."

"Oh, please." Steph gave an exaggerated groan. "Spare us the Boy Scouts stuff. Angus! Where the hell are you?"

"Coming, oh great one." Angus appeared wearing a striking pair of hiking shorts.

"My God," said Dan. "The last surviving member of the Famous Five!"

"Mock me if you will, Daniel Matthews, you know you're just jealous."

"I think you look the part," Laura told him, as Hamish came scampering back into the room. "Here we are. You're all set then."

"Not quite," said Steph. "Where's your lovely guide?"

Laura had half hoped Rhys wouldn't show up. The appointed hour for the walk had come and there was no sign of him. Had he thought better of spending so much time with his lover's husband? The answer to Laura's question came with a knock on the open front door.

"Hi, everyone ready?" Rhys flashed one of his most charming smiles. Everybody smiled back. Everybody except Laura.

After much jostling for position the party set off. Laura and Steph stood in the yard to watch them leave. There was no wind, just a dampness in the air after such a long spell of mist and rain. Laura felt strangely uneasy as she watched the boys trotting off behind Rhys. She shook her head to rid herself of silly notions and turned back to the house.

"I'll make some fresh coffee," she said.

Inside Steph sat down at the kitchen table and flicked idly through the Sunday papers.

"All seems a million miles away, doesn't it?"

"What?"

"Oh, all this news, the rest of the world, real life."

"This is real life. Real for me and Dan, anyway."

"If you say so."

Laura stole a glance at Steph, but she seemed intent on an article. She sensed that her friend had something on her mind. She measured coffee into the percolator and tried to decide if she could risk confiding in Steph. It would be good to talk to someone, but was it fair? She was Dan's friend, too, after all. The decision was made for her when Steph straightened up, looked her in the eye, and said, "So, have you let him shag you yet?"

Laura opened her mouth to protest but was stopped by the knowing look her friend was giving her. She sighed, sitting down heavily at the table.

"Is it that obvious?"

"I'll take that as a 'yes.' He is gorgeous, I grant you, but hells bells, Laura, what are you doing?"

"I don't know. It just . . . happened."

"Oh *please*! What does that mean, exactly? He just *happened* to be passing when all your clothes just *happened* to fall off, and he just *happened* to jump your bones? Somewhere along the line you made the decision to have an affair, Laura. At least admit that much."

Laura closed her eyes and rubbed her temples. "It isn't as simple as that."

"Yes it is. He fancied the pants off you, you got all flustered and flattered. Fine, you could have left it there. But no, you chose to sleep with him. You're cheating on Dan, and you're lying to yourself."

"Look, I'm not trying to excuse what I've done. I'm just saying there was more to it than that."

"Don't tell me you're in love with him! Please don't tell me that."

"No. No, I'm not. It was a physical thing."

"So you're risking your marriage, and you're prepared to hurt Dan, just for a shag?"

"Steph . . ."

"I don't see what's complicated about it. You think I haven't been tempted? That I haven't had offers in the twelve years I've been with Angus? Of course I have. It's an ego boost, it makes the old pulse speed up a bit, you get all wet-knickered at the thought of the guy for a few weeks, but you don't act on it, for Chrissake. You buy some sexy clothes, daydream, watch silly movies, snap at your spouse. Then you wake up one morning and realize the object of your lust is a bit of a plonker anyway, and you'd have to spend ages training him up, and you move on. You don't throw away everything for a crush."

"By everything you mean Dan?" Laura looked up now, beginning to feel cross at the way Steph was reacting. "Let's not forget the crucial difference between your everything and mine, Steph. You have children to consider. I don't."

"Unbelievable! You're actually using your childlessness to justify screwing around? Haven't you forgotten it's Dan's childlessness, too?"

"But I'm the one with the body that doesn't work properly, not Dan! I'm the one every gynecologist in London has poked and prodded and declared inexplicably but irredeemably infertile!" Laura was shouting now. "Well, maybe I needed to feel that I wasn't some dried up hag. Maybe I needed to feel good about my body again. To feel desirable. Not just an object of pity."

"Don't worry, it won't be you I'm pitying when Dan finds out and his heart is broken."

"You just don't understand."

"Too bloody right I don't!"

Laura stood up, her chair scraping on the flagstones. "Well, thanks for your support," she yelled as she stormed out of the house.

By the time she reached her studio, she was crying uncontrollably. She was hurt that Steph had been so harsh, had given her no sympathy at all. But if she was honest with herself, she knew her friend was entitled to be so angry, and that she was right in what she said. She had betrayed Dan for what she knew now had been a passing madness. She should have just told Steph straight away that it was over between her and Rhys, that she felt guilty as hell and hated herself for what she had done. But she had felt cornered. Ashamed. And she was still worried at what might lie ahead. She knew Rhys well enough to be certain he would not take it well when she told him she didn't want to see him anymore. Would he tell Dan?

Laura sat on the stool in front of her easel and let her tired mind change its focus to the painting in front of her. She looked at the girl in the wild woods and recognized something of herself that she hadn't seen before. Not just the physical resemblance—she had been aware of that as she had painted, of course. There was a certain lostness about the figure, a peculiar sense of her being adrift and alone and searching for something that struck a chord. She reached forward and let her fingers wander over the thick paint. It was perfectly dry now. She had thought of working a little more on the picture, but at that moment decided it would be best left in its slightly raw, unfinished state.

A sound behind her made Laura jump. She turned to look. At first she could see nothing, but then she noticed movement in the shadows in the far corner of the studio. She climbed off the stool.

"Who is it? Who's there?" As she waited for an answer she felt goose bumps prickling her arms. She moved forward tentatively, aware of her accelerated heartbeat. She heard another noise and stopped. "Come out!" she said, failing to keep a frightened shrillness out of her voice. She took a deep breath to try and calm herself but nothing could have prepared her for what happened next.

A figure stepped out into the light. Laura recognized him at once. Close up he was taller than she had expected, his long hair coal black and his eyes the blue of a Renaissance Madonna's dress. It was impossible to say how old he was. He had the strength and bearing of a man in his prime, yet there was a wisdom about his face that spoke of age. His dark robe almost completely covered his somewhat drab clothing. The staff he carried bore intricate carvings of strange symbols and hieroglyphics. Laura wanted to run, but found she could not.

"Who are you?" she whispered.

"You know who I am," he answered in a soft, low voice. He moved forward again until he was standing so close Laura could have reached out and touched him, had she had the courage.

"Are you real? Am I losing my mind?" she asked.

His response to her question was to reach out very slowly and take her hand in his. Laura gasped as she felt his strong, warm fingers wrapped around her own. He placed her palm against his chest so that she could feel the steady thud of his heart. She stared at him, trying to make sense of what she was seeing. What she was feeling. Merlin let go of her hand.

"You have no need to fear me. I promise I will protect you," he said, letting a smile spread warmth across his features.

"What do you mean? Protect me from what?"

"So many questions. Be patient and all will be explained."

"This is madness. I'm talking to . . . what? A ghost? A character from a legend? From a storybook?"

"I am as real as you are, Laura," he said.

Something came into Laura's head, something Anwen had said. "He is as real as you or I." Her mind raced to make sense of it all. Surely not knowing the difference between real and imaginary was an early sign of insanity. And yet, here she was, talking to a person who most definitely did not exist in her world, but who was solid and alive and living and breathing and talking right there in front of her.

Merlin seemed to sense her bewilderment. He lifted his hand and, with the gentlest of touches, stroked Laura's cheek.

"OK, enough sulking." The sound of Steph's voice at the door made Laura swing around. "You can't stay in here all day."

Laura turned back, but Merlin had vanished. All that remained was a glow on her face where he had touched her. She put her own hand to her cheek, remembering how she had felt before the exact same mixture of fear and thrill, of almost unbearable excitement, that first day in the bedroom at Penlan. Now she knew who had been the cause of it.

"You're not going to make this even more bloody difficult for me are you?" Steph rolled her eyes. "OK, I admit, I had no right to be so judgmental. I'm sorry."

Laura pulled herself together as best she could. "No, it's OK. You were right. I'm sorry I overreacted. You touched a nerve," she said, wishing her breathing would steady. "And anyway, it's over. I've been making myself miserable with guilt ever since. I know it was a mistake." She was relieved Steph had chosen to make peace with her. She needed her friend's support, now more than ever. There was no way, however, she could begin to tell her about what she had just experienced.

Steph stepped forward and slipped her arms around Laura, hugging her warmly. "You know I'd support you, whatever you did," she told her. "Even if I do have to have a go at you first. I'm just worried for you. And I'm here if you need to talk. You must have been going through some kind of hell keeping this all to yourself. Wow!" Steph noticed the painting on the easel. "Is this some of your new stuff? It's certainly different."

"What do you think?"

"Pretty wild. Quite trippy, in fact. And those colors . . . quite a change from what you usually do, isn't it?"

"You don't like it."

"I do! I do. God, don't be so sensitive. I just said it was different, and it is, right?"

"Yes, it is. I've been trying to do something new. Something that reflects the way this place makes me feel."

"Have you got any more?' Steph moved to a stack of canvases leaning against the wall and began to look through them.

"Not really, nothing finished anyway. Just sketches and stuff."

"What does Penny say?"

"Oh, she hasn't been up here to have a look yet."

"You do surprise me—she's such a dragon. I'm amazed she's let you drift on for so long."

"I am not drifting." Laura gently eased herself between Steph and the rest of her paintings, finding a cover to drape over the stack. "Sorry, have to keep the dust out. It's a bit of a menace in here." She looked up at Steph, her uncertainty etched on her face. "Do you think they're rubbish? Please tell me honestly."

"Laura, you are incapable of producing rubbish, as you bloody well know. I admire your courage—doing something new is bound to be a bit scary. Relax. Everyone will love them, I promise you. Now, come on," she said, putting an arm around Laura's shoulders and giving her another brief but warm hug. "Let's go and have some lunch."

"Lunch? We've only just had breakfast."

"Good grief, you must have been deeply into something in here. You've been at it nearly three hours."

"Three hours?" Laura could not believe such an amount of time had passed. So many inexplicable things were happening to her at once that she could not take any of it in properly.

They ate together quietly, an unspoken agreement not to discuss Rhys further for the moment, enabling them to be friends again. Laura was so shaken by her encounter in the studio, she could barely think straight. She knew that at the first opportunity she must seek out Anwen. She was the only person Laura could discuss Merlin with without feeling she was a complete lunatic. She was so distracted she hardly noticed the cloud descending outside. It wasn't until the fog thickened to the point where the yard wall could no longer be seen from the kitchen window that she began to worry. Where had the walkers got to? It would be a whiteout on the mountain. These were not the conditions in which to be up there with two small boys. She noticed Steph checking her watch.

"Don't worry. Rhys knows the mountains very well. They'll be home soon," she told her.

"I don't feel great about the welfare of my boys resting on his shoulders. Still, I suppose Angus is only an idiot part time. I need a drink," she said, going to the fridge and fetching a bottle of Chablis.

Laura went back to staring out into the eerie whiteness. She had so much to think about it was an effort to keep still. Steph had indeed touched a nerve where Rhys was concerned, but what had happened between them was in the past. Merlin's appearance, on the other hand, was something she knew she would not be able to ignore. Assuming he was who he claimed to be, and assuming also that she was not losing her mind, why had he chosen to manifest himself to her? What did he want? Why did she feel such a strange and powerful connection with him? And what did he want to protect her from? And now there were the boys to worry about. She kept telling herself no harm could come to them. True, the mountain could be testing, even for experienced hikers, but they had three grown men with them. They would appear through the mist any minute—she was certain of it.

Half an hour later the cloud lifted as quickly as it had descended. Laura opened the door and went into the garden, certain she could make out some movement on the edges of the visible hill. Steph joined her.

"Can you see anything?" she asked.

"I'm not sure . . . Yes! There they are!" Laura began to climb the bank but as she did so she could see that there were only three figures slithering down the slope toward them.

"Where's Angus?" Steph called up from behind her.

And where is Rhys? Laura asked herself.

Dan had Hamish on his shoulders and a firm grip on William's hand. All three looked exhausted and the boys were plainly upset. Hamish began to wail the second he saw his mother. Dan passed him to her, not breaking his stride as he hurried on to the house.

"Can't stop, have to get to the phone."

"Dan?" Laura picked up William. "What's happened? Where are the others?" she shouted after him, but he had already disappeared inside. It was William who tried to explain.

"Mummy, Daddy fell over. He hurt his head," he told her.

"Oh, my God." Steph clutched Hamish a little tighter.

"Rhys stayed with him," he went on. "I didn't want to leave Daddy, but Uncle Dan said we had to come home to get help."

"Why didn't you use Daddy's phone?" Steph asked.

"He squashed it when he fell," said William starting to cry. He buried his face into Laura's shoulder, his little body shaking with sobs.

The two women exchanged worried looks.

"Let's get them inside," said Steph.

In the kitchen they found Dan finishing his phone call to the air ambulance service.

"Mountain Rescue say they'll be with him very soon. The mist has cleared now, so the helicopter can get up there and fetch him." He waved a sweet wrapper with numbers scribbled on it. "I wrote down the map coordinates. They know where to look."

"What the hell happened?" Steph demanded.

"Angus had a fall. He hit his head."

"How bad is it?"

"He was unconscious when we set off for home. Rhys stayed with him. We weren't very far away, but the mist . . . it came down so quickly." He ran a hand through his hair. "I still can't work out how one minute we were walking along happily and the next . . ."

"Trust my bloody fool of a husband," said Steph, distractedly taking off Hamish's poncho and dropping it onto the kitchen floor. Laura reached over and gave her shoulder what she hoped was a reassuring squeeze.

"Daddy is going to be all right, isn't he Mummy?" asked William.

"We couldn't wake him up," said Hamish.

Steph's eyes were filled with tears, but she made a fair job of sounding confident and reassuring. "He's going to be just fine. You know Daddy. He's tough as old boots."

"Oh, Steph," Laura whispered. "I am so sorry."

"Please," Steph said as she started gathering up wet gear. "Don't be nice to me, Laura. I can't keep it together if you're nice to me."

Laura took Hamish's hand. "Come on boys, you must be starving. Who wants fish fingers?"

"And Smiley Faces?" pleaded Hamish.

"Sure, why not. You can help me. Come on William, you too." She led them away, pausing only to exchange anxious glances with Dan as he poured himself a brandy.

"Look, don't worry," he said. "Mountain Rescue can handle it. And the helicopter will find him. It's the easiest and quickest way to get him to hospital."

Steph spoke quietly as the boys left the room, but Laura was still able to hear her strained conversation with Dan.

"Tell me how it happened."

"He fell onto some rocks, Steph. It was all so silly. We weren't anywhere dangerous. The mist had come down, but we were on a good path. I was in front, Hamish was holding my hand, then came William, Angus was behind him, and Rhys bringing up the rear. There was a shout. He must have slipped. When I turned round he was lying on the rocks. He only fell a few feet. He landed awkwardly."

"You think it's serious, don't you, Dan? Please tell me the truth."

Dan could not keep the emotion out of his voice as he answered her. "He didn't look good, Steph. I'm so sorry."

Within an hour of Dan's return the Mountain Rescue team had located Angus, and the Air Ambulance had flown him to the nearest accident and emergency unit at Abergavenny. Rhys had returned looking tired and concerned. Laura offered to look after the boys and insisted Dan drive Steph to the hospital. She had not reckoned on Rhys staying at the house and was unsettled to find him still in the kitchen when she came down from putting the children to bed.

"Are they asleep?" he asked.

"Hamish is. William is fighting it, but he's exhausted. Poor little mites. It must have been awful for them, seeing their father like that." She put the kettle on the Aga, not trusting herself to drink alcohol. She felt she needed to keep what shredded wits she had about her. "Do you want tea before you go?" she asked Rhys.

"I thought I might stay here with you." He stood behind her, resting his hands on her waist. "I could keep you company until the others get back. You don't want to be on your own at a time like this. You know I can help you feel better."

Laura wished she could be sure his motives were kind and

altruistic, but she feared he was considering using the opportunity for something more basic. She turned to face him.

"Rhys, you can't seriously expect that we might . . . Look, I'm very tired. The boys might wake up at any moment . . ."

"I know, I know. Hey, I wasn't suggesting anything. I just want to be here for you. What sort of a person do you think I am? I know you won't be thinking about sex while poor Angus is dying in hospital."

Laura let out a scream. "Dying! For pity's sake, Rhys, he's not going to die!" She stared at him, the thought taking shape in her mind. "He's not! Tell me you don't think that."

"I don't want to scare you, Laura, my love. But, well, you didn't see him. He was pretty badly hurt. Head injuries like that . . ." he said with a sigh. "I don't want to give you false hope."

Laura put her face in her hands and wept. It was too much to bear. As she cried she realized how much tension and anxiety she had been under for weeks. She let Rhys hold her and rub her back as she sobbed, but she was surprised to realize she would actually prefer it if he were not there. Somehow, his presence was not appropriate. It was unsettling, unnecessary and, in some way she did not fully understand, in poor taste to have him there. She sniffed, pulled away a little, and wiped the tears from her eyes.

"I think it would be better if you went," she told him.

"What? But that's silly. I can help."

She shook her head. "I'm sorry, Rhys, it just doesn't feel right, you being here. Not now. Not like this. I'll be fine, really. I'll come up tomorrow and tell you how Angus is. OK?" She looked at him with as bland a smile as she could muster. She didn't want him to know how disturbed she felt, didn't want him to get any further inside her head than he already was.

He looked back at her for a long moment, seemingly sizing her up, trying to read her face. At last he shrugged and said a little tetchily, "All right, if that's what you want. I'll go." He stooped to pick up his things. "Look after those wonderful boys, won't you?" he said, recovering himself enough to smile.

She nodded and smiled back, relieved he was not going to protest further. When the front door shut behind him she felt as though a great weight had been lifted from her. Realizing this, she made herself a promise. As soon as Angus was better, as soon as things returned to somewhere near normal, she would tell Rhys it was over between them.

❧ 10 ❧

MEGAN BEGAN TO wake up. She had the strangest sensation, that she was underwater, and that some heavy weight was holding her down. She fought to free herself, gasping for air as she opened her eyes. She was in an unfamiliar room. A fine room, with carved furniture and elaborate tapestries on the walls. At first she saw everything as if looking through the very water in which she had been drowning. Nothing was clear. Nothing would remain still long enough to be properly seen. Megan tried to sit up. Kind hands urged her to stay laying on the large, high bed. A pain stronger than any she had known before gripped her head as if it were in some torturer's instrument. Megan gasped, her hands flying to her skull to find it tightly bandaged.

"Be still." The woman's voice was familiar.

"Bronwen? Is that you?" Megan had known Dafydd's wife for many years, and knew she sometimes worked as a maidservant in the castle. Now she recognized the bedchamber as Lord Geraint's own. "What has happened to bring me here?"

"Do you not recall, Megan?"

As Bronwen's face began to form more sharply before Megan's confused eyes she could see the grave concern written there.

"I can't remember . . . I was riding. Not Hazel. Midnight? Why was I riding Midnight?" Despite Bronwen's protestations Megan sat up. "Merlin? We were being chased . . ." At last the memory of that terrible night came rushing back. She let out a cry, "Oh! My father! My poor, dear father!"

"There now, child, do not upset yourself. You took a bad fall. You must rest, give yourself a chance to heal."

"I cannot believe he is dead!" She began to weep. "I should have been quicker to warn him. I knew of the danger. It is my fault."

"No, no, that is not the case, and this you know. It was Lord Geraint's wickedness that brought your father's life to an end." Bronwen glanced in the direction of the heavy door as she spoke. She lowered her voice, "On one count you may rest easy—Merlin made good his escape."

Megan wiped her tears with the back of her hand. "They did not catch him? Oh, thank the heavens!" She paused, searching for more details in her mind. She looked at Bronwen. "Midnight is dead, the trap . . ."

"He could not be saved."

"I killed him, too."

"Now, you must stop this." Bronwen put an arm around Megan's shaking shoulders. "It was Lord Geraint's wish that you be kept here until you are recovered. Then you are to go to him. When I heard I offered to nurse you myself."

"But what of Dafydd? He helped me."

"Lord Geraint assumed you took the horse on your own account. We have not told him otherwise."

Megan sank back onto the pillows, the enormity of all that had taken place, of the consequences of her own actions and her own failings, almost too much to bear. Bronwen offered her a sip of wine but she turned her face away. At last she asked, "Why has Lord Geraint seen fit to keep me here? Why am I not in the castle dungeon?"

Bronwen shook her head. "If I understood the workings of that man's mind I would be a very wise woman indeed. All I know is he is to be informed when you are well enough to speak with him. Beyond that, we can only guess."

"He will be angry that his plan failed, that Merlin still has his freedom. What more can he want of me?" Megan struggled against deepening despair. The loss of her beloved father was such a heavy blow. If it were not for Merlin she would happily go to her death herself. But he at least was safe, and must by now know that she had been taken back to the castle. While he still lived she could not give up. She would not, whatever base motives Lord Geraint had for keeping her in his quarters. A timid knock at the door made both women tense. They exchanged worried glances, Bronwen bidding Megan remain silent with a finger to her lips.

"Who's there?" she asked, her hand on the door latch.

"It is only I, Bronwen," came the soft reply.

"Master Huw?" Bronwen opened the door quickly and let the boy in. "What on God's earth are you doing here, child?"

"I came to see Megan. Is she going to die?"

Megan found herself smiling again at the sight of the dear little boy. "Not just yet she isn't," she told him, propping herself up on one elbow.

"Megan!" Huw ran to her, throwing his arms around her neck.

"Now then," Bronwen said crossly. "Have a care, Master Huw, we want Megan well, not strangled!"

"Don't fuss, Bronwen," said Megan. "What better cure could there be for my ills than the love of this fine young man?"

"I heard such terrible things, Megan." Huw scrambled onto the bed beside her. "Midnight lost a leg and bled to death. The soldiers were out riding all night, but they did not catch the magician. And you were brought home near dead. Oh, Megan!"

"Hush now. As you see, I am all in one good piece, save for a bump on my head, which will no doubt knock some sense into me." Megan realized as she hugged the child how glad she was to be spending time with him again. It was as if something small but good had come from all the terrors of that dreadful night. "You must take care, Huw," she said, stroking his fair curls. "Your father would disapprove of you coming to see me."

He sat up and looked at her with wet and anxious eyes.

"What will happen, Megan? What will Father do next?"

"That I do not know." She pulled him close again and closed her eyes against the fear that was building inside her. "We must bide our time and be prepared to face whatever comes."

Two hours later Megan followed Bronwen down the passage that led to the great hall. As instructed, she had been dressed in a fine gown, her hair washed and braided, and in every detail prepared to look her best. If this were some trick to make Megan feel ever more uneasy and less herself, it succeeded. The strange garments and fine ribbons made her feel brash and immodest and were most definitely not befitting a maid who was in mourning for her father. The amethyst ring Lord Geraint had pressed upon Megan was cleaned, polished, and replaced on her finger.

As beautiful as it was the sight of it made her stomach turn. As they passed the open windows in the main part of the castle she glimpsed the mountains outside. The autumn sun gleamed gold on the hilltops, and she longed with all her fractured heart to be out there, riding free, with the cool October air on her face. As if reading her mind the two armed guards behind her stepped a little closer, reminding her that escape was impossible. She wondered how far away Merlin was, and whether they would ever be together once again.

There was a sizeable fire in the hearth in the great hall. Megan was surprised to find Lord Geraint was not alone. She might have expected Llewelyn, or one or two of his Lordship's manservants, but it was unusual for Lady Rhiannon to be present on such an occasion. Megan was all too aware of her mistress's harsh gaze upon her as she was made to stand in front of Lord Geraint's chair. He looked at her for a moment before speaking, openly appraising her. Megan felt repulsed by the intimacy of the examination, more so, somehow, because it was in front of his wife. At last he stood up with a sigh.

"Well, Megan, I have to say I am disappointed in you."

"My Lord." Megan could not trust herself to look him in the eye. The memory of her father's decapitation, while she had watched helplessly, and the knowledge that it was done at her master's behest, made her hate the man with such intensity she wanted to leap at him and claw his eyes from their sockets.

"I had you marked as that rare creature—a woman of good sense. It seems I was mistaken." He stood close to her, spittle landing on her face as he spoke. Megan refused to let herself so much as flinch. "You might salve your conscience by blaming me for the

death of your father, but I warned you. You knew what the consequences would be if you did not act as I wished. You brought
about your father's execution, Megan, not I. I cannot allow my
authority to be so challenged and go unpunished. You surely must
see that. I was acting only in accordance with my position. You,
however—you acted out of your own selfish desires, out of your
wanton longing for the mad magician. How does it feel to know
your father paid for your lust with his life?" He paused, enjoying
her discomfort. While he waited for a reaction he walked slowly
around her, running a hand down her back and over her buttocks.
Still she did not move. Lord Geraint came to stand before her
again.

"So, it seems I must make the best of the situation. My soldiers were not able to capture Merlin. It is clear he does not intend to be of assistance to me. I must ensure he does not instead
go to the aid of my enemy. Therefore I have a plan I believe will
bring me to him, and you are going to help me. I understand the
magician is a man of honor. He will not suffer to leave you here
indefinitely. One way or another, he will no doubt come for you.
And when he does, I shall be waiting for him. He will not escape
me a second time. You, Megan, I shall allow a little choice. You
will remain here, of course. It is up to you to decide how . . . *comfortable* your stay is to be. I can have you incarcerated, shut away
from all daylight. Or I can install you as my mistress." He could
not resist a smile as Megan raised her head to look at him now,
eyes blazing. "Personally, I prefer the latter option. Aside from my
own pleasure, I believe news of your position would inflame the
seer beyond endurance. What say you, my dear? Prisoner or
lover?"

Megan could not remember ever having felt such fury. This vile man had murdered her father, was planning to use her as bait in a trap set for Merlin, and was now suggesting she share his bed. She glanced at Lady Rhiannon. The purpose of her presence was clear now. By making his intentions plain in front of his wife Lord Geraint was showing Megan that there was no one left for her to turn to. Any appeal to her mistress for help would fall on deaf ears. Either the woman cared nothing for her husband's infidelities, or she would not show any such feelings if they existed. Megan was merely being used in a game which had little to do with her and everything to do with the way Lord Geraint exercised his power, be it over his servants, his army, his villagers, or his family. Megan took a steadying breath and met her master's eye.

"I have seen my father cut down before my eyes, at your command. I have seen the man I love driven from this valley, at your command. Lock me where you will. I would rather share a bed with death than with a man possessed of such a black heart. My Lord."

Lord Geraint's face hardened at her response. Megan fancied she saw Lady Rhiannon smiling behind her hand. She was reminded that her mistress was as much under Lord Geraint's rule as anyone else. Megan thought back to what Merlin had told her about Huw's parentage. How much did Lady Rhiannon have to bear in order to protect her son?

Lord Geraint snapped his fingers and the guards who had brought Megan to him stepped forward once more.

"Take her away," he instructed with a weary gesture.

Megan felt rough hands grasp her arms and she was marched from the great hall. Bronwen reached out a hand to her as she passed, her eyes filled with tears. Megan struggled to remain composed. She was determined not to allow Lord Geraint the pleasure of witnessing her fear. Whatever lay ahead, she would endure it, knowing she had made the only right choice. She could never give herself to the man who had so brutally slain her father. On the matter of Merlin she was now completely torn in two. She prayed that she would not be the cause of his entrapment. And yet, the thought of never seeing him again was more painful than any torture Lord Geraint could devise. The thought of Merlin, and of what they shared together, made her desperately want to live. Would he come? Could he outwit Lord Geraint and save her, even here in the castle? As she was taken down into the darkest recesses of the great house she wondered if she would ever see the sun kiss the mountains again. At last they reached a place she had never known existed until this moment. Beyond the jails, at the far end of the dungeons, was a small, windowless corner. A stone mason was working, building a wall that would form the closing part of a triangle, creating a tiny room. Megan felt the blood drain from her face as she realized what fate awaited her. The guards placed her on the far side of the low wall, then retreated to stand behind the mason. All Megan could do was stand and watch and wait as her tomb was completed. It was impossible to tell if it were day or night in the dungeon, as no natural light descended the spiraling stairs, and no windows allowed air or sun to intrude. By the time the wall was nearing completion her eyes had become accustomed to the dimness, but it was clear to her, even in her terrified state, that once she was without candle or torch, and her merciless prison was built around her, she would have no further use for her poor eyes.

❦

LAURA STOOD IN the oak woods watching the children play. The weather had changed again, so that each day was now a little colder. She found she preferred the bright, frosty days, prepared to put up with the cold if it meant being rid of the damp fogginess of autumn. She leaned against the sloping oak and stuffed her hands deeper into the pockets of her duffle coat, reminding herself to buy warm gloves next time she went to town. Watching the boys now it was hard to believe they were all in the grip of a tragedy. Together they had decided to dam the icy stream. William fetched heavy stones while Hamish stuffed mud and twigs into the gaps. She marveled at the capacity children had for continuing, for functioning normally, when all around them their world was crumbling. Their very choice of activity seemed an affirmation of hope, of rebuilding, of survival.

Angus still lay unconscious in the hospital. The doctors were unwilling or unable to give an idea of how long he might remain in a coma. The only thing they were certain about was that he must not be moved. Steph had been keen to get him to a London hospital and get herself and the boys home, but she had been told such a journey would seriously compromise his chances of recovery. His head injuries had been severe, and his problems had been worsened by complications brought on by having to wait on the mountain for rescue. He had so far shown no signs of being able to hear anything that was said and no one would be able to tell if he had suffered any brain damage until he woke up. If he woke up. The idea that he might not had been something none of them had been prepared to accept at first. But, as time went on and days became weeks, it had become harder to ignore the possibility. Steph had worn herself to the breaking point, torn between keeping vigil at Angus's bedside and being with the boys. Dan had eventually returned to work, lending at least an illusion of normal life to the house. Laura had spent most of her time with the boys. It was no sacrifice. There was no way she could shut herself away in the studio when they needed her, even though she would have found painting therapeutic. She wanted to help. At least looking after the children made her feel as if she were doing something for Angus. And Steph. Poor Steph. All the joy and light had gone out of her. She was neither eating nor sleeping properly and she looked to have aged years in a matter of weeks. Laura had tried to talk to her. She had been receptive to words of comfort and to positive thoughts about the future. She would not, however, listen to anything on the subject of a possible bad outcome. As far as Steph was concerned Angus was going to get better and that was that. Laura wished with all her heart that she could share her friend's conviction. She wandered over to join the boys.

"Can I help?" she asked.

"If you like," shrugged William, not pausing in his task. He had become wary of the adults, knowing that at any moment they might insist on knowing how he felt about what had happened and about his father doing so poorly. For William, talking about his father's condition was unthinkable. He could talk about things they had done together in the past, or things they might do in the future. He could even visit his father and sit with him in the hospital in a quiet manner that showed a maturity beyond his years. What he absolutely could not do was listen to the possible extent of his father's injuries, or discuss the fact that he might be dying. Despite his giving the impression of being totally absorbed in what he was doing, Laura could see pain etched on his beautiful, young face.

"No, not like that, Auntie Laura!" Hamish had very definite ideas about dam building. "Here, you've got to stuff the mud right in, like this."

"Oh, I see. You're making a good job of that." She smiled at him. When he smiled back she felt a sharp stab of pain at the thought of what grief might lie ahead for this little one. Hamish must have read her expression, for his own face showed concern. "Don't worry," he said. "Daddy will be alright. We had William's special mountaineering kit, didn't we? That must have helped. And he got to ride in a helicopter. Daddy likes flying."

Laura pulled herself together. "You're absolutely right, Hamish. He's been very well looked after. He just needs a bit more rest to get better, that's all."

"Are you two going to help or just talk?" William demanded crossly. "I'm not going to build this thing all on my own."

Chastened, they turned their attention back to the wall. There was something strangely comforting about the steady manual labor on which they were all now focused. Their hands were red with cold from being in the bubbling water, but it didn't matter. The river stone had been washed smooth by the water, yet strangely still felt rough because of its slightly porous nature. The low November sunshine skimmed across the little rock pools like a well-thrown stone. They were all so deeply engrossed in what they were doing that none of them noticed Rhys approaching. When he spoke they all swung around to face him.

"Don't let me interrupt," he said, holding up a hand. "I can see important work is underway."

"We're making a dam," Hamish told him.

"And a very fine one it is, too."

Laura found her overriding feeling was one of irritation and impatience. She resented his intrusion. She had been putting off telling him that their affair had to end. She had meant to do so immediately after Angus's accident, but there had been so much to do, so many people who needed her. She knew she had been finding excuses to avoid telling him. Not because she had any doubts about it being the right thing to do, but because she feared what his reaction might be. She had enough difficulties to cope with right now. And besides, however mad it seemed, if she thought of anyone in her few private moments, it was Merlin, not Rhys. In truth, Rhys had become an embarrassing reminder of her own weakness. She cursed herself now for giving in to lust, for letting herself, as Steph had pointed out, be flattered into betraying Dan. She just wanted to put the whole episode behind her. Somehow. Her tactic had been simply not to see him. If ever he came to the house the boys were there, and sometimes Steph, too. It had been easy to brush him off with excuses about being needed elsewhere. But still he insisted on visiting, on occasion, like now, searching for her. She did not enjoy being pursued in such a manner. At another time, in different circumstances, she might have been flattered. Now she found his persistence off-putting. It made her feel hunted. And it frightened her. It did not bode well for what his reaction to her finishing their relationship might be. She knew, in her heart of hearts, there was a strong chance he would be furious and end up telling Dan everything. There might be no way she could avoid it, and she would have to face the consequences. But not now. Now there were other people to think about and far more important things to worry about. She would simply have to play for time.

She straightened up and brushed the mud from her hands.

"We just came out for a bit of a walk," she said. "Steph's trying to catch up on some sleep. We're all going to the hospital later this afternoon." This seemingly pointless piece of information was designed to make Rhys realize she did not have time to be with him right now. She smiled at him brightly, trusting his ego to assume she was as disappointed as he was.

"It must be difficult for her," Rhys said. "She is lucky to have friends like you and Dan."

"You think? If it weren't for us, Angus would never have been up that wretched mountain." Out of the corner of her eye Laura caught sight of William's expression at the mention of the fateful walk. She moved a little way away from the boys, confident Rhys would follow. She could not talk to him safely within their earshot. She couldn't trust herself to not say something insensitive, it seemed, and Rhys was definitely too unpredictable and unguarded.

"Those are two fine boys," he said. "Enough to make anyone want to start a family of their own."

Laura could not think of a suitable response to such a remark, given the circumstances. She rubbed her hands together to try and restore some warmth to them. Rhys took them and cupped them in his own, blowing on them. A part of her responded to his touch. A part of her still wanted him. Still recalled the thrilling, dangerous sex they had enjoyed together so much. But that was then. And, if she was honest, he did not arouse the same response in her now. She had suffered too much from remorse, had regretted what damage she might already have done to her marriage and, in truth, she had became wary of Rhys. No, more than wary, she was, she at last acknowledged, more than a little afraid of him. She pulled away her hands.

"Look, Rhys. It's good of you to be so concerned for us all, but I'd find it a lot easier if you didn't keep coming to see me." She did not look at him as she spoke, but picked up a twig and began to work at a patch of moss on the tree beside her.

"I know, my love. It's hard for me, too, seeing you, and yet not being able to . . . But to not see you at all. . . . I couldn't stand it. Besides, I want to be here for you. You're having a rough time."

"This is not about me, though, is it? Or you, Rhys. Angus is the one lying in a hospital bed with his head all broken. Steph is the one facing the possibility of losing him. The boys are in torment. Dan blames himself, ridiculously, of course, but I sort of understand. You and me, well, this just isn't the time. Surely you can see that?"

"I suppose so," said Rhys slowly. "As long as that's all it is."

"What do you mean?" Laura remained apparently focused on the mossy bark.

"I mean that's fine, if you can't cope with seeing me right now because of what's happening I understand. Yeah, it's a tricky situation. As long as you're sure it's not more than that."

"More? What more do you want? A very dear friend is in

trouble and needs me, isn't that enough?" Laura failed to keep the edge out of her voice.

Rhys did not answer immediately. He stepped forward, taking Laura's hands again and turning her to face him. He leaned toward her so that his face was only inches from hers. She could feel his warm breath on her chilly cheek as he spoke.

"Laura, my beautiful, perfect Laura. So precious. So special. Now that I've found you at last I won't lose you. You must know that. I could never be without you again. And I know that, deep down, in that passionate heart of yours, you could never give me up. Could you?" His voice was barely more than a whisper, but still his words carried a frightening force.

Laura felt vulnerable, just her and the boys there in the woods with him. This was not the moment to confront him. She mustered a smile. "Just give me some time, Rhys. Please be patient. Things won't be like this forever."

"No, you're right about that," he said. He stepped back and grinned at her. In a second his face relaxed and his mood was lighthearted once more. "Come on, let's help Will and Hamish finish that magnificent dam."

❧

THE FOLLOWING DAY Steph took the boys with her into town to do some shopping. They had only come with luggage for a weekend and were badly in need of new clothes. Dan was continuing his working week in London and would not be home until evening, so that when Laura waved the others off she was pleased to at last have some time to herself. The old Laura would have hurried back to her studio, hungry to be painting again. But not now. There was something else she had to do. She stepped into her Wellingtons, shrugged on her duffle coat, and jammed one of Dan's ski hats on her head. The temperature had plummeted further, and the subzero air stung her cheeks as she crossed the yard. By the time she reached the oak woods, however, the exertion of the brisk walk had sent hot blood rushing around to warm every extremity. This was not a walk for a walk's sake. Laura moved with purpose, focusing on the frozen ground so as not to stumble as she negotiated the thicker parts of the woodland. Within thirty minutes she could see Glyn the Bryn's farm through the trees. In the bleakness of early winter it looked even more shabby and unkempt. She squinted at the buildings but could see no sign of the quad bike. There was a rusty Land Rover parked beside the farmhouse, but no other vehicles were visible. She knew he could be out on the quad, or it could be parked up in one of the barns. She waited a few moments. Nothing moved. At last cold and determination drove her on. If he was in she would just have to deal with him. It was Anwen she had come to see. If he answered the door she would have to be persistent. She had a desperate need to question Anwen, and who knew when the opportunity to do so would present itself again?

She quickly climbed the fence, crossed the field, and strode up the garden path. She hammered on the front door. Silence. She tried again. At last there were noises inside. She could hear sounds of a key being turned, and the door was pulled open. To Laura's great relief, it was Anwen who stood on the threshold.

"Hello," said Laura, not quite knowing how to explain why she had come. "I'm so glad I found you in." She smiled, but was unsure of the reception she was going to get, after the incident with the spell.

"I've been waiting for you," Anwen told her. She turned and began to walk back into the house. "Don't stand there all day with the door open," she called back over her shoulder. "Glyn doesn't light the fire to warm the garden."

At the mention of his name Laura glanced nervously about her. The narrow passageway was dark, but she was sure the horrid dog would have made its presence felt by now had it been in the house. "Sit yourself down in there." Anwen gestured toward the open door of the sitting room. "Kettle's on. I'll be there now in a minute."

The sitting room was similar in size and shape to the one at Penlan, but higher ceilings and smaller beams suggested it was in fact several centuries younger. The fireplace had obviously been installed quite recently, for it boasted hideous cream tiles and a hearth too small for logs. At least the coal burned brightly. It was the only cheerful spot in an exceedingly gloomy room. Ragged curtains, neither closed nor open, hung limply at the north-facing window. The carpet was of dark green with dizzying gold swirls. Faded wallpaper of more than one design clung to the damp-looking walls. Laura pulled off her hat and undid her coat. There was a filthy armchair close to the fire, a seventies coffee table, and a sagging sofa. The only other piece of furniture in the room was an enormous Welsh dresser proudly displaying cups won at sheepdog trials, a lumpen clock, a bottle of whisky, a harvest jug, and a calendar featuring photographs of wild birds. She moved three weeks' copies of the local paper to one side and sat gingerly on the sofa, wondering if it was the preferred place of the revolting dog. She was surprised not to see any sign of a woman's hand in the home. It was as if Glyn had been in charge of interior design, and Anwen had not so much as added a single pretty cushion. Laura could well imagine Glyn was a difficult man to stand up to, but it seemed out of character for the cheerful old woman to live in such dreary surroundings.

Anwen came shuffling into the room carrying a tray which she set down on the coffee table.

"There we are, then," she said, landing heavily in the armchair, sending up a small cloud of dust. "You be, Mam, it bothers my legs to stoop for more than a moment."

Laura did as she was told, pleasantly surprised to see chintz china cups and saucers and even a teapot to match.

"This is gorgeous china, Anwen."

"Glyn keeps it locked away. For best. Ha!" The old woman laughed her distinctive merry chuckle. "I'm blessed if I know what *best* the silly old fool is expecting! Two sugars in mine, please. And plenty of milk. That's right, *cariad.*" Anwen took the tea from Laura, her shaking hand causing the cup to rattle alarmingly in its saucer. She stirred thoughtfully, then said, "Well, well, this is very nice, Laura, but you didn't come to see me to talk about china and drink tea." She slurped noisily, peering at her over the top of her cup.

Not for the first time Laura had the feeling Anwen knew a frightening amount about what was going on in her life. And indeed in her head.

"Well, first I want to thank you for stopping me. That dreadful spell. I had no idea what I was doing."

Anwen nodded. "If I thought different we wouldn't be sitting here together now," she said. "But, no matter. No harm was done. This time."

"Trust me, I won't be trying anything like that again!" She paused, looking for the right words. "Actually, there was something else I wanted to talk to you about. Something happened. Something I don't understand, or even quite believe, and yet I know that it did happen. I thought you might be able to help me make sense of it."

Anwen nodded again but this time said nothing.

"I was on my own in the studio when I heard a noise," Laura went on. "And I sort of sensed something, *someone*, was behind me." She hesitated. However real the encounter had seemed to her, she still felt ridiculous trying to talk about it. Even to Anwen.

"He spoke to you?" Anwen asked.

Laura looked at her closely. It was almost as if the old woman had been expecting something like this. She did not seem in the least bit surprised. "Yes," she said. "He spoke to me. And . . . he touched me."

Anwen nodded, "So you believe he is real now, then, don't you? How simple folk can be. You thought your mind was playing tricks, yet you are quite happy to believe what your fingertips tell you. Where does your true sense lie, Laura? In your mind or in your body?"

Laura was thrown by the question. She had been ready for Anwen to be astonished, amazed even, and for her to question what had happened. She had not expected her to be so quick to accept what she was being told, and then to be berated for not believing Merlin was *real* until she had touched him.

"This is hard for me, Anwen. I'm doing my best to convince

myself I am not losing my mind. There are a lot of other things going on at home just now. Difficult things."

"Ah." A shadow passed over Anwen's dimpled features. "You're speaking of Rhys."

"Not just Rhys. I know you don't approve. And after the spell . . ." she said, rubbing her brow, feeling suddenly achingly tired. "Actually, its over between us. There never was anything really, at least, nothing that mattered. I was stupid. Stupid."

"Have you told him that yet?"

"No. It's not a good time. As I said, there are other things going on, my friend had a bad accident. He's in hospital . . ."

"For one who is able to see what others cannot, my girl, you are very poor at seeing what is plainer than the nose on my face!" Anwen's sharpness was in such contrast to her gentleness of seconds before that Laura spilled half her tea into her saucer.

"Please, don't talk in riddles, Anwen. Not today. I know I'm probably being dim, but I need your help. Can we talk about Rhys another time?"

"Open your eyes! These things are all one and the same, all connected in the most elemental of ways. You might as well waste your time separating the clouds from the sky as separating those two men."

Laura shook her head. "None of this makes any sense. You think Rhys and Merlin are the same person?"

"What I think doesn't count for tuppence. It's what Rhys thinks that matters. That's what makes him do the things he does."

Laura put down her tea with a sigh, feeling utterly confused.

The old woman seemed to sense her despair. She leaned back in the armchair, letting her cup and saucer rest in her ample lap.

"I know you came here for answers, Laura, but there are some things you have to discover for yourself. But, still, I meant what I said. You have nothing to fear from the wizard. He has sought you out because your destiny and his are bound together."

"How on earth can that be?" Laura asked. "Why me? I'm a city girl, I don't come from here. I don't believe in spooks or ghouls or things that go bump in the night. I've never experienced anything remotely supernatural in my life before. Why would some long dead, mythological ghost want anything to do with me?"

"There's that word *ghost* again." Anwen tutted and shook her head. "Pour me another cup, and I will try to make things clear for you."

She did as she was asked then leaned forward, elbows on her knees, desperate to hear what the curious creature in front of her had to say.

"You probably heard about Merlin many years ago. Storybooks, was it? History lessons? That thing over there?" She waved a pudgy hand at the television Laura had not, until that moment, noticed lurking under a tea towel in the corner of the room.

"I suppose so," she said. "I've known who he was for as long as I can remember."

"Exactly! And before that someone else knew about him all their lives. And after you others will read about him, too. And so he goes on. Don't you see? As long as his story is alive, then so is he. People who exist in stories and legends can never die, not if those stories continue to be told, in whatever way, from generation to generation. I'll wager you tell stories to those two young pups up at the house."

"William and Hamish? Yes, they love to be read to."

"Of course they do. What was the last tale you shared?"

Laura cast her mind back to the previous evening. "Hansel and Gretel," she said.

"Oh those two! They've been about a fair number of years. And they will still be with us when your boys are telling their story to *their* children. Don't you see?"

"Well, yes, I see that the *story* still exists. But not the people in it. You surely can't mean every character from every book is running around somewhere on some sort of endless loop."

"Not every story. Just the good ones," she said with a little chuckle. "The ones that mean something. The ones that get passed on, that stand the test of time. Myths, if you like. Legends."

"OK, if I accept that idea, why haven't I been tripping over golden geese and Red Riding Hood and God knows who for years? Why just Merlin? And why now?"

"Better ask, why here?"

"Here? This place? All this has something to do with my moving here?"

"You said yourself you never experienced anything similar before you came here. All stories are rooted in a place. A landscape. It's the magic ground where the characters live their lives. And some people, if they spend time in those places, if they are really lucky and maybe just a little bit special, with a special way of seeing, well, they can see the wonderful characters around them, forever living out their story, year after year, century after century, never growing old. Never dying."

Laura was quiet for a moment, trying to take in what the old woman was telling her. She was very sure if someone had tried to get her to believe such a theory six months ago she would have laughed at them. But now, after what had happened, after actually meeting Merlin . . . There had to be an explanation, why not this one? A thought occurred to her.

"But, you said our destinies were linked somehow. Mine and Merlin's. That sounds like more than just tapping into this . . . this other world that's going on here. I didn't go looking for him. He found me."

The old woman smiled at this, her dimples deepening.

"Now you're beginning to see things for yourself, *cariad*!"

"But why? Why would he seek me out?"

"To know the answer to that, Laura, you must look to his story."

"But there are so many different ones. People have been writing stories about him for centuries. Where do I start?"

"I always find it's a good idea to start out from wherever you are in the first place."

"Now you're talking in riddles again."

Anwen laughed, her whole body wobbling like a blancmange, her apron strings threatening to snap at any moment. "You'll work things out, eventually," she said. "I have faith in you."

"I don't know why."

"I trust Merlin's judgment. He has chosen you. That's all the recommendation I need."

"You speak as if you know him." Laura's face lit up suddenly. "Do you see him, too, Anwen? Is that it? Does he talk to you? Oh, please tell me he does—then I won't feel quite so much like I'm going completely mad."

Anwen pursed her lips and said nothing. She closed her eyes

and appeared to be deep in thought. The silence was so long Laura began to think she might have fallen asleep. Then, suddenly, her eyes sprang open again, her beady gaze fixed on Laura.

"Let me ask you something, Laura. What is the thing you long for most in this world, the thing that would make your heart sing and your life shine?"

Laura hesitated. She was certain that Anwen already knew the answer to this; she knew so much about her.

"A child," she said at last, her strained voice giving away the constant emotion that went with the subject.

"Some people, clever people, sharp, quick-witted people, will see that need. They will recognize your longing as both your strength and your weakness. Your strength because disappointment and heartbreak have made you tougher and more determined. Your weakness because you could be made to do almost anything to get what you want. Your task, my dear, is to see who truly has the answer to your prayers. Even if it is a different answer from the one you expect." Anwen pushed at the arms of the chair and rose slowly to her feet. "Now, if you'll forgive me, I've chores to be doing."

"Of course." Laura stood up and gathered her things. She could see the old woman was tired, but there were still so many things she wanted to talk to her about. "Can I call again? Would you mind? You've been so helpful, and there's really no one else I can turn to."

"Well, of course, you're quite wrong about that. But, yes, you come and see me again. I enjoy our little chats."

As they reached the front door, Laura remembered the corn dolly.

"That corn dolly you gave me, Anwen, it was to protect me. It was to protect me from Rhys, wasn't it?"

"I think, in your heart, you already knew who it is you have to fear," said Anwen. Before Laura could question her further she had disappeared inside the house and shut the door.

♪ 11 ♫

THAT EVENING LAURA was poor company. She knew she
should be spending more time with Dan, and with Steph,
but her conversation with Anwen was still spinning around in
her head. After supper she gathered together all the books she
had on Merlin and on local legends and settled down in a corner
of the sitting room. Dan was trying to watch a documentary on
snow leopards. Steph, unable to sit still, was in the kitchen emp-
tying the dishwasher. Dan had got a good fire going and opened
the doors of the wood-burning stove, the very sight of the flames
being warming. Laura wondered how many other women had sat
in that same spot, gazing into the fire, searching for answers. She
picked up one of her books and flicked through the pages. It felt
like an impossible task, looking for clues in so many thousands of
words. It was all very well Anwen saying she needed to discover
things for herself, but it would have been a lot simpler if she could
have just explained things plainly. There were two questions in
particular Laura dearly wanted to know the answers to. First,
why had Merlin chosen to show himself to her, to make contact?

Anwen had said she would find what she needed to know if she looked to his story, but Laura was worried she might not see the reason even if it were on the page in front of her. The second thing that would not go away was Anwen's insistence that someone was a threat to Laura. She had seemed to suggest that it was Rhys, but could that really be true? He might not want their affair to end, and Laura had already accepted the fact that he might react badly and tell Dan everything. But beyond that, a threat? A danger? She shook her head and went back to the book.

A sudden burst of laughter made her look up. It was a rare sound in the house now. Dan had given up on his program and joined Steph in the kitchen. Through the open door Laura could see the two of them enjoying a small joke. As Steph's laughter subsided she wiped away a tear or two. Dan stepped forward and put his arms around her, pulling her close in a friendly, comforting embrace. She thought how lucky she was to have such a caring and sensitive man for a husband. The thought made a small knot of guilt tighten in her stomach. She sighed and forced herself to concentrate.

Local legend had it that Merlin had spent a summer in the area before going on to Camelot and the court of King Arthur. He had lived high in the mountains, and the more Laura read, the more she was convinced the dwelling described as his was in fact Rhys's croft. She paused, looking into the flames once more. So, not her own house. What was his connection with Penlan? She read on. The story told how Merlin had fallen in love with a local girl, the daughter of a breeder of horses. Her name was Megan, and she had returned Merlin's affections. However, the local noble, and her employer, Lord Geraint ap Gruffydd, had a feud with

Merlin and tried to have him killed. Laura turned the page. Her hand shot to her mouth to stifle a cry. There was a picture she had not noticed before. It was small, only a quarter of a page, but still the detail was clear. It showed Merlin kneeling on the ground, in his arms a young girl, clearly either dead or dying. The girl had fine, angular features, long limbs, and waist-length, wavy auburn hair. She resembled Laura so closely it could have been her own portrait. Looking at the picture Laura realized how much her own appearance had altered since arriving at Penlan. Who or what had brought that about? Rhys? Merlin? The place itself? In any case, the result had been to transform her from city artist to the image of a medieval heroine. The image of this girl. Merlin's lover. As Laura turned the book a little to allow more light to fall on the illustration something slipped from the pages and fluttered to the floor. She picked it up. It was half a white envelope, torn lengthways to make a bookmark. Laura checked the cover of the book again. It was one of the ones she had borrowed from Rhys's collection. She studied the grubby strip of paper, cursing the fact that she had let it drop out before seeing what page it had been marking. The name Rhys Fisher was typed on the front, along with a Cardiff address she did not recognize. She was about to throw it in the stove when something in the words of the red postmark on the envelope caught her eye. The print was quite faded and faint, but still readable. Lawnsdale Hospital, it said on the first line, then, underneath in smaller letters, Peterborough Mental Health Trust.

"Something riveting?" Dan asked, handing her a fresh glass of wine.

Laura snapped the book shut with the bookmark inside it, hoping she did not look as shaken as she felt.

"Oh, more local history. Helps me paint the place, the more I know about it." She took the glass from him, wondering if she would ever be able to explain to him the real reasons for her interest—and fighting growing anxiety at what the envelope could mean.

"I forgot to mention," Dan's tone was light, but his expression gave away his concern, "Penny rang earlier. While you were in the bath."

"Oh?"

"Yes. She was keen to speak to you."

"Must have been, phoning so late."

"She said she's left messages endlessly. You haven't been returning her calls."

"I've had a lot on my mind lately. We all have."

"Of course, but . . ."

"But what?" she snapped, not enjoying having Dan mention something she already felt a niggling guilt about. She knew Penny had been phoning, but hadn't the gumption to call her. What was she supposed to say? She was miles off from being ready for the show, and she wouldn't be able to lie to Penny about it.

"I think she's a bit concerned," Dan said gently. "You know, the show being only a few weeks away. And she hasn't seen your new work yet, and . . ."

"Yes, OK, don't go on."

"I wasn't. But she does have a point. You're usually so much more together about your exhibitions. This time you seem to be getting more stressed out and grouchy and not getting any actual work done." He sighed, shaking his head. "So much for a more peaceful life in the countryside. Whatever happened to that rural idyll you talked me into?"

"Dan, why don't you come right out and say it?"

"Say what?"

"That moving out here was all my idea. That if we'd stayed in London none of this would have happened."

"Nobody is blaming you."

"Aren't they? Aren't you? Just because you don't actually say it doesn't mean you aren't thinking it."

"OK!" Dan was shouting now. "OK, if that's the conversation you want then let's have it! Yes, this place was what you wanted— your idea, your dream. And no, I didn't want to come here, but I was prepared to give it a go because you wanted it so badly."

"Give it a go? You spend more time in London than you do here. You haven't done anything about looking for a job nearby."

"No, I haven't, and d'you know why? Because I reckon that if I wait long enough you'll get bored with all this rustic living crap and come to your senses. Then we can buy a house back in London and get on with our lives again."

"I knew it! You never intended to commit to this move. You were just pretending, waiting for me to get some . . . some whim out of my system!"

"What choice did you give me? You were never going to be satisfied until you'd bought a place like this and dragged us out here. I told you from the beginning I didn't like the idea, but you wouldn't listen. What Laura wants, Laura damn well gets!"

Laura opened her mouth to respond but in that instant all the fight went out of her and she felt close to tears. Head down, she pushed past Dan and strode upstairs.

Later, as they were getting undressed, Dan came to stand close behind her. He stretched out a tentative hand and touched her hair.

"Look, I'm sorry," he said. "I didn't mean it. Any of it."

"Please be straight with me, Dan."

"I am. I do want this to work. I just need a bit more time. And, well, what with Angus . . ."

"I know."

There was a moment of silence. Laura found herself wishing he would just let the whole thing drop. She really didn't feel up to a serious discussion about their future plans. Her head was too full already to take in anything more.

Dan leaned forward and wrapped his arms around her, nuzzling gently into the back of her neck.

"I really am sorry," he whispered. "I'll make it up to you."

"It doesn't matter now," she said. "Please let's not fight. I can't cope with any of this if we're hurting each other."

"Hush now," he said, pulling her closer.

They stood without moving for a long while, silently drawing strength from a closeness and familiarity born of years of intimacy. She felt tears sting her eyes at the thought of what she had done to Dan. She blinked them away, wishing that, just for a few moments at least, she could pretend everything was as it had been before. What a difference a few short months had made to all of them.

"You know I love you, Laura," he told her. She fancied she could hear tears choking his voice. "I will always love you. No matter what."

No matter what? What did he mean? Did he know about her

and Rhys? Had he known all along? Or was it what had happened to Angus that had made him say such a thing? Laura dearly wanted to say something meaningful back, something honest and loving. But the words wouldn't come. Instead she lifted one of his hands and kissed it fondly.

"Are you OK?" he asked. "Really OK, I mean?"

Laura nodded.

"And us, Laura? Are we OK, too?"

How could she answer? She closed her eyes. She so wanted to be able to say yes, they were fine. They would always be fine. But so much had happened, there was so much she still did not understand about herself, about what she was experiencing, and about what sort of future she and Dan could have together. She took a deep breath.

"I think we will be," she said carefully. "I'm sure we will be. Soon."

Dan's body tensed but he did not move. There was a silence in which Laura could sense him struggling to take in what she had just said. So few words, and yet so loaded was each one they were almost too heavy to bear. She had, in fact, admitted that they were not OK, and if he had harbored any suspicions about her fling with Rhys then she had just as good as admitted everything. But, beyond that, she had tried to reassure him. To give him hope. She waited for him to react. At last he kissed her shoulder and stepped away.

"That's good," he said, his back to her as he walked toward the bathroom. "Good enough for me. Think I'll take a quick shower."

She watched him close the door and heard the water turned

on. Now she could breathe again. Dan was a good man, a man who knew how to love somebody. He could have quizzed her there and then, he could have cornered her and pressed her for answers, but he had not. He had said he would love her no matter what, and he had clearly meant it. He was prepared to wait for her to come out of whatever she was going through. She silently cursed herself for her own stupid selfishness.

MEGAN SAT ON the rough floor of her prison and accepted the fact that however accustomed her eyes became to the darkness, she was never going to be able to see so much as a chink of light. The stonemason had done his work well, so that no glimmer of a torch reached her from the dungeon, and the outer wall of the castle was at least the thickness of two oak trees. No sunlight could force its way through. She closed her eyes, finding her own darkness less frightening. The initial horror at her entombment had subsided, and now she found herself devoid of feeling and unable to think clearly. She longed for Merlin, to hear his voice, to feel the comfort of his strong arms about her. And yet, above all, she wished him safe, and for him to come to the castle would be to put himself at great risk. For a moment Megan wondered what it would be like, to die of thirst and of hunger. Would she simply get weaker and drift into a final sleep? Would she become raving and delirious? Would there be pain? Would she be able to breathe for more than a few hours in this airless place of endless night? She stood up quickly, hugging herself, rubbing her arms. She must not give in to despair. Whether she wished it or not,

Merlin would not abandon her. He would come. He would find her as he had promised he would, and they would be together again. She must endure and be patient. She paced the small space, her hands out in front of her, becoming familiar with the curve of the outer wall and the straightness of the inner one. Round and round she walked, calming herself with the rhythm of her steps. Her head still hurt, though Megan had been able to remove the bandage. She was exhausted from all that had happened and from fear and grief. She moved to the far corner of the room and lay down on the cold flagstones. She could feel the dirt beneath her hands as she folded them under her head for a pillow. She imagined the grimy state of her beautiful dress now. At least it was thick and warm, though she knew all too well that it would not be able to keep out the bone chilling cold of her tomb for long. She closed her eyes and wished for sleep. Peaceful, renewing, safe sleep. At last, she felt herself drifting and relaxed into the blissful moment before slumber would remove her from her torment.

A scratching noise at the inner wall reached her ears. At once she was awake again. She sat up, instinctively looking toward the sound even though she could see nothing. It could have been a rat or a bat or a mouse, but there was something in the purposeful nature of the noise that suggested a human hand. Megan waited and listened.

"Megan?" The voice was no more than a whisper, and at first Megan thought she had imagined it. Then it came again. "Megan? Are you there?"

"Huw!" Megan flung herself against the wall, straining to listen for more words. "Huw? Can you hear me?"

"Oh Megan! You *are* in there!" the little boy said in a mixture of sobs and whispers. "Poor, poor Megan! Why has Father done such a terrible thing? I shall go to him and tell him he must let you out. He must!"

"No! No, Huw. Do not tell your father you have been here." She kept her own voice as level and calm as she could. "If he knew you had spoken to me he would stop you coming again, Huw. You can help me, but you must be careful."

"Tell me what to do, Megan. I will do anything. You have only to ask."

Megan was deeply touched by the child's affection for her and his determination to help. She was reluctant to involve him, knowing that there were limits to his father's feelings for the boy. How angry might he be if he discovered Huw had been helping her? But she had no choice. At this moment, he offered her only chance of survival.

"I need water, Huw. And some food. Can you fetch them without being seen?"

"Yes. Yes, I can do that."

"Wait! One more thing, Huw. Bring a tool, something sharp. We will have to make a small hole in the wall. Not a hammer though. We would be heard. Do you understand?"

"Yes, Megan. Fear not, I will look after you."

Huw scampered away, and his absence after such brief but vital contact left Megan feeling even more alone than she had before. At least now she had hope. There were means of staying alive. That her life now depended on one small boy was a frightening thought, but it was just possible that Huw could indeed make the difference between living or dying. She felt along the inner wall again, searching with her fingertips for the smallest crevice, the tiniest flaw in the mason's handiwork. At last, at a low point where the new wall met the old, she found an indent where two stones where not well matched. The lime mix between them was still not completely set. She started to scratch at it but could make no impression at all with her nails. She needed something sharp or hard. She felt about on the floor for any stray pieces of stone, but there was none. Exasperated, she stood up again. She could not leave everything to Huw. There must be something she could do, she thought, rubbing her hands together to keep them warm. Of course! Her ring! She wriggled it off her finger, her skin cooler now than before. She unthreaded a ribbon from the neckline of her dress and wrapped it around the silver of the ring giving her a better handle and leaving only the sharp gem protruding. She began to dig at the wall, timidly at first, then, feeling that she was making progress, with more vigor.

By the time Huw returned she had made some inroads into the gap between the two stones.

"Megan? I have some water and bread," he told her breathlessly.

"Are you sure you were not seen?"

"I am sure."

"What tool did you find, Huw?"

"I took a knife from the kitchen. Will that do, Megan?"

"That will do very well. I have started to dig. Look down to your right, no lower than your knee." She tapped the place from her side of the wall. "Can you hear that?"

"Yes." He started to scratch with his knife. "Oh, it is very slow."

"Don't let that concern you, my brave little friend. Work

steadily, and you will make progress. Only take care that no one hears you."

"The guards are all up having their breakfasts. Brychan is out riding. I said I was feeling unwell and would stay in my bed awhile. No one will miss me for some time."

"You are a true hero, Huw," said Megan, marveling at the idea that it was breakfast time. There was not the tiniest indication in her little tomb that morning had broken. How long could the human spirit endure such unnatural conditions, she wondered?

Together they toiled on, pausing only for the occasional word of encouragement. The more she dug the more Megan became aware of the dreadfully solid, near impregnable nature of her prison. Near impregnable, but not completely, she told herself as she worked on. She knew they did not have unlimited time, for if Huw's absence was noticed he would be searched for. With unexpected abruptness a sliver of light stabbed through the wall.

"Huw! It's working. I can see the light from your candle!"

Huw scratched with renewed enthusiasm. At last Megan could see the end of the knife poking through the narrow opening.

"Good boy, Huw!"

"But it is such a small hole, Megan. Such a tiny space." He began to cry softly. "I wish I could just get you out, Megan. I don't like you being in there."

"Hush now, little one. This is not a moment to be sad. We could not make the hole bigger or it might be noticed. As it is, this little space will save my life, with your help."

"I'll pass the bread through in small pieces."

"Dip it in the water first, not too much, though, or it will be too soft to force through. That's it." She took the morsels as she felt them pushed into the gap. As they passed between the stones they blocked out the light momentarily, and Megan had to fight to quell panic. How crucial was that glimmer to her sanity.

After some time Huw said, "That's the last piece. It is enough?"

"It is plenty. Thank you, Huw. I never smelled a more delicious loaf."

"But, Megan, what about the rest of the water? No cup or bowl could ever fit through the tiny opening we have made."

"You must simply pour it through the hole."

"But you have nothing with you to hold water."

"I will drink as you pour this time. Next time you come see if you can find me a small piece of leather. That will come through our portal, and I can fashion a bag of it with ribbon. It will hold water well. Now pour slowly."

Huw did as he was told and Megan lapped the gritty, lime-tainted water. It tasted bitter and dirty, and grit threatened to choke her as she drank, but she knew she must drink it or die.

❧ ❧ ❧

THE FOLLOWING SATURDAY morning was cold, bright, clear and, as far as Laura was concerned, inappropriately cheerful. It had reached a point where everyone at Penlan seemed worn out by the relentless worry and upset. It was decided that the boys would spend the morning with Dan clearing part of the garden and building a bonfire. Laura drove Steph to the hospital. They made the journey in silence, each lost in her own thoughts. The day before Laura had finally found a moment to use the Internet without being observed and had looked up Peterborough Mental

Health Trust. Lawnsdale was indeed a psychiatric hospital. After searching her mind for a way to confirm her fears she had summoned her courage and telephoned the number given. She knew they would never give out information about an ex-patient. Unless she could trick them into doing so. Of course, it was just possible Rhys could have had a job there, rather than being an inmate. But in her heart she already knew which was the more likely answer.

"I'm phoning from the surgery in Abergavenny" The lie had made her voice thin. "We are still waiting for the notes for Mr. Rhys Fisher to be forwarded on to us."

"Oh? Just a moment, please." The young woman from the hospital administration department had disappeared for what felt to Laura like an age. At last she returned. "Mr. Fisher's notes were sent on to the surgery at the Holly Road Hospital, Cardiff, last year. I have a copy of the accompanying letter from Dr. Hindmarsh. He was Mr. Fisher's psychiatrist for the whole eight months he was here. You'll have to take the matter up with Holly Road, I'm afraid. Which surgery did you say you were calling from?"

Laura had wriggled and waffled and made her excuses before ringing off as quickly as she could. She had found out what she needed to know. What she had suspected. Rhys had been an inpatient in a mental hospital. More than once, by the sound of it. She googled Dr. Hindmarsh and was further alarmed to find that his specialty was delusional psychosis. She felt ill at the thought of just how dangerous Rhys might be, and that it was she who had let him into their lives. It also accounted for his reluctance to talk about his past.

As they arrived at the hospital Laura did her best to forget about Rhys. She was here for Steph and for Angus. However often she saw her dear friend, the sight of him still so inert and so dependent on medical intervention was shocking. She looked at the tortured expression on Steph's face.

"Oh, Steph," she said, taking hold of her hand. The two stood in silence together, looking down at poor Angus, both unsure if life would ever return to anything approaching normal ever again.

"They still won't let us move him," Steph said. "I know it's silly, but I want to take him home. Well, back to London, I mean. Don't get me wrong, you and Dan, you've been great. It's just, the boys would be better off back at school. And all this hanging around . . ." She shook her head slowly. "Wake up, Angus, you lazy old sod," she said with a sniff. "This is no time for a lie in."

Laura squeezed her hand. "He will be OK, Steph. You have to believe that."

Steph nodded, "I know. The boys keep asking me when Daddy is going to wake up. How can I tell them he might not? Or that if he does, he might not be the Daddy they remember."

"You don't know that."

"I try not to think about it but . . . Oh, Laura, what am I going to do?"

Laura wrapped her friend in her arms, noticing how angular her body had become after weeks of worry and not eating properly.

"I wish I knew what to say to make you feel better, Steph. We just have to stay positive. Angus is a fighter. He'll come through this. OK?"

Steph nodded again, dabbing at her eyes. "OK," she said in a small voice almost unrecognizable as her own.

"I'll go and find us some coffee," Laura said. 'There must be a machine here somewhere."

"Right." Steph mustered a tired smile. "Only fair that we should suffer, too."

Laura leaned against the coffee machine and felt close to tears. *Ridiculous,* she told herself, *Steph needs your support. She does not need a sniveling wreck. Pull yourself together, woman.*

She punched buttons and waited for the cups to fill. Two young doctors joined her, waiting for their turn. Laura recognized one of them as the intern who she had seen with Angus soon after he was first admitted.

"Hello," she said. "I'm here visiting Angus Keane. He's a close friend."

"Ah yes, the climbing accident, I remember. How is he?"

"Not very good, I'm afraid. You know, he wasn't really climbing. Just going for a mountain walk."

"Nasty head wound."

"He just slipped off the path. Hit some rocks. It seems such bad luck, to have such a serious injury from a simple walk." She took the coffees and stood aside to let the others make their selections.

"He was unlucky," the young doctor went on. "Must have landed pretty hard. But then, he's quite a heavy chap. And of course the conditions didn't help. Damp and foggy, wasn't it? Took a while for the air ambulance to get to him."

"Yes, but he was being looked after by an experienced hill walker."

"I'm sure he did his best, but once the body goes into shock all sort of things can be affected." He fed coins into the machine.

"Can't you prevent shock?"

"To an extent, if you can keep the patient warm." He picked up his drink and turned to leave. "Well, must get on. I hope your friend makes a good recovery. Everyone here will do their best."

"Thank you." Laura stood and watched him walk away, then a thought struck her. "Wait!" She trotted after him. "You say he needed to keep warm. What if the walkers had had one of those survival blankets with them? You know, the tinfoil type things? Would that have made a difference?"

"God, yes, huge difference. A sad reminder of how it pays to be well prepared. If he'd been snuggly wrapped up in one of those he wouldn't be in the condition he's in now. A not particularly serious head injury is one thing, but add complications brought on by shock and you're dealing with something quite different." He was interrupted by a beeping from his coat pocket. "Sorry, being paged. Gotta go."

Laura's mind was racing. All she could hear was William's voice telling her how he was so well prepared for the walk. With his special bag. And the survival blanket.

As soon as she returned home Laura went into the utility room and searched through the coats. She found William's hiking bag and rifled through it. No survival blanket. It must have been taken out and used when Angus had his fall. So why wasn't he still in it when he was taken to the hospital? None of it made any sense. Rhys had been with him, looking after him while they waited for Mountain Rescue. He must have known how important it was to keep Angus warm. What possible reason could he have for taking off the survival blanket? Anwen's words came back to her. Laura knew she considered Rhys dangerous in some way. But why would he want to harm Angus? And was he really capable of such a terrible thing? She went into the kitchen and hurried over to the shelf beside the telephone. There were dozens of scraps of paper with numbers written on them among the local directories and Laura's own phone book. At last she found what she had been looking for. She unfolded the crumpled sweet wrapper. There, in Rhys's flamboyant hand, were the map coordinates for the spot where Angus had been injured. She stuffed the paper into her pocket. She had no clear idea of what she might find, but at the moment she felt she was trying to do a puzzle with only half the pieces. Maybe the mountain would reveal some more.

❧❧❧

Monday morning was more grey and windier and generally not as pleasant as the weather of the previous week. Nevertheless, Laura was determined to seize the opportunity to go up onto the hill. Dan had left for work. Steph took the children to see their father and was expected to be gone some time. She had decided to try to get Angus moved to a London hospital so that they could go home and the boys could return to school. A meeting with Angus's consultant had been arranged.

Laura dressed warmly, took a map, a compass, and a sketchbook, and set off. She was fairly confident about finding the right spot. It was the mountain mist that had caused problems for the walkers that day. In truth, they had not gone a great distance, nor chosen a difficult route, out of consideration for the children. On a clear day, with the map reference, her own familiarity with parts of the hill, and what Dan had told her about where the accident happened, she reckoned she stood a reasonable chance of success.

It felt good to be out of the house, away from the gloomy atmosphere which could only normally be escaped for a moment or two before someone said something, or did something, or looked a certain way that brought Angus's condition back into vivid focus. Here thoughts could spread away, snatched up by the wind. Here was space and peace and timeless nature, constant in its beauty. The cold air rasped the back of Laura's throat as her breathing labored on the steep incline. She pressed on, stomping out every second heartbeat as her boots thudded onto the frozen ground. After the better part of an hour she stopped and checked her map. The site of the accident must be close now. She looked around, realizing that her best hope at this stage was to use her eyes. Dan had described a narrow sheep track winding up the side of the hill. They had passed several rowan trees with branches so low on the path that the men had been forced to step off it, while the boys had enjoyed scurrying underneath. Then there was a stream, and after that the path became slightly stonier. They could have gone no more than fifty yards beyond the stream when Angus fell. Laura spotted some small trees and went to examine them more closely. The path did indeed run beneath them, and there was too little head clearance for her. She followed the track around a small bend and bingo! A stream. Laura felt foolishly pleased with herself for finding the right place. Jumping the stream, she started to count her paces. When she got to forty she slowed down, scrutinizing every rock, looking for the four "steps" Dan had mentioned. They were helpfully obvious. They consisted of four flat pieces of stone which weather and sheep had beaten into perfectly flat rectangles which did indeed look like man-made steps. Laura stood on the top one and scanned the area. This had to be the spot. The ground fell away steeply from the path and, about fifteen feet down, there was a small group of rocks sticking out of the wiry grass. Below that was a sea of winter bracken, brown and bent and almost impossible to walk through. She sat down and tried to understand what must have happened. It was a narrow path, but not dangerously so. Why would Angus have fallen? She could only think that the thick cloud that had reduced visibility to a few yards must have caused him to misjudge a crucial step. Even so, he would have had to hurl himself onto the rocks below or he couldn't have sustained such a terrible injury. Unless he had been pushed. As the idea formed in her head Laura felt a shiver twitch down her back. But why? She always came back to the same question: Why would Rhys hurt Angus? She stared down at the stones, finding it hard to believe Angus could have smashed his head so badly and crushed his mobile as well. There were only a few rocks, and if the phone was in the pocket of his shorts it could not have connected with a stone at the same moment his head was doing so. And then there was the question of the survival blanket. What had happened to that? Laura had been half hoping she might have found it on the ground somewhere, having fallen out of William's bag or been overlooked in all the drama. But, no. She sighed heavily, taking off her ski hat and running her hands through her hair. Whatever answers she had expected, none were forthcoming.

Suddenly, she knew beyond any doubt that Merlin was close. Her whole body tensed. Slowly, she turned and found him standing on the path only a few yards from where she was sitting. Laura could hear her heartbeat echoing in her eardrums. Merlin smiled at her and came to sit beside her. Laura gave a little laugh at the casualness of his actions, as if they were for all the world old friends out for a walk together, taking a break to admire the view.

"Did you follow me here?" she asked.

"No, but I knew where to find you. I always know where you are, Laura."

She was surprised to find this a comforting thought. If Rhys had said it she would have been unnerved, but from Merlin it was reassuring. As if he knew when she needed him and would be there for her. She waved her hand at the path and the rocks.

"Something bad happened here," she said. "Actually, I think something bad happened here because someone made it happen."

"Do you know who?"

"I think I do."

"Do you know why?"

She shook her head. "I can't figure it out. I can't see any possible reason why Rhys would want to harm Angus."

"Rhys is a man of strong passions, and he will act on those passions."

"Have you been talking to Anwen? Are you going to speak in riddles, too?" Laura was exasperated. "Look, it's been a dreadful few weeks. I'm trying to make sense of all this"—she glanced at him—"and to make sense of . . . us." She paused, then went on, "If you know what is going on in Rhys's head will you please, *please*, just tell me?"

"Rhys yearns for something more than he has ever wanted

anything in his life before." Merlin sat, looking into the far distance as he spoke. "He wants something so special and so precious to him he will stop at nothing to get it. In truth, he desires what I desire."

"What?" asked Laura, momentarily distracted by this small glimpse into Merlin's heart and mind. "What do you want?"

He turned to face her now, his unforgettable eyes seeing right through to Laura's very soul.

"You," he said.

Laura could not move. She was transfixed by his gaze and both thrilled and alarmed by what he had just said. In that instant she could not think of Rhys, or even of what had happened to Angus. She could not think at all. All she could do was feel the power of the connection between herself and this specter, this being from another place, another reality. She took off her gloves, lifted her hand and very slowly reached out and touched his face. She let her fingertips trail over his fine features, then trace the outline of his mouth, then run down his throat and onto his chest. Even through his heavy cloak and warm garments she could feel the steady beating of his heart. She had never felt so close to anyone, ever. The knowledge of this made her feel elated and at the same time desperate. How could she ever really be with this man? She was falling in love with an impossibility, and it could only end in heartache.

This is no ghost, she told herself, *this is the most incredible person I have ever met. A magical man, someone who has done great things and existed in the hearts and memories of millions of people over hundreds of years. And he chooses to be with me. He has sought me out.*

"The answers you seek are not here on this mountain," he told her. "You must look into Rhys's mind. But have a care. He will not risk losing you."

"He has already lost me. I was never his in the first place."

"That is something we both understand, but he does not. Protect yourself, Laura. He would not directly harm you, but you must protect the ones you love most in this world, for he sees them as standing between you and himself."

"Dan? Do you mean Dan? I would never forgive myself if Rhys did something terrible to him because of me. Oh, God, I've been such a selfish idiot." She buried her face in her hands to hide her tears. "How did I make such a mess of everything? This was supposed to be a new life, a new start for us, maybe even a baby." She took her hands away and rolled her eyes. "Ha! How ridiculous that sounds. I've lied to my husband, betrayed him and neglected him, all for a stupid, stupid fling with Rhys. Just because he made me feel good about my useless bloody body again. Lust, plain and simple. Nothing more to it than that. And now it looks as though I've brought some sort of dangerous lunatic into our lives." She let out a weary breath, shaking her head. "Is what happened to poor Angus really down to me? Did I cause that to happen? Because I got involved with a man I hardly know? And then there's you." She turned to look at him again, wiping tears from her eyes, trying to pull herself together. "I go years being perfectly content with Dan, then I run around like a hormonally challenged teenager with Rhys, and now I feel this unbelievably powerful connection with someone no one else can see. Am I going mad?"

"When are you most yourself? When are you happiest and most free?" he asked.

"When I am here, in this incredible place. When I'm inspired by it and painting it. This landscape, these mountains, this whole high valley . . . it feels like home," she said.

"That does not sound like madness to me."

Laura sighed. In front of her the mountains rolled away twenty miles in every direction, with barely a house to be seen. It was such a magical place, was it any wonder magical things were happening? She longed for all the worry of the past few weeks to melt away. For Angus to be well again. For Rhys to be gone. And then? Could she really just go back to some sort of normality with Dan? At last the heavy grey of the sky had begun to lift and the sun started to force its way through the veil of cloud and light up the valley thousands of feet below.

"I read some more about you," she said. "About your summer here. About the woman you loved." She saw Merlin's expression alter minutely. "Her name was Megan, wasn't it?"

"Yes. Her name is Megan," he repeated softly.

"I saw a picture. An illustration. I look at lot like her, don't I?"

He nodded.

"Is that why you've sought me out? Is that what it is? Do I remind you of her? Do you think I *am* her . . . maybe, I don't know, reincarnated, or something?" She waited anxiously for his answer. She had made the question sound as casual as she could, but it was hugely important.

"Megan is like me, Laura, she exists in legend now and always. She cannot, as you suggest, be reborn as another." He put his hands on her shoulders and looked at her earnestly. "Know this: It is you I have crossed worlds to find, you I have stepped out of my rightful place for. For yourself. For all that you are, and for what you will be long after I have left you."

"Left me?" Laura's voice was small and frightened.

"We do not have forever, but I will not leave you alone. Don't be saddened by what I have said. All will be for the best," he said with a small smile.

Laura wanted to believe him, but she could not see how things would ever be all right again. She had to somehow get rid of Rhys and the threat he presented. And she had to make a decision about her marriage. She didn't know how she was going to manage any of it. All she did know was that if Merlin disappeared out of her life her heart would break. An idea came to her.

"Will you let me draw you?" she asked. Seeing him hesitate she pressed the point. "Please, it would help me, when you're not here, to have something . . . tangible. Just a few sketches. Please?"

At last he nodded, then turned to gaze out at the view, sitting still as a stone for nearly an hour while Laura filled page after page with images of the most beguiling man she had met in her life.

❦ 12 ❧

MEGAN HAD NO way of knowing how many hours had passed since Huw had brought her the bread and water. Reason told her that it had not been more than a day, but already it seemed an eternity. She could be patient. She had to be. But there was, under the loneliness of waiting, the ever present fear that he might never return. He was, after all, a small boy, barely seven years old. It might happen that he was too afraid to come again, that he found it too upsetting, or that he was fearful of his father's anger. It could even be that the children had been taken away for a visit somewhere. What would happen then? How long would it be before she gave up all hope? She began to pace the small room again, briskly this time, as much to keep frightening thoughts from her mind as to dispel the cold that was already seeping into her bones.

She knew she must do something to stop herself descending into despair. Closing her eyes she thought of Merlin. She had heard his voice at the start of her incarceration but, though she had opened her mind to him and listened for his whisper in her ear, he had been silent of late. Could it be that he no longer knew how to reach her in this terrible place? That the stone fortress in which she was imprisoned had somehow become impenetrable even to his far-seeing eye? Could it be that he was dead? She refused to believe such a thing. It was only a matter of time, surely, before she would hear from him again and feel the comfort of his presence.

She took a deep breath and let her thoughts drift back to another time, another place. Her body might be captured, but surely her mind was still as free as the skylarks up on the mountain. She pictured herself back at Ty Bychan, on a glorious autumn day. She remembered just such an occasion when she had stolen away from the castle to spend a few short hours with Merlin. How quickly they had learned to be completely at ease with one another, to walk in step, to breathe in rhythm, to have harmonious thoughts and feelings. How wonderful it had been to find such companionship and love. They had taken some food and a flask of ale and sat beneath a chestnut tree that still held its autumn leaves of gold and copper which gleamed and shimmered under the high September sky.

"You risk a great deal by coming here," he had said, laying beside her, resting on an elbow to look at her.

"No more than you risk by not leaving this place. Lord Geraint will not wait forever for your cooperation, Merlin," she reminded him. She picked up a late daisy and twirled it between her fingers. "You know it would be better if you left Ty Bychan, left the valley altogether."

"Better for whom? For his Lordship? For me? For you, my love?" He leaned forward and planted the lightest of kisses on her brow. "How can I leave you?"

Megan reached up and slipped her hand behind his neck, pulling him gently down. "Then give me the kiss of a man who is truly unafraid. Kiss me with all the truth of your love and your belief in us. How else can I know this is not another dream, another vision you are sending me?" Her voice was serious but the hint of a smile in her eyes gave away the fact that she was teasing him. He smiled back, then placed his lips on hers and kissed her full and slow and not at all in the manner of one who is hunted or on the point of fleeing. Megan's body responded to him and, in the amber light of the waning year, they consummated their love for one another.

Megan returned from her daydream cheered by the thought of her lover, but frightened by what might lie ahead. It was not only for herself that she feared. The small hole she and Huw had worked so hard to obtain allowed a dull light to fall in one corner of her prison. She knelt there and let her hands slide over the warm fabric of her gown, caressing her still-flat tummy, imagining the baby which was growing inside her. If she did not get more food and water her unborn child would die before it had ever seen the sunshine on the mountains or the snow on the branches of the sloping oak. She was glad she had shared her news with Merlin, so that he, too, could hold the thought of their child in his heart. She knew he would never give up on them. She must be strong and wait. Only wait.

❧

THE SMALL STOVE in the studio was cheerful, but it was no match for the biting cold that forced its way in through every drafty gap. Laura shoveled on a little more coal and opened up the flue. Despite a lifetime of modern central heating she had quickly become adept at dealing with open fires, be they coal or wood. She took a certain pride in lighting the stove herself and tending it as she worked. Even so, she began to think she would have to take to painting with thermal underwear beneath her warm clothes. She wondered if she could hold her brushes properly in fingerless mittens.

She was making the most of a rare opportunity to paint. Dan had taken Steph and the boys for an outing to Llangors Lake, and Laura had excused herself on the grounds of needing to do some work. Dan had been right to be concerned. The exhibition was barely a couple of weeks away and she had nowhere near enough canvases. It was also fair to say that she longed to paint, to be absorbed totally by her work, to create something in her own special way by expressing herself in her most eloquent manner. In fact, she knew she was not in the right frame of mind. It occurred to her that, on top of everything else, this was becoming a real cause for concern. In the past, whatever her problems, she had always been able to lose herself in her art, to escape to that other place in her mind. The place she was most sure of and most proud of. Now, however, with every additional worry and complication in her life, she seemed to be moving further and further away from her creative self. Was her talent simply dwindling in the face of such momentous turmoil? Would it ever return?

She glanced over her shoulder before moving some canvases to unearth the pictures she had done of Merlin. She hadn't let anyone else see them, fearing the questions they might ask and not trusting her own responses. There were dozens of sketches, some done when he was with her, others drawn from memory. She had found it comforting to work on his portraits, particularly when she was missing him and feeling alone. She moved the sketches to one side and looked at the paintings. At least when she had been working on these she had been utterly absorbed and focused. And she knew the results were good. Such a strong face, such presence and charisma, and she believed she had captured it as near as was possible in two dimensions.

With a rare moment of clarity Laura saw that these were the paintings she should put in her show. Up until now, she had gone out of her way to hide them, but at that moment she realized they were the best, the most sincere, the most striking work she had done in a very long time. Excitedly she stood the pictures up around the room. There were only five paintings, but she had time to produce a few more, maybe, and she could include the sketches and drawings. Together with the landscapes and self-portraits she very nearly had a show and, standing back to take in the collection, Laura could see it worked. Merlin needed to be surrounded by the landscapes to be in context. She could not say how such a subject would be received. She could only follow her heart and trust her artistic instincts. If Penny didn't like it, well, that was too bad. It was far too late to produce alternative paintings, and Penny would rather pull out her own eyelashes than cancel a show.

Laura heard the door open and turned, her heart leaping for a moment at the thought that it might be Merlin. But Merlin did not need to open doors. Rhys stood before her, looking strangely haunted and wired.

"I saw the others leave," he told her, stepping forward to take hold of her. "I've wanted to come and see you so much. It's torture, having to stay away."

"They won't be gone long." Laura lied, resisting the impulse to push him away. However little hard proof she had of him being a violent and dangerous man, in her heart she had convinced herself, and she knew she must tread carefully. She let him kiss her, then slipped from his arms, smiling. "Your hands are cold. It's freezing out there. Let me make you some coffee." She set about fixing the drinks. Rhys was about to say something when he caught sight of the paintings of Merlin. He hurried closer.

"When did you do these?"

Laura was thrown. However she felt about going public with the pictures, Rhys was the last person she wanted to discuss them with.

"Oh, over time. Some a while ago. Those two more recently," she said as casually as she could. She continued to make the coffee, but all the while watched him out of the corner of her eye.

Rhys studied the paintings up close for an age before turning back to her. His face was quite lit up.

"They're fantastic, Laura. I knew you were good, but these . . . And I'm deeply touched."

"You are?"

"Of course, who wouldn't be? To think, I've been in agony, not seeing you, having to stay away, thinking maybe you didn't want to see me anymore."

"Oh, no . . ."

"I know. Silly of me. When there you were, all this time, painting these wonderful, loving portraits of me. She stared at him. He wasn't joking. He truly believed the pictures were of him. She didn't know whether to be relieved or horrified. She really did not want him thinking she was so caught up in him, so fixated. On the other hand, if he thought it was his face she had been adoringly reproducing all these weeks he wouldn't ask any awkward questions about Merlin.

Something odd caught her attention. There was something different about Rhys's face. She looked closer and wondered why she had not spotted it the instant he walked in. One of his eyes was brown. The effect was disconcerting. It took Laura a moment to work out that the contact lenses he wore must be colored. The bewitching blue was not his own, but artifice, an illusion, a deliberate attempt to change himself in what seemed to her a very fundamental way. As he clearly had not noticed the lens was missing it could serve no other purpose than a cosmetic one. It struck Laura as deeply odd that a man purporting to live a simple existence should do something so unnecessary, so vain. She looked away, trying to refocus on the matter of the portraits. At all costs she wanted to keep Rhys placated at the moment.

"I'm glad you like them," she managed to mutter at last.

Rhys found a stool and perched on it, watching her now.

"So," he said, "your husband and your best friend off together without you. Again."

"I've got to get on with some work."

"I'm sure they'll have a fine time without you."

Laura turned to frown at him. "What's that supposed to mean?"

"Just what I said. They get on very well, those two, don't they? Doesn't it bother you?"

"Why on earth should it?"

"You wouldn't mind? If they were screwing each other?"

"Dan and Steph? Oh don't be ridiculous!"

"He seems pretty pleased to have her staying here all this time. I notice he's been taking time off to be here more, to take her out. They're always going off together."

"With the boys," she pointed out.

"But without you."

Laura shook her head. "You couldn't be more wrong. They are fond of each other, of course. We've all been friends for years. But there's nothing more to it than that. Besides, as you said, she's my best friend. And Dan would never . . ." She didn't finish the sentence.

"Cheat on you? He must be more in love with you than you are with him, then."

"You're imagining the whole thing, Rhys. It's ridiculous," she snapped.

Rhys shrugged, "You know them best." He slipped off the stool and ran a hand down the curve of her back. "I've been watching the house," he said. "Just waiting for a chance to come and see you. Have you any idea how much I've missed you?"

"Of course. It's been hard for me, too." She avoided looking at him. "But what can we do? Things are still very uncertain for poor Angus."

"Will he live?"

It was such a bald question and devoid of any warmth or concern. Laura shuddered as she thought of how Rhys must have pushed Angus off the path and onto the rocks. And then what, while the others had gone for help? Had he really been so cold-blooded as to strip him of the vital survival blanket and sit waiting for him to die? A man who could do that would be capable of almost anything. And how would she ever be able to prove any of it?

"Let's hope so," she said, spooning coffee into cups. She tried to steady her nerves by remembering what Merlin had said. *He would not directly harm you.* Was he right? If she told him it was over between them might he not turn his violence toward her? She sought for ways to deflect his interest in her, to distract him. "He opened his eyes yesterday." She was glad she had her back to him as she lied.

"Really?"

"Yes. Just for a moment. But that must be a hopeful sign, don't you think?" She handed him a mug.

"Did he say anything?"

"No." Laura realized she was playing a dangerous game. She sipped her coffee, trying to hold his gaze, wishing her tired brain could come up with a way of dealing with such an alarming situation. She gestured at the prepared canvas that sat on the easel. "I came in here to try and do some work. With all that's happened I've got horribly behind. If I don't produce something worthwhile soon I'll be having an empty show. An exhibition of blank walls." She wandered around the studio, idly peering at paintings stacked here and there. She heard him follow her. Soon she could feel his breath on the back of her neck. He put down his coffee and moved her hair to one side, nuzzling into the nape of her neck.

"I've missed you so much, my beautiful, beautiful Laura. I want you so much," he said as his hands finding their way to her breasts.

Laura was horrified. The thought of having sex with him now

made her feel physically sick. Where once his touch had inflamed her with desire, now she felt repulsed. She fought panic. Of course he would expect her to want to make the most of the opportunity, too. They had not been alone together for some time. He would be bound to notice the change in her response to him. She turned to face him and forced herself to kiss him with as much conviction as she could manage. His probing tongue in her mouth made her want to retch. She pulled away, breathless, but for all the wrong reasons. She held his face in her hands, a gesture she hoped he would interpret as one of tenderness, when in fact she was simply trying to avoid another kiss.

"I've missed you, too," she said. "But . . . we can't . . . not today."

He frowned. "Why ever not? It's the best chance we've had for days. Weeks, for Chrissake."

"I'm sorry. I've got so much work to do. Dan's expecting me to be on top of things, to show him what I've done, do you see? I have to work."

"Fucking brilliant," he said. It was the first time she had heard him use such language, as if a mask were slipping and she was glimpsing another face beneath. The real face. The real, frightening Rhys.

"Things will get easier, soon. A few days perhaps."

"Will you come to me then? Straightaway?"

"If I can . . ."

"Say you will. Promise me you will." He was gripping her arms tightly now.

"How can I?"

"Wait until everyone is asleep. They won't notice you are missing. There's a full moon two nights from now. Come to the croft after midnight. Promise!" He squeezed her arms until they hurt.

"I promise," she said, determined not to show how scared he was making her. "Thursday night. I'll come to the croft."

He held her for a full minute, then, at last, seemed satisfied and let her go. He stepped back, smiling, relaxed, playful now.

"That's my girl. Don't worry. I'll make it worth the walk." He went toward the door, pausing on his way to blow her a kiss. "Until Thursday night, my love."

"Bye." She gave a feeble wave and a smile to match. As he closed the door behind him she leaned heavily against the door, her heart pounding, her palms sticky with sweat.

❧❀❧

MEGAN SLEPT FITFULLY in the gnawing cold of her prison, and as she slept she dreamed. Her dream took place in a dark forest, somewhere she did not recognize. Tall trees loomed above a party of riders as they threaded their way through the wood. The men numbered three dozen or more. The horses wore breastplates and some had armor over their bridles, so that the dull thud of their hooves was accompanied by the clanking and jangling of beaten metal. As the vision became clearer the riders revealed themselves as soldiers bearing arms—heavy swords, bows, knives, spears, and axes. The lead rider stood out from the others. His destrier was frost white and very fine beneath gleaming armor and rugs of gold and blue. The rider himself wore chain mail and a shining breastplate. His visored helmet and elaborately tooled sword marked him out as a noble or a knight. To one side of him rode the standard bearer, the flag unfurling in the wind to reveal a red dragon and a falcon. On the far side of the nobleman rode a tall figure on a mount the color of ripe corn. The rider was dressed in dark hooded robes and wore no armor. He did not carry a sword but a staff, and close to his courser's hooves loped a large, grey wolf.

The path narrowed between ever denser trees and descended a steep hill, the horses dropping back on their hocks as they slithered and slid down toward a clearing at the bottom of the incline. They had not descended more than halfway when the first arrows whipped through the air toward them. As the sharpened heads found their mark the men screamed in pain, while their captain shouted for them to rally and fight. Within seconds they were set upon. They had unwittingly ridden into a deadly ambush. With terrifying shouts and roars upward of fifty soldiers sprang from their hiding places, swords raised, axes swinging. The clash of weapons and the cries of the stricken riders echoed through the trees as they were outnumbered and overwhelmed. The nobleman wheeled his destrier about, slashing at those who ran toward him. His own soldiers marshaled themselves and fought back, even though the situation was hopeless. The hooded rider urged his horse into the fray, wielding his staff with deadly accuracy, sending men flying backward into the undergrowth, where they lay like rag dolls, their skulls cracked and their senses gone. Beside him the wolf defended its master, biting the throat from a soldier who raised his knife to attack. But the ambushers were too many, and one by one the riders fell. At last the nobleman bid his men retreat, and those who were able turned and fled into the cover of the forest. The hooded man turned his courser to follow them, but behind him a well-armored soldier drew a dagger from his hip and threw it. As he did so the wolf lunged at him, tearing his hand from his arm. But the soldier's aim had been good, and the knife sank into its target's back to the hilt. The rider cried out and slumped forward, clinging to his mount's mane. The courser raced away, bearing its rider out of the reach of further harm, not stopping until all sounds and smells of the gruesome battle were well behind it. When finally the animal came to a halt, breathing heavily, its neck running with its own sweat and its master's blood, the rider slumped to the ground.

All was silent, and a preternatural stillness surrounded the fallen man. The wolf found its master and circled him, whining pitifully. A movement disturbed the animal, which backed off warily. From the trees emerged an old woman, stout and ruddy, walking on thick legs, bundled up in a muddle of clothes against the winter cold. She stooped over the wounded rider and used her foot to turn him so that his face was clearly revealed. The dream ended with a lingering image of the crone's dimpled features as she peered down at the bleeding man at her feet.

Megan awoke with a cry.

"Merlin!" she shouted aloud. "Oh, my poor Merlin." She let the tears fall unchecked down her face, shaking her head, realizing that this had been more than a dream. She knew now why he had been silent for so long, why she had not heard him or sensed his presence. But was he dead? Or had he survived his terrible wounds? Had the old woman sought to help him or to turn him in to his enemies? Megan felt herself giving way to despair. He had been riding from some distant place, toward her, she had no doubt of that. And now he lay mortally wounded, and death could be claiming him at that very moment. And she was power-less to help him. She beat her fists against the cruel stones, tears of grief and anger and frustration lending vigor to the futile ges-ture. At that darkest of lightless moments the sound of a small boy's voice was indeed sweet music. "Megan? Megan? Are you well?" whispered Huw.

"Oh, Huw! Yes, yes. I thought you might not come again."

"And leave you here alone? Never. Here, I'll pass through the leather and the food. I've brought cheese today. I was given it for my supper, but I hid it and saved it for you."

"You are a brave and clever boy." Megan wiped the tears from her cheeks and squared her shoulders. All was not yet lost. She drank more gritty water and caught some in the leather pouch before hungrily devouring the food. "Huw, have you heard news of Merlin?"

There was a worrying silence on the other side of the wall.

"Please tell me what you know, little one. I must hear the truth." Megan kept her voice level but was terrified at what the response to her question might be.

"Oh, Megan . . ." Huw began to cry. "There was a battle. I heard Llewelyn discussing it with my father. They did not know they were overheard. Merlin had gone to the castle of Lord Idris and raised help. He was on his way to fight for your freedom. But one of Lord Idris's men betrayed them, and my father laid an am-bush. Lord Idris escaped, though most of his men were slain."

"And Merlin? What of him?" The bread had turned to sawdust in her mouth.

"It is only known that he was wounded by Llewelyn, who him-self lost a hand to a monstrous wolf that fought alongside Idris's men. Merlin fled, but I heard Llewelyn assure my father that he . . . he could not have lived. I'm so sorry, Megan," said Huw through heavy sobs.

"Hush, hush now." Megan clutched instinctively at her stomach, as if to protect all that she had left of Merlin. Huw had confirmed what her dream had told her. What neither of them knew was the extent of Merlin's wounds. Megan reasoned that the vision had been sent to her, and that must surely mean he lived. The old woman must have taken pity on him and staunched the flow of his blood. Llewelyn had failed to bring home a corpse, so he would naturally seek to convince Lord Geraint of the success of his mission. Megan believed the truth was very different, and she clung to that belief with all her fading might.

❧

LAURA WOKE WITH a jolt. Her dreams had been vivid and disturbing, with images of Angus bleeding onto the rocks, of Rhys naked, and of the boys lost in a fog somewhere, with Steph shouting out their names over and over. At the end of it all Laura had heard another voice. Merlin's voice. He had been calling her name.

She looked over at Dan. He was sleeping soundly, though she knew he, too, was tortured by what had happened on the mountain that day. She slipped from the bed, shivering despite the heavy white cotton nightshirt she had taken to wearing. Bright moonbeams fell through the gap in the curtains. She went to the window and looked outside. The landscape was illuminated by a fat full moon. There was not a breath of wind, and a sharp frost was crystallizing on the grass. Again, even though she was now fully awake, Laura was sure she heard Merlin calling her. She pulled on a long, warm skirt, quickly fastening its belt, slipped her feet into the nearest pair of sandals, and crept downstairs. Now that the wood-burning stove had gone out even the sitting room was cold. She took a Welsh tweed rug off the sofa and wrapped it around her shoulders before heading out the front door.

The luminous moon was so bright she had no need of a torch. She had never before seen such perfect moon shadows. Her own followed her now as she crossed the yard and walked through the meadows in the direction of the woods. Bats swooped low past her head as she walked. She was aware of small animals ahead of her scuttling away, startled by the unexpected human presence. Soon she had left the lights of the house behind her and entered the shady woods. From the roots of a lightning-scarred oak came the snortling grunts of a badger, his temper ruined by this un-welcome disturbance. The coolness of the air removed almost all of the forest scents, save for a pungent patch of fungus on a rot-ting beech trunk. Laura felt strangely unable to process the infor-mation her eyes were sending to her already unsettled mind. The light was so unusual, so opposite to what she ordinarily sought out for her work, that she had few points of reference with which to connect. What was normally burnt umber autumn fern was changed to a much paler yellow ocher. The moss beneath her feet was no longer Hooker's dark green, but a soft sap green. The sky was dark beyond knowing, yet the stars were so brilliant it made her squint to look at them. The artist part of her brain, forever shouting to be heard, demanded she commit this ethereal scene to canvas at the earliest opportunity.

She walked on, not knowing where to, but certain she was

following the sound of Merlin's voice. She wanted to find him now. She needed to see him again. Alone and away from anyone who might remind her of the insanity of what she was doing. She passed the sloping oak and stepped out into the small glade beyond it. She stopped, waiting, completely sure he would appear. After a moment she could not resist speaking.

"Merlin?" It felt strange hearing her own voice, little more than a whisper, calling out his name. "I'm here," she said.

"I knew you would come."

Laura started. She had been searching the trees for the slightest movement, yet she had not noticed Merlin enter the clearing.

He reached forward and touched her hair. Then he stroked her cheek. Blood suffused her skin at that strangely familiar touch. They stood wordlessly regarding one another. She looked closely at Merlin, trying to read him, to know him. Nearby, an owl screeched and took flight.

"What is it you expect of me?" she asked him. 'You say our destinies are linked . . . but you don't say how. I still don't understand."

"You will. In time, everything will become clear." He was silent for a moment, his expression distant. When he spoke again his voice faltered, and Laura noticed with astonishment that he was trembling. "There was a time, here, in this place, when my fate was entwined with that of another. Our future together was uncertain, but we were full of the hope that love brings. Alas, such obstacles were strewn in our path, such wickedness pitched against us. . . . But now, with you, Laura, destiny has offered another chance. A chance for what was meant to be."

"But, we can't be together, you and I," she said.

"No. Though I confess I wish that it were possible." He smiled and then asked, "Tell me, do you believe in magic?"

She gave a nervous laugh. "I'm here talking to you, how could I not believe?"

Merlin took her hand and placed it on his own heart. Then he gently set his palm against her stomach. "Close your eyes," he told her. "Close your eyes and make a wish. A single wish, for what it is you long for most in the world."

The second her lids fell shut Laura felt a dizziness take hold of her. She staggered a little to keep her balance, but Merlin held her. She had the sensation she was falling, tipping backward and drifting down, down, down. Her head filled with the sound of distant thunder, starting low and then building to a tremendous wave of sound. She gasped, a little afraid. And then, suddenly, it all stopped. She felt Merlin's gentle touch against her cheek once more, and then . . . nothing. When she opened her eyes she was standing alone in the glade. Alone save for the owls and the badgers, and the myriad tiny eyes watching her from their hiding places. Brushing tears away, she turned and hurried back toward the house.

ᘒ 13 ᘓ

THE NEXT MORNING Laura found it hard to focus on the demands of everyday life. Dan had taken another day off work, and he and Steph were flying a kite with the boys in the high meadows. As Laura watched them from her studio window, she wondered that no one had apparently noticed anything strange about her. She felt herself irrevocably changed by the events of the night before. Her mind was still reeling, still marveling at what had happened. It was as though she no longer inhabited only the real world, but had stepped over into another alternative version that was constantly swirling about them. At the moment she stood astride the invisible divide, a foot in each reality, but how long could that last? Merlin's hold over her, the bond she felt with him, her need for him, was making it impossible to stay grounded in her own life, with her husband, her home, the boys, and her art.

And then there was Rhys. She rubbed her temples, unwilling to even think about him now, yet knowing she had no choice. He was expecting her to go to the croft that night, and she was afraid of what he might do if she did not show up. She watched Steph in the field, laughing as Dan steadied her arm to help control the kite. They looked close and, for that moment at least, happy. Surely there couldn't be any truth in Rhys's suggestion? Steph and Dan—it was unthinkable. Just another convolution of Rhys's bizarrely twisted mind. Another attempt to turn her away from Dan, and toward himself. How could he have known that there was someone else who held her in his thrall? Laura was beginning to question her own sanity. She only knew that the presence that had somehow drawn her to Penlan in the first place was Merlin's. That the connection she felt with him was something real and unique and far beyond any passing lustful crush she had had on Rhys. But Merlin had said their time together was limited. That although their destinies were linked, they would not, could not, ultimately be together. It was a cruel fact to have to face. But face it she must. And when Merlin did finally move out of her reach, there would be Dan, waiting for her. Laura shook her head, certain, at that moment, that she did not deserve him. Watching Dan now she felt a stab of deep, deep sadness. This had been their new beginning. Somehow she had lost sight of that. Something strange and wonderful had happened to her. Something no one else could possibly understand. Something that had changed her forever. How could she ever go back to the way things were, to who she was before?

At least she was able to think clearly enough to know that she still loved Dan. And of course she loved Steph and Angus and the boys. It was for them that she would have to deal, once and for all, with Rhys. If she did not face him and tell him herself that it was over between them he would never believe her, she was sure of that. And it just might be that she was the only person who could deliver such news without him reacting with violence. However warped his sense of right and wrong, he loved her. He was besotted with her. She had to trust his obsession to keep her safe. She had thought long and hard about going to the police with what she knew, but how could she possibly make them believe her? Rhys had no feasible motive for hurting him. On top of which, she could not prove Rhys had pushed him or that he had deliberately removed the survival blanket. She could hardly back up her theories with the tangled rantings of an old woman and the word of someone who had, at least to everyone else, been dead for several hundred years. And if she voiced her thoughts to Dan and Steph, what then? Where would she start? She could never fully explain. She had brought the situation about, and it was up to her to stop things before anyone else got hurt. And if that meant squaring up to Rhys, then so be it. And maybe, just maybe, she could find some sort of proof for her theories. Something more than her own conjecture, so that she could go to the police. Perhaps then they could be rid of his dangerous presence once and for all.

MEGAN DRIFTED IN and out of a feverish sleep. The cold and the damp had assaulted her body, which now trembled and sweated and shivered, at once hot and chilled. She knew that such an illness could well be sufficient to kill her. She was already weak, and Huw's visits over the past endless stretch of time had grown further apart and less frequent. On the last occasion he had failed to bring food and given her wine to drink. It had temporarily eased her suffering, but left her more in need of water than before. She feared for the tiny life inside her. How much more of such brutal privations could it survive? Would she herself hold out long enough for Merlin to find her? He had been badly wounded, of that she was certain. The small hole in the interior wall allowed not so much light in, as an impression of a less dense darkness. It was just enough to indicate morn from night. Because of this she was aware that many slow days had passed since her dream, days that could be added to form weeks. She had not heard his voice in all that time. Had the old woman failed to save him? Megan stroked the now grimy fabric of the dress over her belly and spoke to her child.

"There, my precious little one. Rest gently. We will wait for him together." So saying she curled herself up like a cat on the rough floor, closed her eyes against the grimness, and rode the swell of her fever into sleep once more. Sometime later she heard unfamiliar noises. At first she thought she might be dreaming again, but no, these were sounds from the waking world. She sat up, staring at the inner wall, listening to the rhythmic thudding and scraping coming from the other side. Someone was digging.

"Megan?" Huw's little voice squeezed through the gap they had made together.

"Huw? What is happening?"

"All is well, Megan. Fear no more. He is come to save you!"

"He?"

"I am here, Megan, my love. I am here."

At the sound of the words—the voice—she had waited so long for, Megan was almost overcome.

"Merlin!" she sobbed. "Is it really you?"

"Stand back from the wall," he told her. "I must use a heavy hammer."

She did as he instructed, raising one arm to protect her eyes from the dust and dislodged masonry, while the other cradled her belly. The hammer blows sent shudders through both the wall and her entire body. She wondered no one in the castle heard them, or indeed felt them. Merlin worked on. She felt rather than saw the great stones begin to move. At last, handfuls of lime and stone began to fly free, and in a few more moments dust-filled light entered the space. Megan held her sleeve over her mouth now as the unbreathable air threatened to choke her. Yet more hammering, and a man-sized lump fell into the room, leaving a void behind it. Through the swirling dust stepped Merlin. Megan thought she might faint away from a mixture of delirium, exhaustion, and happiness. He reached in and pulled her gently from her tomb, steadying her as even the dim light of the dungeon hurt her eyes.

"There." He supported her while he held a flask of water to her cracked lips. "Drink. You are safe now."

She coughed as the water washed more grit from her mouth, then drank deeply. When finally she let him take the water from her, she smiled through her unsteady vision and said, "I have never tasted anything so sweet, nor seen any sight so welcome."

"I would never have had this happen to you. And for such a time. I should have come to your aid much sooner, my love. Forgive me."

"There is nothing at all to forgive. You are here now. All is well." She looked over at Huw. "And besides, I have had my brave, brave little soldier to care for me."

Huw beamed and blushed and rushed forward to embrace

Megan. He looked so much less a little boy than when she had last seen him, even though it had only been a matter of a few weeks. It was as though his experiences had robbed him of his innocence and his childhood, and at such a tender age. She kissed his cheeks.

"Thank you, Huw. I am forever in your debt, my tiny hero."

"I would do anything for you, Megan, anything."

"Come," Merlin said as he picked up the torch. "We must leave. I have subdued the dungeon guards, but we might be discovered at any time."

"Indeed you might."

All three turned as one, shrinking back against the ruined wall. Lord Geraint stood before them, sword drawn, four soldiers flanking him.

"Well, well," he said slowly. "I admit to deriving some small satisfaction from seeing a plan come to fruition. It seems all things do indeed come to he who waits."

"Let us pass." Merlin's words were in the shape of a demand, not a request. "You have no fight with this maid. She has done nothing, and you have treated her with cruelty beyond measure. I have come to take her from this hellish place."

"Did you in all truth believe you could walk in here, take the girl, and walk out again? Had you really imagined that using your foul magic to addle the senses of a few lowly guards would be sufficient to breach the defenses of my castle? You insult me, Magician, and not for the first time. I was ahead of your reckless plan to involve Lord Idris."

"We were betrayed."

"There will always be men more loyal to gold than to that jumped-up peasant boy who calls himself noble. It was a costly skirmish, and one for which you must bear responsibility. Good men lost their lives. Llewelyn lost a hand, though God knows I should take the other for his failure to capture you. And Idris made good his escape, damn him. You cannot imagine I would let you have your freedom."

"Please, Father, let Megan go. Please don't hurt her anymore." Huw stepped forward, holding out his hands to his parent in a heartfelt entreaty.

"Stand aside, boy! You are no son of mine."

"Father!"

"It comes as no surprise to see where your allegiance lies. For years I have raised you as my own, when it was plain to all with fingers to count and eyes to see the color of your hair to know you were not. And this is how you repay me. Treachery! Betrayal!"

"You are cruel and wicked!" Huw shouted, clenching angry fists. "It is no wonder mother chose Lord Idris over you!"

Lord Geraint flinched as if the child had struck him, and then he let out a bellow and lunged forward. Megan saw in that instant that he was going to kill Huw. With a scream, summoning strength she thought had long ago left her forever, she flung herself in front of the boy. The sword's point found its target, digging deep through flesh and muscle, but the breast it pierced was not Huw's but Megan's.

The dungeon was filled with cacophonous cries. Huw screamed as Megan fell at his feet, blood pouring from her wound. Merlin sprang forward with the roar of a wild beast. He grabbed Lord Geraint by the throat before the man had a second to evade him. With superhuman speed and power, he lifted him up and slammed him against the wall. The soldiers hesitated to go to their master's aid, seeing the strength and fury of the wild man in front of them. One summoned the courage to charge with his sword. Without so much as glancing in his direction, Merlin used his free hand to send an unseen thunderbolt cracking into the swordsman's chest. The young man shrieked in pain, and his body flew backward, crashing against the far wall. The other soldiers backed away. A terrified silence replaced the noise. All that could be heard were the gurgling noises from Lord Geraint's throat as Merlin let him slowly choke in his iron grasp.

"Mercy!" he croaked, his hands clawing at Merlin's wrist, his feet kicking. "*Mercy!*"

Merlin watched him struggle. "When in your evil life have you ever known the meaning of that word?" he asked. At last, Lord Geraint's eyes clouded over, his tongue lolled from his mouth, and his futile struggling came to an end. Merlin released him, and the body slid onto the rubble of the dismantled wall. Lord Geraint lay broken and twisted and grotesque, unloved and unmourned. Merlin turned to the soldiers, who cowered under his gaze. "Let him stay where he lies," he told them. "Let no man move him, so that he rot here—the fate he had intended for Megan." He dropped to Megan's side. Huw was desperately pressing his bundled shirt to her wound, but already it ran scarlet, and a pool of blood grew at their feet.

"Megan! How have I brought you to this?" Merlin took her hand and kissed it. "What use is my magic now? What use at all, when I do not possess the power that could save you?"

"Hush now." She stroked his cheek. "This is not your failing. Evil men will do evil, and the hapless innocent will sometimes get in their path. It is the way of things."

Merlin pressed his face to her belly, tears spilling from his eyes, his voice cracked and hoarse. "Do not leave me!" he begged her. "You are my life, both of you!"

Megan winced with pain, grateful at least for the fever, which was blurring the edges of the agony she should otherwise be engulfed by. She struggled to speak.

"Take me out of this place," she said. "Take me up to the sunlight once more."

Merlin looked at her, his own heart as broken as hers, and nodded. Gently he lifted her up and turned to leave. In front of them the remaining soldiers shuffled nervously. Without a word he subdued them, so that they stood aside, heads bowed, as he carried Megan out.

Slowly he wound up the twisting stairs. In his arms Megan moaned lightly. She was so happy to be close to him now, at the end, that she felt no fear, only sadness for him and for their child. He took her onto the parapet of the nearest tower and knelt down, cradling her in his lap. It had been a bright day, and now the sun was just touching the horizon, sending crimson and scarlet slashes through the forget-me-not sky.

Megan sighed as she looked out at the mountains. It was good to see them again, to feel the fresh, clean air on her face, to be free once more, for however brief a moment. She heard Huw sobbing softly behind her and looked up into the tortured eyes of her lover. With some effort she raised a bloodstained hand and touched Merlin's face.

"Do not weep for me, my love. We were the favored ones, to have found each other and shared one sun-kissed summer. I am only sorry I did not give you the child you long for. It was not meant to be. Instead, I will take it with me to heaven to keep me company. And you will find another."

"No . . ." He shook his head.

"Yes, you will. One day. And she will ease your aching heart and give you your child." She wanted to say more, but she felt faint and distant, her vision unclear. Suddenly she was high above the castle walls, floating above the crenellations of the tower. Looking down she could see Merlin holding her in his arms, weeping silently over her limp body as Huw stood a short way off. How curious it was to see herself thus, to be a distant observer of her own death. A sound distracted her. She turned her head the better to catch the voices she believed she had heard. At last they were louder. It filled her with joy to hear her father's voice again. And her mother's, too! Gently but persistently they called her name. Megan took one last, lingering look at the man who clung to her earthly body, then turned away and was gone.

14

IT WAS A little after midnight when Laura crept out of the house and headed for Rhys's croft. A cloudless night made the journey easier than it might have been, but still she needed her torch to pick her way along the hill path. She was sure she would not be missed. The evening had been an emotional one, where talk had turned to how life had been before Angus's accident. Every memory was punctuated with a swig of wine, so that it was hard not to become teary as the hours passed. Steph had eventually headed for bed, promising that this time she would forgo the sleeping tablet that had become the norm for her. Laura and Dan had not been in bed more than five minutes before he was snoring gently. She knew him well enough to be certain he would sleep soundly until morning.

All the same, she quickened her pace. She was dreading the scene that lay ahead and wanted it all done and over. Her breath clouded in the torchlight, and she could feel the cold seeping in through her gloves. At least the exertion of the uphill climb was keeping the rest of her warm. When she reached the cottage it looked almost cozy with its lamplight falling through the curtain-less windows. She took a breath and raised her hand but the door was opened before she could knock. Rhys stepped out quickly and pulled her into a tight embrace.

"Laura, my beautiful Laura, I knew you would not let me down."

She fought the impulse to push him away but wriggled free as soon as she could.

"Let's go inside," she said. "It's freezing out here."

"Of course, sorry, my love, I wasn't thinking. It's just so good to see you and have you to myself again at last." He led her by the hand to the open fire. "Sit down, I'll get you a drink." He fetched wine while she peeled off her warm outdoor clothing and sat nervously on the edge of the sofa.

"Here," he said, passing her a large goblet of red wine. "Drink. It'll warm you up."

Laura sipped reluctantly. She needed a clear head and had already drunk more than she should have before leaving the house.

"Rhys," she said hesitantly. "We need to talk."

"You are so right," he said, nodding with enthusiasm.

"I am?" He surely could have no idea what was on her mind.

"I love you, Laura. We are meant to be together. It's obvious. We can't go on letting other people get in the way of that any longer. It's time."

"Time? Time for what?" Laura felt her mouth drying and took another sip of wine.

Rhys knelt in front of her and took her hands in his.

"Time to tell everyone about us. Time for you to move in here with me. It's what we both want. Let's not put it off any longer."

"But . . ."

"I know it's hard for you, I understand. Of course you feel bad about Dan, but he'll get over it. I told you, Laura, he's already getting close to Steph. Leave them to it. Think about yourself for a change."

"Actually, I think I've been doing rather too much of that lately," she said, pulling her hands away. "That's what's got us into this situation."

"Situation?" There was an edge to his voice now. "You and me, we are not a *situation*."

"Look, I'm sorry, Rhys. I'm making a mess of this."

"Don't put yourself down. You know I don't like you doing that."

"You don't understand." She stood up and stepped away from him a little. "Rhys, I came here tonight to tell you that it's over. You and me. Us. It was wrong. It never should have happened in the first place. I can't do this anymore."

"Of course you can't. I wouldn't expect you to, all this creeping around and feeling guilty. That's why we're going to be together properly. No more hiding."

"No!" She had not meant to shout, but she had to make him listen to what she was saying. "I can't be with you, Rhys. Not anymore, not secretly, not living with you, not now and again, nothing. It stops now. I'm sorry, but that's the way it has to be."

There was a moment's silence. Laura began to stop feeling nervous and start feeling scared. She could sense the anger building in Rhys as he stared at her in disbelief.

"You don't mean that." He spoke softly, but there was ice in his tone.

"Yes, I do."

"You love me. We are destined to be together. This is not some whim, some passing fancy. This is what has to be," he said, grabbing her hand. "Come upstairs."

"What?"

"Come upstairs—there is something you should see. Something I need to explain."

Laura hesitated. Rhys's bedroom was the last place she wanted to be right now, but what choice did she have?

"Please," he said, stroking her palm with his thumb.

She followed him, cursing herself for not handling things better, anxious that he was stubbornly going to refuse to listen to her.

Upstairs the little room was in darkness. Rhys lit a candle by the bed, then an old oil lamp. He carried the lamp over to the wall with the Indian hanging and beckoned Laura. She stepped a little closer. Rhys reached up and detached the fabric, removing it completely. The wall behind it was covered in pictures. He held up the lamp, and as the light fell on the images Laura stared open-mouthed. There were drawings, paintings, pictures cut from books and magazines, computer printouts, and photocopies. They were all different in size and quality, but they were all of the same person: Merlin. Laura was aware of Rhys watching her, waiting for some reaction.

"Wow," she said feebly. "This is . . . impressive."

"Look." He gestured at one image, then another. "This is Merlin when he was a boy. You don't see many depictions of him at such a young age, and this is him at the cave near Carmarthen, and with Arthur, and working as a shaman."

"I never realized you were quite such a fan." Laura regretted the flippancy of her remark the second she had made it.

"Fan! I am not a fan. For pity's sake, Laura, can't you see?" He stood close to one of the larger images, one that made Laura long for Merlin with all her heart. "Open your eyes," Rhys told her. "What do you see?"

"You look very alike," she said.

"Not just alike. The same. *The same!*" In the lamplight his eyes glinted and his face was animated. "I have known for so long. I've studied him for years, and that's when I began to realize the connection. That's why I came to live here, where he was. I've come home. Do you see that now? And look, there's something else." He grabbed her hand again and pulled her to the wall. "Look at her."

Laura looked and saw a delicate watercolor print of Megan.

"Don't you recognize yourself?" he asked.

"Rhys, that is not me."

"But it is!"

"No, she looks like me, but she is somebody else."

"I know it's hard for you to take in, but you have to trust me, Laura. I know. Merlin has been reborn in me, and Megan, the love of his life who he lost so tragically—she has been reborn in you."

"Rhys . . ." Now Laura was really frightened. If she had clung to any thought that she might have been wrong about Rhys she let it go now. He was clearly seriously deluded. Dangerously so, she believed. How could she ever reason with such a person?

"Don't worry, my beautiful Laura, in time you will come to accept what is true. You must. We don't have a choice in these things. We are the way Merlin and Megan will be reunited and have the family they longed for."

Laura shook her head. "Rhys, you know I can't conceive. You *know* that."

"There are other ways to acquire children."

"Acquire! What are you talking about—you can't go out and buy babies! Listen to yourself, Rhys. You must know what you say is impossible."

"No, it isn't! I admit when you told me you couldn't get pregnant I was thrown. Here was my Megan, but how could we have a child together? And then the boys came."

"The boys?"

"William and Hamish. Two fine boys. We can raise them as our own. Soon they will forget they ever had other parents before us. We can live here and teach them everything they need to know."

Under the pulsing light his features had taken on a fierceness that now, in his maniacal enthusiasm, looked truly terrifying. Laura tried to stay calm.

"Rhys, William and Hamish belong to Steph and Angus. Not to us."

"But they could!"

"No! This is madness. A fantasy."

"I can do this for you, Megan, for us."

"My name is Laura! And I don't want you to do anything for me!" She turned and ran toward the stairs, but he darted across the room and blocked her way.

"You have to have courage, my love. I will do what needs to

be done. Don't worry. Then we can all be together," he said as he dropped down the stairs, slamming shut the door at the bottom.

Laura flung herself against it as she heard him push the bolt home.

"Rhys! Let me out! What are you going to do? Rhys!" she screamed, as she hammered on the unyielding wood. "Let me out!"

"Be patient, my love," he said.

Laura heard the front door open and close and then there was silence. She kicked frantically at the door in front of her, but it did not give at all. She went back up the stairs, her mind in turmoil, terrified at what Rhys might be planning, at a loss to see what she could do to prevent it. He had taken the oil lamp with him so that the only light in the bedroom came from the solitary candle by the bed. She picked it up and made her way slowly around the room, searching for a way out. The window was tiny, and locked. Had he planned to trap her in here all along? She kicked at the small panes, but the frame was tough hardwood, and there was no way she was going to be able to break it—or squeeze out, even if she succeeded. The thought of what Rhys might be planning spurred her on. She put down the candle and picked up the bedside cabinet. She manhandled it to the window then heaved it at the glass with all her strength. One of the panes cracked, but beyond that nothing. It was futile. She picked up the candle again, near despair, clinging to the tiny light as to the small hope that Rhys was not going to do anything terrible. He said he would do what needed to be done to get the boys. What could that mean? Was he going to snatch them from their beds? They weren't babies—he couldn't just carry them away. And even if he did, Steph would just call the police and get them back. A new thought made her feel sick. What if there were no Steph? She searched her memory. Had she ever told Rhys that she and Dan were down as the boys' potential guardians? Had she mentioned that if anything happened to Steph and Angus they would have legal custody of the children? With cold dread swamping her she remembered that she had told him. She had shown him a way he could indeed "acquire" children. But to do that he would have to get rid of Angus, which, after all, hadn't he already tried? And perhaps succeeded? And now he would have to kill Steph. And Dan, if his plan were to be properly carried through.

"Oh my God," Laura shouted aloud. "Help me! Somebody! Help me!" she screamed, and the breath from her cries blew out the candle. "No!" But it was too late. She was in darkness, save for the moonlight from the now half-blocked window. She felt herself beginning to panic. Here she was, locked in a dark room while a madman went to kill her husband and her best friend believing he was doing it for her. "Stay calm, Laura," she told herself. "Your eyes will get used to the dark, then you will be able to see." She waited and, sure enough, dim shapes in the room began to edge into focus. And the most striking of these was the girl who now stood in front of her. Laura let out a scream and staggered backward.

"Do not be afraid," said the girl softly.

"Megan?" Laura's mind was reeling.

"Come," she said. "Follow me."

Laura stepped cautiously after her, feeling her way around the room. Megan descended the stairs to the door. She lifted the latch and opened it as if it had never been locked. Laura followed her into the kitchen, from where she could see the front door was open.

She turned back to thank Megan, but she had vanished. Laura wanted to call her back, to talk to her, but there was no time. She blundered over to where she had left her things and groped for her torch.

"Yes!" she said as she found it. She considered her coat for a moment, then decided it would slow her down, and ran out into the night.

As she ran she thanked God for her sturdy boots, the dry ground, and the pools of moonlight falling on the path. Small clouds were snagging on the mountaintops now, but there was still a fair amount of natural light to back up the narrow beam of her torch. She ran as fast as she dared, but the short journey seemed to take an age, as if she were running in a dream, on leaden legs. At least the downhill slope meant she did not have to pause for breath but could charge on, not allowing herself to think about what she was going to find when she reached Penlan. Nor what she would be able to do about it. Nothing in her wildest imaginings could have prepared her for the sight that awaited her once she turned the last bend before the house. Smoke. Lots of it. Billowing up from Penlan.

"No!" she screamed, running on, heart pounding, hurling herself down the hillside. As she got nearer she could hear the fire, a low, terrifying rumble like a gathering avalanche. She could see figures outside the house. She tried to make out who they were, and how many. Only three. One tall, and two small. Rhys and the boys. Where were Dan and Steph?

"Rhys!" she bellowed as she raced into the yard. "Where are they? What have you done?"

"It's all right! I've got the boys out!" He held on to the terri-

fied children who were too shocked to do more than cling to him
and stare at the burning house.

"We've got to get the others out!" Laura ran toward the door.
Rhys sprinted forward and intercepted her, grabbing hold of her
shoulders and pulling her away.

"You can't go in there, Laura."

"Let me go, you madman!"

He tightened his grip and started to shout at her, but the
sound of breaking glass distracted them both. Looking up Laura
saw Steph at the little bedroom window, coughing and gasping
as she used a small chair to break through the frame and glass.

"Mummy!" William screamed. Hamish started to cry loudly.

"The porch roof, Steph!" Laura shouted to her, thanking God
Steph had not taken her usual sleeping tablet. "Lower yourself
onto the roof!"

Steph did as she was told, holding on to the tough twists of
the honeysuckle. Somewhere in the distance another noise could
be heard. Laura looked down the valley and saw small lights coming up across the meadows. The lights of a quad bike. Rhys saw
them, too. Laura seized her moment and wrenched herself free
and dived into the house. She heard Rhys curse and blunder after
her. The heart of the fire must have been in the kitchen, for though
the sitting room was filling with smoke, there were no flames.
Laura raced to the stairs, hoping that the thick door would have
slowed down the progress of the deadly fumes.

"Stop, Laura!"

Rhys had caught up with her and grabbed her around the
waist.

"No! Get off me you bastard!" She beat at him with her torch as she used the other hand to pull open the door. Something at the top of the stairs glinted in the light from the small window. A pair of eyes. Golden, ancient eyes. The smoke cleared for a second to reveal the enormous wolf in the instant that it sprang. It leaped over Laura's head and landed fully on top of Rhys. She heard him scream as she dragged herself on up the stairs.

"Dan!" She coughed as she hammered on his door. She felt for the latch in the smoky darkness. A piece of wood had been used to jam it. She worked at it frantically until at last the door sprang open. Inside, the bedroom was dense with choking smoke. Dan lay on the bed, horribly still. Laura shook him, trying to wake him, but he had breathed in too much smoke. She was having difficulty breathing herself now, spluttering and gagging as she heaved Dan off the bed. At least near the floor there were still a few inches of breathable air. She tried to drag him toward the stairs, but he was far too heavy. Her muscles burned with the effort, but still she could only move him an inch at a time. Too slow. Much too slow. Tears of fear and frustration began to mingle with the soot on her face.

"Merlin!" she wailed. "Help us!"

For a few seconds nothing happened.

"I won't leave him!" she screamed. "I will not. Do you hear me?"

There was still no sound or sign of Merlin. Laura thought that she and Dan would die together as the house burned around them. Then, imperceptibly at first, a breeze began to stir the smoke. The air moved more quickly, until there was a strong wind howling through the room, forcing the smoke out and clean air in. Laura tried to move Dan again.

"Dan, wake up! Come on!" She shook him again. This time he groaned in response. "Yes! That's it, come on."

As the fresh air reached his lungs Dan coughed and retched, fighting for breath. At least he was now conscious enough for Laura to be able to help him to his feet. Together they all but fell down the stairs, which, had they not been stone, might not have been standing.

As they staggered into the sitting room Laura saw a figure coming toward them. For a moment she feared it was Rhys.

"Come on there." Glyn's reedy voice cut through the smoke. "Let's 'ave you out of this place!" He ducked under Dan's arm to take some of his weight, and the three of them charged for the door, the terrifying sound of tumbling timber lending wings to their heels.

Once in the yard Laura and Glyn laid Dan gently down on the grassy cobbles. Steph and the boys hurried over to them.

"Is he OK?" Steph asked, clutching Hamish with his arms wrapped around her neck, William hanging on to her free hand.

Laura nodded as she coughed, unable to find enough air to speak.

"I saw the smoke," Glyn said. "The fire brigade are on their way."

Laura scanned the yard, but there was no sign of Rhys.

"Where is he?" she demanded of Glyn. "Where is Rhys?"

He shook his head. "I never saw him."

"I did," said Steph, her words tense with fury. "He ran out of the house, screaming. He went that way." She gestured toward the mountain.

Laura was too traumatized to know whether to be relieved

he had gone or terrified that he was out there somewhere and might come back. She crouched down next to Dan and took his hand in hers.

"Dan, I am so sorry," she said.

He tried to answer her, but the smoke still had his voice. Instead he mustered a weak smile and shook his head, squeezing her hand.

Sirens could be heard echoing through the lower reaches of the valley. Laura turned to look at the burning house, the flames now feeding on the roof which cracked and groaned as it began to fall in on itself. The fire burned with terrifying ferocity, lighting up the night sky with a dizzying display of spark and flame. Within minutes timbers that had sheltered generations for hundreds of years were consumed and replaced by a cavernous, orange hole.

EPILOGUE

OUTSIDE THE VILLAGE shop the colors of the plants lined up for sale spoke joyfully of spring. Laura considered the vermilion climbing rose and the china-white daisies before settling on a vigorous looking honeysuckle. Mrs. Powell appeared in the open shop doorway.

"Ooh, hello there. Lovely to see you again. My goodness, it's been a few months, hasn't it? Are you keeping well?"

"Yes, thank you. I'm fine. Just a little tired sometimes."

"Oh, that's to be expected, isn't it? And after that terrible fire, well, well. Was Glyn the Bryn called the fire brigade, wasn't it?"

"That's right. Actually, I was buying this to take to Anwen."

"Who, dear?"

"Mrs. Morgan. Glyn's wife?"

Mrs. Powell laughed merrily at this. "Glyn have a wife? Oh, my goodness, the idea. Who'd want to be married to that grumpy old beggar?"

"I'm sorry, I don't understand. I thought . . ."

"Glyn's been up at the Bryn on his own since his father died in 1978. Or was it 1987?"

Laura stared at Mrs. Powell, trying to take in what she was saying. At first she thought there was a simple misunderstanding, or that the postmistress was getting forgetful and would remember Anwen in a minute. But no, the more she thought about her, about what an ill-match Anwen and Glyn had always seemed, about the strangeness of the old woman, and about the fact that there had never been anyone else around when Laura had seen her, the clearer the truth became. It made more sense, in fact, that Anwen should be like Merlin, a being who inhabited that liminal realm of stories and legends. It seemed too obvious now; Laura felt foolish for not having seen it sooner.

"No wife?" she asked Mrs. Powell once more, handing her the money for the plant.

"No, dear. No wife."

Laura looked at the honeysuckle and then smiled, deciding in that moment what to do with it. An idea had come to her. She put the plant in the passenger footwell of her car and settled herself carefully behind the wheel. She fidgeted with the cushion she had taken to using in the small of her back when driving, then set off for Penlan.

It had indeed been several months since she had been to Wales. It was good to see the countryside in its spring finery again. With a pang she thought of the first time she had seen the house, exactly at this time of year twelve months ago. Such a lot had happened in that time. So many things to so many people. She drove slowly up the twisting lane, not wanting to take any of the bumps or potholes too quickly this time. A mixture of excitement and

nervousness took hold as the house came into view. How different it looked now. All around it the timeless landscape remained
constant, shifting only with the seasons, year in, year out, but remaining otherwise as it had been for centuries. In its sheltered
position in the lea of the hill Penlan still nestled snuggly against
any threatening winds that might come, but the makeshift corrugated roof and boarded-up spaces where the windows had been
made it a forlorn sight. She parked the car and climbed slowly out.
At least now that the better weather had arrived the rebuilding
work could resume. Soon there would be a new roof and new windows, and the house would be made whole and beautiful once
more. But it would never be like it was before. However sympa-
thetic the restoration, a lot of work would be needed, and something of its history, of those connections with past lives, would
be lost. The main A frame had survived, as had the bigger of the
beams. They were of such stout and dense oak that even such an
intense fire would have needed longer to consume them. Many of
them had been irredeemably blackened, though, and most of the
floorboards were gone, along with the lovely wood paneling, and
many of the details which had given the place its charm. Laura
had known straightaway after the fire that she would never want
to live at Penlan again. It was ruined for her, and not just because
of the fire damage. The main part of the house being stone was
still standing, and to the casual observer there would be little
difference to see. But too much had happened. Too much had
changed. She could never make her home there after what had
been done. After all that she had experienced. After all that she
had so nearly lost, and for which she would always blame herself.
Even now, so many months later, she could vividly recall the

terror of that night. What if Megan had not helped her escape from the croft? What if she had not gotten to the burning house in time? Dan had so nearly died, and all because of her. He had been so understanding, so generous and loving and forgiving. He was prepared to try again, to save their marriage. He promised there would be no more guilt, no more recriminations, just moving forward, together.

Standing still was beginning to make Laura's back ache, so she fetched the honeysuckle from the car and walked slowly down across the meadows toward the woods. The May blossom was spilling from the hedgerows, and the first of the bluebells were blooming in shady spots here and there. A small flock of long-tailed tits bobbed by, and a squirrel chattered in an ash tree as she passed. As she entered the woods and stepped over the stream she thought of William and Hamish and how much she had loved spending time with them here. At least they had their father back now. It would be some time before he was completely his strong and irrepressible self again, but he had woken up on Boxing Day, giving Steph and the boys the best late Christmas present they had ever had. Laura still felt horribly responsible for what her best friend and her family had been through. No one had openly blamed her, but she knew the very sight of her must bring back painful memories, thoughts of what had happened, and of what nearly happened. Laura counted herself lucky that her friendship with Steph had been strong enough to endure all that had tested it. She was certainly going to need her friend more now than ever before.

She made halting progress but eventually reached the sloping oak and the clearing around it. The glade looked every bit as enchanting as she remembered, with wild garlic and violets and silvery lichen and a hundred different mosses, not one of them actually moss green. She put the plant pot down and hunted for a sharp stone with which to dig. The ground was dry but soft beneath the topsoil. She scraped and scratched away until she had dug what she hoped was a deep enough hole, then upturned the honeysuckle and planted it. She stood up, aching as she always did now if she stayed in one position for more than a few moments. She brushed the dirt from her hands and regarded the enormous oak tree, imagining what it might look like in a couple of years with the honeysuckle twining its way up the trunk and through the branches, with fragrant, drooping blooms attracting bees and butterflies for miles around. She wondered if perhaps she would come back to see it, but she doubted it. In her heart she knew that this was good-bye. It was a moment she had been putting off, but it had to be faced. At least she did not fear coming across Rhys. The police had tracked him for two days after the fire. He had eventually been found, hiding out on the mountain, raving and incoherent. Laura had spent many difficult hours telling the authorities everything she suspected, everything she knew, everything that had happened. He was ultimately charged with abduction and arson, the police feeling they did not have enough evidence to prosecute him for what happened to Angus. There was little doubt that he would be convicted, though it was more likely he would be sent to a secure hospital than a prison. Laura pitied him now. Pitied him, and despised herself, for her own selfish weakness, and for the danger she had brought to those she loved. She quelled a shudder at the thought of what he had done, and at the thought of how close she had let him get to her.

She still missed Merlin. She had grown accustomed to the constant, physical ache just below her heart, and even the vivid dreams where he seemed so very close and so very real. But the thought of never seeing him again, the endlessness of that, was something she would never get used to. It had taken her weeks to realize that he had gone. Forever. At first she thought it was just because she wasn't living at the house any more. But she would come back, to oversee clearing up, or sort out builders or insurance men, and each time she would look for him. And each time she came away weeping. She could not understand why he had left her. For a while it felt as if she had lost everything worth living for. Her imagined future with Dan at Penlan. And Merlin. She had never in her life felt so alone. But then, gradually, with the passing months, she had come to understand at last what Merlin had meant about their fates being linked. She remembered that he had told her they were not destined to stay together, but that all would be well. The thought of a future without him being a happy one had seemed an impossibility to her at the time, but now she understood. She put her hands on her swollen belly and closed her eyes, trying to picture the growing baby inside her. Of course to Dan, to everyone else, this little person would be a miracle the two of them had conjured, without help. Laura knew different. This child was indeed miraculous. A magical gift. Merlin had been robbed of his own baby, but he had used his unearthly magic to see to it that Laura would at last have a child. Her baby, hers and Dan's, but one brought about by an ancient power, a spark of legend that had been rekindled in her. Now she understood her part in the continuation of Merlin's story. And there was something else he had given her; a second chance with

Dan. She had known, at that moment when she came so close to losing him, that she still loved her husband, still wanted their marriage to work. If Merlin had still been in her life she knew she would have found it harder to fully commit to Dan. There were more ways of being faithless, she had learned, than with your body. Now, with the baby on the way, they had the opportunity to start again. She knew she was lucky to still have him.

The move back to London had been painful, but now they were settled once more. They had found a large flat not far from Steph and Angus. It was part of a warehouse conversion, with ample space for a studio, so that she could continue to work from home. The exhibition that winter had been a success and had renewed her belief in herself as an artist. People had been captivated by her new style; by the atmospheric paintings she had produced at Penlan, and in particular by the paintings of Merlin. She had kept one and it hung on the wall of her new studio, so that she worked beneath the steady gaze of those unfathomably blue eyes. One day she would tell her child of its wonderful origins. Of how an ancient soul possessed of strong magic had given her his blessing, a blessing that enabled her to at last conceive a baby of her own. One day, when it was old enough to understand. It was up to Laura to make sure that that day came, that she raised her boy or girl with an open mind and a special way of looking at things. A special way of seeing. Anwen had called it her artist's eye. Maybe the baby would inherit her mother's predisposition. Maybe as it grew to adulthood it, too, would be able to see what others could not. Maybe there would, after all, be a time when Laura returned to these woods, to show her son or daughter this very special place that was so filled with magic and wonder.

A movement at the edge of the glade caught her eye. She froze, watching. Into the clearing, on silent paws, padded a large, grey wolf. It stood squarely, raising its nose to sniff Laura's scent and gazing straight at her. She watched it without fear. She knew whose wolf it was. It seemed she was not the only one who needed to say her good-byes. The wolf looked at her steadily for a minute longer, then turned and trotted away, disappearing noiselessly into the woodland undergrowth. Laura gazed after it until her swollen ankles began to complain, took one more look at the oak and its new adornment, and then started her steady walk back to the car.

A Note from the Author

My inspiration for this book came from the house I was living in at the time, and the landscape surrounding it. Although born in Dorset, I grew up in Wales, and have returned here to rear my own family in the hills of my childhood. This is truly a magical place. With my partner, I moved to an ancient, unmodernized longhouse high in the Brecon Beacons in 1999. The house had no electricity, no phone, and no cell phone signal. You can see for miles in every direction, but not a single light from another dwelling is visible. The weather is often extreme and highly unpredictable, which is where the idea for the sudden thunderstorm came from, as well as Megan's wild ride through the night.

There is a tangible sense of timelessness about the place. Generations have lived and died in the house, which has changed little over centuries. The flags have been worn thin and the stone stairs blunted by hundreds of feet down the years. It is impossible to feel lonely in such a house, despite its isolation. It does not take a great leap of imagination to hear whispers or glimpse shadowy shapes, though happily my family always found these presences to be peaceful and friendly. I would not call them ghosts, more echoes of lives lived long ago, and stories softly told.

Discussion questions follow.

St. Martin's
Griffin

1. When we meet Laura and Dan their relationship is under great stress because of their thwarted longing for a family. What do you think about Laura's theory that moving to Blaencwm might help her conceive? Do you think Dan is right to go along with her wishes when he is clearly so reluctant to leave the city for the wildness of Wales?

2. Laura immediately feels an affinity with her new home, and is sensitive to all manner of presences there. Why do you think she is so easily able to connect with people from a different time or a different reality? Do you think the fact that she is an artist makes a difference to the way she experiences her new mountain home?

3. Rhys is a complex character, and Laura's response to him is influenced by many aspects of her life that are not really to do with him. What were your own feelings about Rhys when he first came into the story, and how did they change through the course of the book?

4. Laura makes some poor decisions, but knows when she has been foolish, and suffers terrible guilt. She tries to make amends and set things right, but some things cannot be undone. Do you feel sorry for her, or angry with her?

5. Have you ever been to a place where you felt a strong connection to past lives? Would such a connection as Laura has with Merlin, for example, terrify you or thrill you, do you think?

6. Who is your favorite character in the story, and why? Do you think most women are attracted to "bad" men, or only in fantasies, rather than real life?

7. Megan is vulnerable because there are people she cares about—her father, Merlin, Huw—but she is also a resilient person who is fiercely loyal. Given this, do you believe there is any way she could have changed her own fate?

8. Anwen is furious when she finds Laura casting a spell. "You are playing with the very fires of the underworld, my girl, and its heat will consume all those you love if you persist along this path." Anwen plays a crucial role in Laura's new life. What do you make of her? Laura asks her a lot of questions but rarely receives straight answers. What would you have asked her?

9. Not everyone makes it to the end of the story. Which death affects you the most? Often readers are more upset by the suffering of animals in a book rather than humans. What do you think that says about us? Is this the case for you with this novel?

10. Now that you know how the story ends, what do you think might happen next?